THE RED CHAMELEON

THE RED CHAMELEON

ERICA WRIGHT

PEGASUS CRIME
NEW YORK LONDON

THE RED CHAMELEON

Pegasus Books LLC
80 Broad Street, 5th Floor
New York, NY 10004

First Pegasus Books edition June 2014

Interior design by Maria Fernandez

Library of Congress Cataloging-in-Publication Data is available.

ISBN: 978-1-60598-568-8

10 9 8 7 6 5 4 3 2 1

Printed in the United States of America
Distributed by W. W. Norton & Company

For Adam G. Province

THE RED
CHAMELEON

CHAPTER ONE

The bartender was cutting a cigar for me when my target stumbled toward the men's room downstairs. I had been paid to keep an eye on him all night, but I decided that didn't mean I had to visit the john. In my favorite black dress and new red wig, I wasn't dressed for urinals, so I watched the bartender light my Belvedere and pass it over. Most of the cigar bars in the city are nice, but Hamilton's outclasses them all with its crystal tumblers and soapstone whiskey rocks. Oak-paneled walls and chandelier lighting make it look like a king's hunting lodge. If all the king's men were Upper East Side trust- and hedge-funders. I took another sip of my pinot noir and checked myself in the mirror.

The once-over had become a professional habit, an unnecessary one that I needed to break. My chameleon-like appearance was one reason I had excelled in the New York Police Department, and after my premature retirement at the ripe age of twenty-five, it was the main reason I survived as a private investigator. When my undercover identity had been blown three years prior, the gang members had disagreed about everything from my height to my eye color. They all agreed that my hair was jet black, but a quick trip to Walgreens had turned it back to light brown, which I kept boy-short in order to occasionally pass as a teenager named Keith.

My parents, God rest their souls, knew what they were doing when they named me Kathleen, a.k.a. Katie, Kat, Kitty, Kathy, Kate, Katya. It was as if they knew their daughter would one day need multiple personas and the driver licenses to go with them. My real name is Kathleen Stone, but that night I was Kathy Seasons. I think of Kathy as a young-looking thirty-five, which is the upper limit of my possible age range. She works in real estate and likes to have a drink or seven before heading back to her high-rise apartment where she lives with a goldfish.

I was sharing these made-up but well-rehearsed details with a gentleman to my right while listening intently to the front door, making sure no one came in or went out without my knowledge. It wasn't too hard since Hamilton's was quiet on a Tuesday night; there were only six customers in the front room, a handful of others in the back. When my target, Stephen Kramer, hadn't returned by the time my bar neighbor finished his divorce story, I started to worry and excused myself to visit the little girl's room. I extinguished my cigar in the spotless ashtray that had magically appeared in front of me and headed down the stairs. I don't normally wish for men to be relieving their bowels, but it was an unusual night. I was crossing my fingers for bad Chinese food because Mr. Kramer's suspicious wife was not someone I wanted to irritate. Partly I wanted to keep her in a good mood because I had already spent the deposit and needed the remaining fee for rent. Partly she frightened me. I worked up a giggle and stumbled my way into the men's room, silently praying for stall doors. In the end, it didn't matter.

Mr. Kramer had presumably locked the stall behind him, but someone hadn't been very impressed with that level of security.

The door was wide open, and Mr. Kramer was facedown beside the toilet, pants around his ankles, and blood was seeping from his skull onto the tiles. Squares of toilet paper floated in the puddle like they were trying to stanch the world's largest shaving nick.

I didn't flinch, which made me perversely proud. The first time I saw someone shot, I had vomited onto the shoes of the killer and got knocked around for being "a pussy." This time, I steeled myself and examined the scene in relative calm. There appeared to be only one bullet hole and no signs of struggle. The bathroom didn't have any windows, which left a whole bar of patrons and employees as suspects. I would probably be on that list if anyone saw me and knew of my association with Mrs. Kramer. There wasn't a good enough wig in the world to keep me from questioning.

I retreated up the stairs as quickly as possible and paid my tab. My newly divorced friend wanted to buy me another glass of wine, but I told him I needed a rain check and exited in the direction of the nearest payphone to call in an anonymous tip. I ducked into an alley to unpin the wig and slip out of my heels. I threw these accessories into my briefcase and extracted a pair of jeans and sneakers. I wiggled into them and pulled the dress over the top of my head, revealing a Yankees tank top. Instant Kat.

Whenever possible, I avoid quick changes, but I needed to get some more information and didn't want to be detained. Without a doubt, everyone at the bar would be detained when the police arrived. The problem with the quick change is what to do with the evidence. More to the point, I didn't want to throw away my pretty new wig or my favorite dress, but knew there was no alternative. I walked around to the back of an apartment building, found the trashcans, located the inevitable busted bag, and buried my briefcase in discarded cans, cat food, and dinner scraps. All I had on me now was a Metrocard and a twenty-dollar bill. I walked back up the alley and looked toward Hamilton's. Several police cars had already arrived, and a small crowd of rubberneckers was stopped on the street. I wiped the remaining trash muck on my jeans and joined them.

A tall man in khakis and a collared shirt was happy to explain what all the fuss was about. "I think someone got killed in there. Can you imagine? I was headed in for a nightcap. It could have been me, you know?"

I didn't think that was likely since it seemed clear Mr. Kramer was the intended victim, but I shook my head sympathetically.

"Hey, you don't happen to know the score, do you?" the man asked.

"Yankees are up 3-2 in the eighth."

What can I say? I can be slick on occasion. I had noticed the score before I went to check on Mr. Kramer in the bathroom.

"Nice. Well, I guess I'll head home." He didn't go anywhere, though, and neither did the other spectators, even when the police asked them to step back so that they could stretch yellow warning tape over the entrance.

There were two officers in uniform, and one plainclothes detective inspecting the area. I would recognize his face anywhere, but his eyes didn't register me at all as they slid over the assembled crowd. I felt a painful twist in my stomach, then told myself it meant I was good at my job.

Ellis Dekker, now Detective Dekker, and I had been in the cadet corps together while getting our degrees at John Jay College of Criminal Justice. We were friends, and I wasn't even jealous when he had excelled at everything from sharpshooting to answering phones. It was no surprise when he was promoted a few months after our graduation. It was around the same time that I was sent deep undercover, where I would remain for the next two years of my life, living among small-time coke dealers. Ellis had wanted an undercover assignment as well, but he looked like a narc.

Being inconspicuous at 6'2" with white-blond hair had never come easy. I used to tease him that he could infiltrate the Icelandic mafia. His light blue eyes would have disappeared into his face without his trademark tortoiseshell glasses. I was glad to see that he had upgraded to a more stylish pair since college. Not that he hadn't looked good back then, but today he was downright Clark Kent-ish, and I wondered what he was hiding under his blazer. Of course, Ellis had always been more Bruce Wayne, the only one of our friends with a blueblood upbringing. He was hardened now—leaner and colder—but the scar running from the corner of his lip to his forehead made him too memorable for my line of work anyway. I told myself this last bit to feel better about my life, but in reality, I mostly caught men having sex with their nannies. I wasn't saving lives anymore.

I retreated across the street to a Starbucks to watch who exited the crime scene. I settled in at a window table with a cup of coffee. After an hour or so, a gurney came out wheeling the dead body. In another half hour, Hamilton's patrons started being released. The divorced man I had been talking to came out first and immediately lit a cigarette. He took one long drag with his eyes closed, then dropped the butt into a sewer drain. It reminded me of a habit my father developed while trying to kick his nicotine addiction. He never went cold turkey, preferring instead to wean his way off, leaving more and more of his cigarettes un-smoked until he could take one solitary puff and be satisfied. Or at least, less likely to snap at my mother over something inconsequential, the way the laundry was folded or where she'd left the remote. My father always struck me as well-meaning, but surprised to wake up one day with a family.

Distracted, I almost didn't notice when the divorcé climbed into a parked BMW. I could just make out the license plate number and jotted it down in case I needed an alibi. I watched for another half hour, during which two women and five men exited. When no one left during the next fifteen minutes, I decided it was like popcorn—this scene was cooked. The question was where to spend the night.

After living in a building favored by rats and lunatics, I was overly fond of my clean studio in Washington Heights. It also had a real bed instead of a stiff couch, but my office was closer and consequently won the debate. When I exited the subway station and regained service, my cell phone had a message, and I was pretty sure I knew who had called. It wouldn't take long for someone like Mrs. Kramer to demand explanations. She was used to getting what she wanted and not used to waiting.

"Ms. Lincoln, this is Mrs. Stephen Kramer, and the police have been here. I'd like to set up an appointment for tomorrow at 8 A.M. to discuss our arrangement. Specifically, I'd like to know what the hell you were doing when my husband was killed."

I had my day all planned out. I would get yelled at in the morning, visit my wigmaker before lunch, then, if necessary, trace a license plate in the afternoon. I pulled on my meeting-clients wig, which was styled into a permanent brown bun, and my meeting-clients outfit, which was a simple black suit. I kept a few of these at the office like a bona fide superhero, or at least an OCDer. The one real perk of the office was that I could keep a couple of potted plants because the floor secretary would water them if I didn't show up for a few days.

I didn't announce my occupation with any signage, and I let people think that I worked in real estate like my alter ego Kathy Seasons. Of course, the secretary suspected otherwise considering my erratic hours and strange disguises, but Meeza was Queens street-smart and wouldn't say anything. I also brought her bagels as hush money.

"To carry or not to carry," I mused aloud. My killer instincts had sort of been squashed out of me since leaving the force. Finding a dead body the night before made me cautious, though, and I slipped my Smith & Wesson .22-caliber handgun into my purse. I had a perfectly legit-looking permit to carry, which I folded into my billfold along with my Katya Lincoln I.D. and credit card. I locked the door behind me and headed toward the lobby. At 7:30 A.M., all of the other rented offices were quiet, but Meeza was sitting behind the front desk reading the *New York Post*.

"You're going to have back trouble from sleeping on that couch," she said, barely glancing up.

Meeza is younger than me, with the longest eyelashes I have ever seen. With her flawless Indian complexion, she looks like a doe, and I had watched grown men blanch at the sight of her, unable to state their business. Of course, she also got her fair share of lechers, but she didn't seem fazed by them either. Her parents sent her on a string of blind dates, hoping she would meet a nice Indian man and start a family. I guessed her age to be about twenty-two, but she exuded a maturity that made me second-guess myself.

"I bought that couch specifically for sleeping," I said by way of defense. "It's a futon."

I craned my neck around to see what story she was reading. It looked like Stephen Kramer was front-page material, with a headline joking about being canned in the can and a lead-in implying gang connections. *Please don't let this be gang-related*, I thought as Meeza slid the paper in my direction.

"It's important for a real estate agent to be up-to-date on local murders," Meeza said.

I glanced at her and managed to suppress a smile.

"You bet. Maybe his widow needs a nice condo to get away from it all."

"Uh-huh. Maybe I could assist with the pitch. You know, get a cut of the commission."

"I'll think about it," I said, which was my standard response when Meeza asked to be included, which was fairly often. Whatever she thought I did for a living, she had decided it was more lucrative—or at least more interesting—than reception work. "Who was last night's contender?" I asked to change the subject.

Meeza shook her hair away from her face. "Oh, jeez. He drove a livery cab and smelled like patchouli. At least fifty. Where do they find these schmucks? 'It's time to settle down, *ladli beetiya*'," Meeza said in what I assumed was a convincing imitation of her mother.

Another office-space renter pushed open the lobby door and complained to Meeza about the steam pipe noise, a banging that is par for the course in old Manhattan buildings. I took that as my signal to leave before Meeza quit on the spot. She seemed destined for better things than either an arranged marriage or a desk job. Then again, maybe I was letting my imagination get the best of me. I had never actually seen Meeza outside of the office.

Mrs. Kramer lived in a Park Avenue penthouse with marble floors that looked dangerous for heel-clad widows, but the one I was visiting navigated the icy rink with ease. She met me at the door in a suit that resembled mine only in color and motioned for me to follow. I was led past a portrait of her from maybe twenty years earlier and noticed that plastic surgery had made the structure of her face look different, as if the present-day Mrs. Kramer were related to the earlier one but not the same person. I pondered whether this tidbit could come in handy for my line of work as my hostess opened a door and gestured toward a brocade sofa. The room was larger than my apartment and office combined times ten. It looked big enough to host a Restoration-era ball complete with orchestra and butlers. Now, there was an occasion for which I didn't have a costume. All that was missing were three or four Malteses.

"Oh, I hate dogs," Mrs. Kramer had replied when I asked about pets the week before.

"I'm sorry for your loss, Mrs. Kramer," I began.

She waved off my sympathies. "Gloria, please, and I suppose you want the rest of your money."

She pulled out a pen and checkbook from a mahogany writing desk. She brought them both over to the sofa and sat down beside me. I couldn't decide if her businesslike demeanor was a coping mechanism or creepy. She didn't seem any different than she had a week before, and I studied her face closely for dark circles or other signs of worry.

"Oh God, I know. I'm heartless. Everyone says so. But I've been trying to divorce Stephen for years. Without being able to prove infidelity, I would be left with nothing. Can you imagine? Twenty-five years of marriage, and I'm still treated like a gold-digger. I made that man and deserve better."

She stared at the large diamond on her left hand for a moment, then slipped it off and put it in her pocket.

"Done," she said.

I tried not to smile, because it seemed possible that Gloria had paid for her husband to be killed execution-style in a men's bathroom, but I couldn't help it. There was something about her no-nonsense approach that impressed me. I even liked her Anna Wintour bob.

"Why did you want to see me, Gloria?"

"Now, dear, that's an attitude I like. The police won't tell me much, but they don't seem to know that Stephen was being followed and I'd rather keep it that way."

That sounded fine by me.

She wrote out my check—adding an extra zero to the end—and held it out to me. I'm pleased to say that I didn't reach for it right away. I weighed the possibility that I was abetting a crime for a moment or two, then slipped the largest paycheck I had ever received into my bag. It took a full twenty seconds to damn myself to hell. Three minutes, if you count the time it took to shake my client's hand, retrace my steps to her entrance, and let myself out. Of course, it only took another three minutes, when I was halfway down the block, for the guilt to kick in. *What if she is the murderer?* I decided it wouldn't hurt to look into it, make sure someone else seemed like suspect *numero uno* and then use my reward for a nice long vacation in the Bahamas.

An international trip would mean I could stop looking over my shoulder for a week. Three full years had passed since my cover was blown and a couple of big-league drug lords had been sent away for a long time, but there were still plenty of people who would like to see my throat slit, for old time's sake. I slid my hand over my wig. Spain would be nice this time of year.

CHAPTER TWO

I n New York City, everyone is proud of knowing where to get the best you-name-it: pizza, haircut, escort, etc. I never go in for these cock tests, but I am positive beyond a shadow of a doubt that I know the best wigmaker. Her name is Vondya Vasiliev, and she was spitting rapid-fire Russian into her phone when I entered her second-floor shop on Neptune Avenue near Brighton Beach. There was only one customer in the store, and I would recognize him anywhere even without his platinum stage wig. That afternoon, the biggest draw of Big Mamma's Burlesque Revue was sitting cross-legged in one of the salon chairs. He had on white jeans and a pink V-neck sweater that revealed baby-smooth mocha skin.

"Hiya, Kitty Cat," he said, inspecting his mascara in the mirror. He had barely glanced at me.

"You know that freaks me out, Dolly. How can you tell?"

"How can't everyone?"

Darío "Dolly" Rodriguez could recognize me in any getup, even when I was trying harder than I was that day. Even when I had spray-tanned, added lifts to my shoes, and put on a brand-new wig, Dolly would greet me like it was no big thing. He used Vondya's shop as a makeshift living room, and I missed him when I stopped by and he wasn't there.

"I can alwayz tell itz you, too, Katerina," Vondya said, putting her hand over the mouthpiece for an instant before yelling again.

"They sent her a shipment of synthetic wigs and won't take them back," Dolly explained.

"The bastards."

"Ain't that the truth? Everyone knows Vondya only sells genuine human hair. One of a kind."

"I'm kind of hoping that's not true just this once."

Dolly swiveled around in his chair to look at me and see if I was kidding or not. When he was sure I wasn't, he laughed. "I hope you don't want another one of those you're wearing, because it does nothing for your complexion. It looks like something Davy Crockett would wear when his best raccoon was being dry-cleaned."

I would almost swear it didn't look that bad.

"No, I had to trash a nice red number that I really need replaced."

Vondya slammed the phone down and didn't bother to fake a smile.

"*Chush' sobach'ya.* These fuckerz do not know who they are dealing with."

I decided it wasn't the time to tell Vondya that I had passed her on the street more than once, and she had never looked twice. I also decided it wasn't the time to ask about a duplicate wig, but it's an awfully long train ride to Brighton Beach for idle chitchat.

"Vondya, the last wig you sold me was a big hit," I said, starting with the positive. "I found a nice divorcé." *And a dead man.*

"Oh, izn't that nice. You need a good man. Take out that pistol and put some diaperz in your bag."

"Amen," said Dolly, but he didn't look like he meant it.

"Well, I'd like to," I hedged. "But, you see, something happened to the wig."

Vondya rolled her eyes to the ceiling and said something I couldn't make out. She stomped out of sight into the back storage room, mumbling to herself. Dolly laughed again and mentioned how he liked that bit about the diapers. "I can see you now, doing whatever sort of badass spy shit you do, with a toddler on your hip."

"I am not a spy. Can't a girl change her appearance once in a while?"

"A girl can, yes," Dolly said, placing a finger on his chin as if lost in thought. "But not a girl like you who buys the ugliest brown wig in the shop."

First Meeza, now Dolly. Who else suspected? Would I have to change cities soon? That didn't sound so bad, but the thought of changing wigmakers made my forehead break into a cold sweat. This, despite the fact that my wigmaker was banging around in the next room, cursing me in Russian. Eventually she emerged carrying a red bob, saying it was the best she could do. The cut was different, but the color was impressively close. I was sure that Vondya had dyed it herself, because the shade looked natural, with a few honey-toned strands and a few auburn ones. The woman was an artisan, no doubt, and I swelled with gratitude.

"It's great, Vondya. Really. This will work."

"You alwayz make it work, Katerina," Vondya said, patting my cheek, apparently placated by the five hundred-dollar bills I laid on the counter, the last of my savings. Since the best wigs can run upwards of a thousand dollars, I never complained about Vondya's prices. I thanked her and made my way back toward the door.

"You come see me one night, Kitty Kat," Dolly said. "I can teach you some new tricks."

"I just might do that. You won't even know I'm there."

"Oh, I'll know."

The beach looked tempting, and I almost caved in to an impulse to lie in the sand and watch the stragglers enjoy the last mild days of the year. A striped kite blew in the September breeze and seemed to welcome me. If I walked out to greet it, I could see all the way to Coney Island, enjoy the neon lights from the Wonder Wheel without having to listen to machines whirring or barkers screaming for customers. There wasn't time to waste, though, and I turned back toward the train station.

At my apartment, I could run the license plate of the Hamilton's customer and maybe check on the gang connection, just in case. I told myself that my motivations were purely professional, but I won't pretend my face didn't get a little hotter thinking about my contact, undercover agent Marco Medina. Marco was hard to describe, but I was pretty sure that his natural hair color was brown or dark blond and that his eyes were hazel or green or gray. He went undercover the same year that I finished my assignment, and I had been his mentor and then his lover for a few months. I taught him what I knew via hearsay about the complex alliances and vengeances of the group he wanted to join, and he repaid the favor by teaching me about body parts I didn't know could tingle. But that didn't matter because my motivations were purely professional.

Once home, I called my man at the DMV and found out that the license plate of my divorcé belonged to someone named James Clifton who rented a place off of Madison Avenue, only a few blocks from Hamilton's. After my chat with Gloria

Kramer, I needed more than an alibi. I also wanted information from someone who had been there the night before, preferably someone who knew the place better than I did and might have noticed something off. I had a suspicion, or a hope at the very least, that Hamilton's was James Clifton's friendly neighborhood bar. My new red bob would not go untested. I was tempted to slip it on to visit Marco, but knew I couldn't drop by dressed as a woman in any hair color. I hadn't spoken to him in months and didn't know his relationship status. I might not necessarily give away his cover if I showed up looking as feminine as I wanted to, but I could get myself cut. I wasn't crazy about that scenario, so I slipped the red wig onto a mannequin head in the closet. I then removed my practical bun and put it in my bag for the office. *The blonde would be nice*, I thought, and then snapped out of it. Instead, I added some dry shampoo to my real hair and pushed it forward and down into my eyes.

With gel inserts, I could fill the B-cup on my black lacy bra that never saw the light of day. Instead, I took out an Ace bandage and wrapped it tight around me until I was all but flat. I put on a skater T-shirt, ripped jeans, and dirty Vans to complete the look. Keith was actually one of my better disguises. I had never figured out how to convincingly fake acne, but throw an issue of *Maxim* and an iPod into my backpack, and I was all set as long as no one spoke to me. Funnily enough, people don't go out of their way to talk to fifteen-year-old boys.

The front door to Marco's apartment building was propped open with a cinder block, so I walked right in and climbed the three flights. I hunched my shoulders and widened my stance a bit, but the act was unnecessary; the hallways were deserted. A television blared from somewhere, and that was the only sign of life. I knocked on Marco's door and was, I'm ashamed to say, disappointed for non-professional reasons when there was no answer. I was so disappointed that I decided to try one of my lesser talents and pick the lock with my Swiss Army knife. I don't know if deadbolts are tricky for everyone, but I have about a ten-percent success rate. Really, I had no business trying, but I wanted to see Marco and knew I couldn't wait inconspicuously in the hallway for long. Sooner or later, someone would ask questions. Who knows, I might have succeeded with the deadbolt that time, but before I got very far, the apartment door at the end of the hall opened, and a fat, shirtless man aimed a large, scary gun at me. Some sort of limited edition Sig Sauer 9mm, and I had a split second to wonder what he had done to obtain a weapon that must cost at least three grand. The Smith & Wesson in my backpack would have looked laughable in comparison, even if I could have gotten to it before having my head blown off.

"What the fuck are you doing, kid?"

I shook my head and started to back toward the stairwell.

"Wait just a goddamn minute. Don't move."

He cocked the gun and strode toward me, his belly swaying from side to side over the waist of his sweatpants. I froze, as asked, and he grabbed the front of my shirt and pulled me toward him. He smelled like day-old weed and spat when he talked. I wanted to wipe my face, but just shook my head again.

"I asked you a question. What the fuck do you think you're doing?"

All I could do was shrug, and that seemed to piss him off. He pulled me even closer, so that I could add sweat to his list of odors, and pressed the butt of the gun against my temple. I held my hands up to show that I was unarmed, but unfortunately, I don't think Mr. Machismo cared too much. I heard someone walk up behind me, and a pair of hands grabbed me by the shoulders and pulled me back forcefully. I hazarded a glance and stared into Marco's eyes—*definitely green*. They didn't look happy to see me.

"*No lo creo,*" Marco said. "It's my sister's kid, Miguel. Don't shoot him, even if he deserves it. Always a pain in the ass."

"He was trying to break into your place."

Marco laughed and slapped me on the back of my head.

"This *payaso*? He couldn't pick a lock on a girl's diary. Get inside," he said to me.

Marco opened his apartment door, and Miguel lowered his gun. He gave Marco a head-nod and walked away.

Once we were safely inside, Marco stared at me without speaking, and I no longer had such a strong desire to talk to him. I tried not to fidget, but couldn't help pulling down on the edge of my baggy T-shirt. Unexpectedly, his eyes softened, and he grinned.

"You used to be better than that."

"Another minute, and I would have had the lock."

"Fat chance. I think this P.I. shit has made you soft."

"If I'd disarmed him, I would have blown your cover."

Marco studied me to see if I were serious. I wasn't. Some days I liked to imagine that I could still run five miles without panting, shoot the heart out of a paper target, and break someone's nose with the palm of my hand, but mostly I accepted reality. My instincts remained sharp, but I hadn't sprinted away from any bad guys in years. Happily, I could still make my face blank as midnight snow, and I could tell Marco was undecided about my sense of humor. There was a time when he'd respected my skill level.

Not everyone had been supportive when I volunteered for an undercover rotation. A few of my peers grumbled that I was skipping line, and it's true that I got an assignment without the typical three years on a street force team. I would be lying if I said I hadn't thought of that. Fact is, there weren't a lot of female volunteers, and I knew my decision would expedite my career. More importantly, it would also allow me to disappear for a while, and after my parents' deaths I felt like disappearing. The undercover gig was a reset button ripe for the pushing, and who was I to question the opportunity?

When I emerged two years later, I wanted another button, and there was Marco, ready to serve and protect. He had completed his three years of drudgery, and his record was commendable. While his peers might have grumbled, too, they knew he was better than they were. He showed up early and stayed late. He was responsible for more arrests leading to convictions than anyone else in his graduating class. When he single-handedly dismantled a hostage situation, most people expected him to savor his fifteen minutes of fame. After all, he'd earned it. Instead, he respectfully asked for his image to be left out of all news reports, so that he could go undercover as planned. His supervisor bought him a beer the same night and gave him a rough sketch of Los Guardias, a gang cruel enough to satisfy the most dedicated sadist.

The drug lords' trials were over, and I had been out of the safe house for all of a week when I was called in to give Marco a crash course. The next official course began in June, and they wanted Marco embedded by May. Mentoring seemed like a simple enough assignment, and it sure as hell beat the mandatory therapy sessions. On April Fool's Day 2010, I strolled into my precinct at 7 A.M. to go over his file. Marco wasn't the only officer who knew how to show up early and stay late.

When he entered the makeshift classroom ten minutes later, I was wiping spilled coffee off of the folder and using some of the colorful vocabulary I'd picked up from the Costas, the family I referred to as my undercover "hosts."

"Reporting for duty, ma'am."

I looked up expecting a smirk, but Marco is a pro at defying expectations. He stared at me intently with his green or gray eyes, and I couldn't tell if he was judging or being respectful. Either way, I instantly felt exposed and rubbed a hand over my newly shorn locks. That much, at least, I was sure he noticed because he mentioned it later. He said he knew from that moment I must have been good at my job because I was obviously more comfortable undercover than in uniform.

Fast-forward three years, and I still wasn't sure what Marco Medina was thinking. It appeared, whatever he thought now, that he was on my side, and I let myself study him more attentively. He was as fit and handsome as ever, but there were deep creases around his red-rimmed eyes.

"Are you just getting home?" I asked.

"Forty-eight hours of nonstop action. Don't you miss it?"

I shuddered involuntarily. There had been a time when I got off on the thrill of crossing drug traffickers. I felt like a big, bad hero passing along information. Even when my contacts suspected a mole, the suspicion never fell on me. Of course, it fell on others, and that's the part that made me shudder. I spent a lot of time telling myself that the ends justified the means, and I believed it at the time. Afterwards, I tried not to think about it. I was lucky not to be suicidal or addicted to meth like others in my line of work. I had to believe that Marco saw a lot worse than I did. Drug traffickers are nasty beasts, but in the end they're businessmen, trying to make the best deals. The gang Marco was immersed in macheted people for the fun of it. At least, that was the rumor. *Please don't let Kramer's murder be gang-related*, I prayed again.

"An all-nighter means better things for me these days," I said, hoping he wouldn't suspect that I meant sitting in a rental car, drinking lots of coffee.

Marco went to the refrigerator and got out two Bud Lites. He passed one to me, and I twisted the top off and took a drink, trying not to imagine how I must have looked—a kid sneaking his first beer. The apartment was bare bones, but clean. The linoleum floors were scuffed, and there was a bullet-sized hole in one corner. The couch faced the largest, shiniest flat screen imaginable.

"Even cops have to catch a Knicks game from time to time," Marco said when he saw me examining it.

I was still checking out the apartment, but Marco had sprawled on the couch and grabbed the remote. ESPN popped onto the screen, and he took a long swig of his beer with his eyes closed.

"I think I've got about half an hour before I go into comatose mode," he said, pressing the bottle against his temple. "And I don't think this is a social call, unfortunately."

My eyes may have widened at "unfortunately," but I ignored the word choice and plowed forward. "My client's husband was killed last night. Single shot to the front of the head. The *Post* is saying there's some sort of gang involvement."

"The Upper East Side murder? Christ, my pals don't hang around Barney's on a Tuesday night."

"You'd hear if it were another gang, though, right?"

Marco was quiet for a minute, and I was afraid he'd fallen asleep. I put down my beer and leaned forward to check when he grabbed me, pushed me flat on my back, and lay on top of me. He pressed his knee between my legs, then brushed his lips against the base of my neck. My pulse sped up, and then he stopped.

"Your reflexes are slower, too," he said and slid off of me. "I'd know if it were another gang. Everyone likes to take credit."

He headed toward a back room, and I could tell that I wasn't invited. I sat up and peered at him over the back of the couch.

My heart was still pounding, so I waited until I knew my voice would be steady.

"How's your credit?" I asked.

Marco's expression clouded for a minute, then he gestured toward the door. I stood up and walked toward it obediently.

"You'll let me know if you hear something?"

Marco remained silent, and I let myself out. I heard the bolt click behind me. Something flashed to my right, and I was sure Miguel was watching me from his peephole.

—◆—

Hamilton's was busier than the previous night, and I could only conclude that murder had a certain mystique. I tucked a strand of my red bob behind my ear and entered the bar, expecting a respectful silence and finding a noisy hub. The gossip swam at me, and I caught bits of distortion: ". . . surrounded by a pool of blood . . . a real bastard . . . pissing . . . another Jameson over here. . . ." I pushed through the crowd to see if any faces were familiar. The bartender from the previous night was there, looking frazzled as she maneuvered bottles of whiskey, gin, and wine. She looked at me without recognition, and I ordered another pinot noir, hoping to spark her memory. It didn't work. When she poured my wine, I gave her a substantial tip and slipped toward the back of the crowd. If I wanted to talk to the bartender, I would have to wait until the end of the night anyway.

I was really looking for the owner of the BMW, James Clifton. He had been friendly enough that I was sure he would talk to me about the evening—what he saw, what he heard—without getting suspicious. If nothing else, though, maybe I could pick something up from the ambient conversation: ". . . not the way I want to go . . . jerking off in the bathroom . . . machine-gunned, I heard." Maybe not.

I shifted my weight from leg to leg and surveyed the crowd. Nearly everyone wore a suit or a dress, and the average age was around fifty. A couple of twenty-somethings were dressed all in black, including veils, and I would have bet my alcohol that they were Juilliard students having a little swank adventure with Daddy's credit card. An older gentleman tried to talk to them, but they snickered, and he walked away. I would have to keep that neat trick in mind for later: the Vanishing Pick-Up Artist. It had been a while since anyone obnoxious or otherwise had tried to pick me up, but there was always a chance.

"Excuse me," a man said to me. He was also in his fifties, but he didn't look like he wanted to chat me up. He was dressed in a tweed sport coat, gray slacks, and shoes shined to a blinding finish. More importantly, he had a tight grip on my elbow. "I wondered if I might have a word with you."

"Perhaps if you unhand me," I answered.

The man released my elbow and turned abruptly. None of the customers seemed to notice us, which made me hesitate. I glanced around, hoping to make eye contact with someone, but there were no lone gazelles that night. I wondered if customers would descend in pairs to the bathroom, just to be safe. The only thing I knew for sure was that if I caused a scene, I would never get any information from anyone. So I followed the well-dressed man through an inconspicuous door and into a desolate hallway.

There were a few identical doors, making the place look like the set of *Let's Make a Deal*. Which one would we choose? The man didn't pause, though. He yanked open the first door and ushered me inside. There were no chickens or sports car, only a spacious office with black leather furniture, including a couch that looked a lot more comfortable than mine. A mahogany desk sat in the middle of the room, and the man sat down behind it.

"Please, have a seat," he said.

"I'm sorry, but what is this about?"

The man leaned back in his chair and checked me out. I couldn't tell if the once-over was sexual, but it definitely wasn't friendly.

"Nice haircut."

I said nothing, but raised a penciled eyebrow at him.

"My name is Colt Hamilton."

"Do you treat all of your customers like this, Mr. Hamilton?"

"No, only the ones who disappear right after a murder."

I decided I didn't like Colt Hamilton very much, but didn't let it show.

"I read about that this morning. It's a shame, though it doesn't seem to have hurt your business."

Hamilton gestured again for me to sit, and this time I complied, setting my wine down on his desk and pulling the straight-back chair closer. He opened a drawer and pulled out a coaster, which he tossed at me. I wanted to toss it back at his head, but instead, I slid it under my glass, impressed by my own politeness.

"You were on the surveillance tape. You went downstairs right around the time the man was murdered."

The thought had crossed my mind that a place like Hamilton's might have hidden cameras, so I wasn't as shocked as I might have been. Worried, though, is a whole other story.

"Really? I had no idea," I replied. "Do I need to talk to the police? I don't remember hearing anything."

I knew my Kathy role. She was well-bred. She hadn't encountered much violence in her life, so Hamilton's questioning wouldn't make her nervous. She would never suspect that she was being accused of anything.

"No sounds of struggle? No gunshot?"

"No, nothing."

Hamilton stared at me from across the desk, his hands clasped in front of him.

"Don't you think that's odd?"

If I had really been downstairs, it might have been odd. Even so, silencers aren't hard to obtain. The job already seemed like a professional one. Not that shooting a sitting target is particularly difficult, but an amateur would have gone for the chest and probably would have fired multiple rounds like in the movies. Contrary to popular action-adventures, one bullet usually does the trick. And with the price of ammo these days, what professional wouldn't want to conserve?

"I guess so. Do you think I was downstairs when that poor man was—," I lowered my voice, "shot?"

Hamilton met my gaze and held it.

"If you think of anything, you'll let me know."

It wasn't a question, but I nodded anyway.

"Is there anything else?" I asked in as sweet a voice as I could muster.

"Not for now, Miss—?"

"*Ms.* Kathy Seasons," I said, pulling out a business card from my wallet. "If you ever want to franchise, you should give me a call."

I picked up my wine and moseyed out of the office. Hamilton remained sitting at his desk when I closed the door behind me. The noise from the bar was muffled, and I glanced up at the ceiling. I couldn't spot any security cameras, but I was sure that Hamilton watched me walk back into the bar. To put it mildly, I was tired of being watched from behind closed doors. Twice in one day didn't bode well.

The bar was still crowded, and there were no empty seats. I didn't want Hamilton to think he had rattled me, so I wandered around, sipped my drink, and formulated a rough plan. I didn't think I could wait for James Clifton or even talk to the bartender inconspicuously now. The only other item on my to-do list was getting more info on Gloria Kramer. I couldn't loiter on foot for long outside of her swanky building, so I needed to park instead. Unfortunately, car rentals from my guy V. P. typically take at least a two-hour notice. Actually, I'm not sure where V. P. gets the cars, but the word "rental" comforts me more than "g ride," plus I could never use that term with a straight face. I sent him a text asking if I could borrow something in the morning and gave him an address a block from my office. A few seconds later, I received "anything 4 u" and felt better about the next day's observation of Mrs. Kramer who remained, despite my reservations, guilty-looking. From hookers to homicide, "follow the money" is the rule.

I left my glass on a table, sauntered to the door and out into the crisp night. It was hard to believe that earlier in the day I had considered sunbathing, but even the cool temperatures couldn't keep me from yawning. I decided to cut my losses for the night. Thirty minutes later, I was passed out on my office couch, curled up under the fleece throw I kept for sleepovers. In the morning, I awoke to the sounds of someone fumbling with the lock.

CHAPTER THREE

Half asleep, I grabbed my Smith & Wesson from underneath the couch, leaned up, and clicked the safety off. When the door swung open, Meeza shrieked and flung her hands over her eyes. I lay back down and exhaled.

"It's okay, Meeza. You just startled me."

"I startled you? Who's the one with a gun pointed at her head?" I apologized and looked up to see Meeza in her most assertive pose, the one she used with handsy delivery boys. "Real estate agent, my ass. I knew it!"

"Knew what?"

Meeza shook a finger at me. "Don't play all innocent with me. I was just coming in here to water your plants. I even knocked."

My mouth felt dry, my wig was crooked, and I had to pee. I was surprised Meeza wasn't more frightened by my appearance than by my gun. I sat up, clicked on the safety, and dropped the weapon into my bag. I pulled bobby pins out until I could wrest the wig from my head, then unlocked the closet and put the red mess on one of the vacant mannequin heads. I could sense Meeza's curiosity, but to her credit she didn't comment on the bald, eyeless heads. They give me the creeps, to tell the truth, but I can't bring myself to paint them like the ones at the wig shop. It's a little too Barbie-meets-Wilson for me.

"It wasn't actually pointed at your head, and what good would it do to cover your eyes?"

"I don't want to see if I'm going to get shot."

I thought about what I could say by way of explanation, but it was early, and I wasn't thinking clearly. "Fair enough," I said. Then, after a pause and perhaps a momentary lapse in judgment, I asked, "So, how do you feel about surveillance?"

After brushing my teeth and washing up as much as possible in the office bathroom, I slipped into an ash-blond suburban wig, jeans, and a polo shirt. I completed the look with a pair of fake Chanel sunglasses. They weren't so much part of the disguise as a way to hide my bloodshot eyes. My office wasn't as cozy as I liked to pretend in my more bravado-filled moments. By the time I emerged, Meeza had called someone to take over her shift and assured me that the floor would survive the thirty-minute absence of a secretary.

A block away, I was pretty sure I had located my rental for the day: a nondescript Nissan Sentra with tinted windows. I texted V. P. to be sure and received a "y" in response, which I assumed meant "yes, ma'am."

"I didn't know you kept a car in the city," Meeza said.

I slipped my hand under the frame and found a duct-taped key. "It's kind of like Zipcar."

"Uh-huh. Is it a private company?" Meeza asked.

I grinned in response and got behind the wheel. Meeza slid into the passenger seat. Ten minutes later we were parallel-parked in front of Mrs. Kramer's building. We couldn't see into her penthouse apartment windows, so I dialed her landline from my cell phone, which I knew would show up as "Blocked," and hung up when she answered. You know, very sneaky stuff. It would be impossible to tell if someone going into the building was visiting her, but we could follow her if she emerged.

"So, you think this lady had her husband killed," Meeza asked. I had sketched out the basic details on our drive over.

"I hope not." I really wanted to cash the check she had given me. "It doesn't make a lot of sense to hire me to follow her husband and then have him killed."

"But you could testify that it wasn't her. You would have seen her."

"I could testify that she didn't pull the trigger."

"Huh."

Meeza sat quietly for a few minutes and then pointed at someone talking to the doorman. "Should we take pictures of these visitors or something?"

I pulled a small digital camera out of my bag and handed it over to Meeza, who happily clicked away.

"I can't get his face from here. Do you have a zoom?"

I rummaged around in my oversized "Mom" bag and retrieved a lens. Meeza screwed it onto the end of the camera and pointed it toward the entrance.

"I still can't see his face."

Before I could stop her, Meeza jumped out of the car and crossed the street. I started to follow her, then figured that would be even more conspicuous. Meeza disappeared from sight, and I looked futilely around for her hiding spot. It was like she had vanished. I told myself not to overreact and kept my eyes on the apartment building entryway. My first responsibility was Mrs. Kramer, and if she left the building without my noticing, I would not be happy.

After an hour, my legs hurt, and no one I recognized had entered or exited the building. I had asked Meeza along partly for company. Surveillance is better with someone to run out for coffee or at the very least complain to. With Meeza snapping photos from a mysterious location, I was on my own, per usual. I dug around in my bag for my water bottle, which I found, then promptly dropped when someone knocked on my driver's side window. I looked through my window at former friend and current detective Ellis Dekker's big blue eyes squinting at me from behind his glasses. I glanced at the rearview mirror to make sure my wig was in place, then rolled down the window.

I said hello in my most cheerful voice as Ellis flashed his badge.

"Am I illegally parked?"

"No, ma'am, but you've been sitting here for over an hour. I wanted to make sure everything was okay."

I laughed a little before answering. "Never better. This is my favorite part of the day. My daughter has a two-hour dance class around the corner that gives me time to read the paper."

Ellis looked around for the newspaper, and I added, "Or nap, if I'm not feeling up to current events."

I smiled again, but Ellis shook his head. "Not bad, Kathleen, but I knew it was you before you rolled down the window. We ran the plates. Hasn't V. P. been arrested yet?"

I shrugged and climbed out of the car. No one had called me Kathleen in a while, and the name sounded distant, like a great aunt's name, not my own. I hopped in place for a bit to restore circulation, then leaned against my V. P.-special vehicle. Ellis stepped closer to me, and I willed myself to stand still. Meeting Ellis's gaze has always been a gamble. His eyes are so clear that you can imagine they belong to a prophet or at least a decent psychic. Mind-reader, possibly. I managed to look directly into them this time, even while expecting him to shake me or cuff me. Neither would have been a complete surprise. Instead, he said, "We have your assistant in the van, and I think we need to talk."

I locked the Sentra behind me and decided against re-taping the key while Ellis was nearby. In any case, I figured my rental lasted at least twenty-four hours. Every so often, a car would disappear while I was sleeping or picking up groceries, but mostly V. P. let me know when he needed to reclaim them. Ellis didn't wait for me and was already halfway down the block before I finished locking the car. I reprimanded myself for always recalling him fondly. That's nostalgia for you. Maybe he wasn't as nice as I remembered.

I hustled to catch up and fell into step with him. I glanced at Mrs. Kramer's window, hoping she wasn't looking down on us, but there was really no way to tell. I doubted she would recognize me from the penthouse anyway, with or without a disguise. Around the block, a mobile police van was parked, and Ellis opened the small side door and motioned me inside. There was a young police officer with a headset on, and I guessed that he was listening to the goings-on in Gloria Kramer's apartment. Was nothing sacred anymore? Meeza was standing beside him, and she gave me a sheepish wave when I walked in.

"Sorry, I thought I was discreet. They didn't believe me when I said I was working with Katya Lincoln."

"That's because her name isn't Katya Lincoln."

I raised my eyebrows but didn't respond to Ellis's words or tone. There was only one other chair in the van, and he gestured for Meeza to take it. She might have batted her pretty eyelashes at him, or that might be what they did naturally. In any case, I was definitely starting to regret bringing her along. Ellis and I leaned against one of the walls. I was feeling awkward and wanted to break the silence, but I wasn't sure small talk was appropriate. Years had passed since we'd been in a room together, and that wasn't exactly a pleasant memory.

Ellis had been outraged that I'd signed up for an undercover mission. I had yelled at him for being jealous, and he had smacked a wall in frustration, causing a vase to tumble and burst on his tiled kitchen floor. "Kathleen, don't you understand how dangerous that will be? Don't you understand—" But he had never finished his sentence because I ran out of his apartment. I had never understood Ellis's attraction to me, but I suspected it was there, lurking underneath his friendship. His rotation of women seemed endless, but there was always the hinted-at possibility that he would give them up for me. Me, who at twenty-one was the biggest mess imaginable. Or maybe I had misremembered his attraction, too. Maybe those lingering hugs had been in my imagination, just another coping method. One of many.

I glanced around the police van again and stayed quiet. It seemed like a definite possibility that I was in trouble, maybe even under arrest.

"Are you working for Gloria Kramer?" Ellis asked.

I blew out a sigh and thought about how much information I should share. On the one hand, I trusted Ellis, or had trusted him in the past. On the other hand, he would tell me to back off, and I wanted to know sooner rather than later if Mrs. Kramer was a cold-blooded killer. Dollar signs were dancing in my head, and I wanted them to dance in my bank account where they might actually do me some good.

"Not anymore. She hired me to spy on her husband."

"Spy on, or kill?"

My body tensed, and I felt the blood rush to my head in a combination of panic and rage. I put a hand against the wall to steady myself. "Shit, Ellis, I'm not a mercenary. I take photographs of husbands and wives in compromising positions."

Ellis mulled this over and nodded his head. He had his arms crossed in front of him, and I could tell that he had put on a few pounds of solid muscle since we'd last met. His skin was slightly sunburned, and up close, I could see a few freckles on his nose. The scar was shockingly white and looked smooth to the touch. Not that I wanted to touch it or anything. He was dressed in dark jeans and a shirt loose enough to conceal a weapon. Not that my eyes lingered on his waistband.

"And did you find Mr. Kramer in a compromising position?" he asked.

"Not even close. I had only been following him for a few days, but he went straight from work to home. Hamilton's was his first unusual stop."

"But she suspected him of cheating?"

"*Hoped* he was cheating is more accurate."

Ellis tapped the younger police officer on the shoulder and asked him to turn on the audio. The officer gave Ellis a surprised look, then slipped the headphones off and flipped a switch. Moaning was amplified in the little space, and I tried unsuccessfully not to blush. Then I tried to look anywhere but at the three other people in the van.

"Enough," said Ellis, and the officer flipped the switch again and put the headphones back on.

When I thought my skin had returned to its normal shade, I glanced at Meeza, who was trying not to giggle. I turned my attention to Ellis, who looked unamused at best, grim more accurately. What can I say, we were a mixed bag.

"Either Gloria Kramer was the one having the affair, or she rebounded awfully quick," Ellis said. "We thought perhaps we might take a look at your photographs."

He held out his hand, and Meeza obediently handed over the camera. I didn't even have time to consider objecting, though

I did suggest that the building probably had security cameras in the lobby.

"This way, we don't have to wait on a warrant," Ellis explained.

"I only got the one shot before you nabbed me."

Ellis smiled encouragingly at Meeza, and I was sure—I definitely regretted bringing her along.

"Yep, but I think your timing might have been impeccable. The rocking started about five minutes after that man entered the building."

Ellis turned the camera on, and I tried to look over his shoulder. He blocked my view for a second, then let me see. The man appeared to be in his late twenties, shabbily dressed in worn-out jeans, a T-shirt, and sneakers.

"I hate to state the obvious, but he looks like he should be her son, not her lover."

"You want to hear more of the soundtrack?"

I blushed again and hoped the new habit didn't stick. "No, thanks. Do you know who he is?"

"We're pretty sure his name is Leif Nichols. They met online. Before today, we didn't have a verifiable photo, just his phony profile one."

"Gloria Kramer is on a dating website? Uh-uh, no way."

Ellis leaned over to the computer keyboard and typed in a URL. A black scene appeared with one pulsing red word: Roll. After glancing at me to make sure I was paying attention, he moved his mouse over the word and clicked. A woman's face popped into view, and she said "hello" and waved. Above her head, new words pulsed: Stay or play? Ellis clicked "play," and a new person's face appeared. He then disconnected and looked at me to make sure I was following.

"It's like Chatroulette?"

"Yes, except that the paying member remains anonymous and gets to choose whom he or she wants to converse with."

"Converse?" I managed not to blush this time and gave thanks for small victories.

Ellis shrugged, and since I couldn't decipher what that meant exactly, I asked another question. "And the non-paying members join for fun?"

"Yep, that seems to be the site's m.o."

"How long has Gloria been a member?"

"Nearly six months now."

The string of swear words just sort of popped out. I am one hundred percent in favor of justice. Really, I am. I wanted my client to be innocent is all, and it wasn't looking promising. A hot, young lover would be a pretty strong motive for a jury.

"You don't know for sure it's him, Leif Nichols." It should have been a question, but I was confident I already knew the answer.

"How'd you like to find out for us?"

My mortal soul may have been in danger, but it looked like I was off the hook with the NYPD. As I climbed down the metal van stairs after Meeza, Ellis grabbed my shoulder and turned me toward him. He stared at me intently, and I expected a parting reprimand.

"It's good to see you again," he finally said. My stomach jumped, but I didn't have time to respond in kind. He had already closed the door between us.

⊰⊱

From time to time, different people from the NYPD had tried to lure me back to work for them on what they called "a consultant basis," which meant "for free." I had always flat-out refused. It turns out, all they needed to do was pair that request with familiar eyes and a get-out-of-jail-free card, and I was toast. Before I knew it, I was following the could-be Leif around town, waiting for the right moment to introduce myself.

His lifestyle was envious. After leaving Mrs. Kramer's around noon, he went to Chipotle and ate a burrito the size of a dachshund. Then he wandered into Central Park and stretched out in a sunny spot for a nap. To me, it seemed a little chilly for that, so I sipped a coffee and watched from a respectful distance.

Park shadowing is the best. No one suspects a thing, no matter how long you sit and stare. Also, if your target is boring, as mine surely was, you can watch other activities like dog-walking and frisbee-tossing. Occasionally a person spray-painted gold or on a pogo stick or both will mosey by on his way to perform for tourists. This time there was even a lady dressed up like the Statue of Liberty for photo ops. I was watching a little blond girl scream hysterically as her mother tried to maneuver her closer to the fake torch when Leif stood up, stretched, and knocked some dirt off his pants. That seemed like an adequate introduction opportunity, but someone beat me to it.

As I was standing to approach, a young man ambled over to him. They shook hands and started walking toward a more secluded part of the park. I kept them in sight but stayed back about a hundred feet, stopping occasionally to pretend to check out the foliage. The two men glanced behind them from time to time, but they never seemed to focus on me. I still looked like a suburban housewife, not particularly threatening. When they entered the Ramble, Central Park's manufactured wilderness, I was less confident in my ability to be discreet, but didn't want to lose them. Drastic measures seemed necessary, and I rushed to catch up.

I asked them if they knew where the path was headed. "I don't want to get lost, you know?"

Leif's companion had large ears that tilted outward and made him look younger than his wrinkles indicated. He was dressed in clothing almost identical to Leif's, old jeans and a

T-shirt. Instead of sneakers, though, he had on work boots that were covered with dust. His hands were callused and bore a simple gold wedding band. He didn't answer or even acknowledge me, but Leif smiled helpfully.

"This is the *Ramble*." He emphasized "Ramble" as if I might not be familiar with the word. "The paths twist around and don't have a destination."

"Sounds exciting!"

"I don't know about exciting, but they're private at least." Leif's companion nudged him in the ribs, but Leif kept smiling at me. "You probably want to stick to the southern half of the park." He indicated south with a sweep of his hand, and I turned to glance at the skyscrapers just visible above the tree line.

"You two men don't want to give me a tour? I'm from out of town." I looked up at him expectantly, and Leif stepped a little closer to me. His friend grabbed him by the arm, though, and pulled him away. He spoke for the first time, to tell me "not today" in a monotone delivery. I nodded and walked away, disappointed that I hadn't gotten either of them to introduce themselves. I was afraid to push it, lest they get suspicious and drag me into the tangled woods to be left for dead and eaten by chipmunks. The wilderness isn't really my area of expertise, even plunked down in the middle of a metropolis. Instead, I called Ellis and told him about the second man.

"Could be nothing."

"Could be, but they were acting weird," I said.

"Unicycle weird?"

"Kids-wanting-to-smoke-pot weird."

Ellis hung up without responding, and I was left with no definite plan for the rest of the afternoon. My surveillance had been put on indefinite hold. Thankfully, the Sentra was where I had left it, so I drove it back to my office and parked a block away. I duct-taped the key back to the frame and texted V. P. that he could pick it up and add the charge to my tab. I took the elevator up to my floor, and the doors opened to an impatient Meeza. She was standing behind her desk, drumming her manicure.

In a low hiss, she said, "Where have you been?"

"I was doing something for Detective Dekker."

"Oh, Lord, I'd like to do something for him." Meeza fanned herself. I started to walk toward my office, but she stopped me.

"Wait! There's someone here to see Kathy Seasons. That's you, right? They want to see you about *real estate*."

"Real estate? That never happens."

"Maybe you should put a fake address on your business cards."

"But I hardly ever give them out," I said, which was mostly true. I thought back to the previous night when I had haughtily handed one over to Colt Hamilton, and vowed that that would be the last time.

"I put him in the empty office at the end of the hall. I wasn't sure you'd want him poking around your office. Another thing, I think it might be that guy from the bar you mentioned, James Clifton."

I froze and looked at her, half-afraid but half-hopeful.

"Why do you think it's him?"

"He introduced himself as James Clifton."

CHAPTER FOUR

Sure enough, the man from Hamilton's was sitting in a folding chair in front of a scratched-up metal desk. I had swapped my Kate wig for my new Kathy and slipped on a suit jacket. It was the best I could do on short notice. Clifton stood when I walked in, extending his hand. In the fluorescents, I could see that he was older than I had originally assumed, closer to fifty than forty, but still spry. He smiled mischievously, which suited his clean but bedraggled appearance, journalist chic you might call it. I sincerely hoped he wasn't an investigative reporter, though, since the room looked like nothing so much as a fake office. Besides the desk and two folding chairs, it was entirely vacant. No computer, folders, photographs, or plants.

"Ms. Seasons," he began. "So nice to see you again. I must admit I had anticipated slightly nicer accommodations."

I grimaced and tried not to glance at any of the dark stains on the carpet. There was no way to hide my embarrassment, so I mixed a little truth in with the lies.

"I wish they were nicer, too. Then again, I usually meet clients on the way to showings. I'm coming from a disappointing one, in fact. No light at all."

Clifton pushed his gray-streaked curls out of his eyes, but they immediately bounced back down, defiant. He nodded at my explanation, but he didn't seem entirely convinced. He bobbed his knee up and down, a telltale sign of a smoker. I kept talking, trying to keep him from bolting.

"I hope you're in the market for a luxury high-rise condo, because I know a gorgeous one in Tribeca. Lower Manhattan is hot right now. Restaurants, clubs, theaters, that swank film festival. Maybe you can be friends with Robert De Niro. Or if you're looking for more space, a two-bedroom opened up in Gramercy this week."

"You do high-end sells, yeah?"

"Only the best," I replied too quickly. I needed him to believe me if I hoped to obtain any additional information, but couldn't help worrying that he would actually hire me.

He stopped looking around the office and met my eyes. For a moment, I thought he might call my bluff. Not that I was posing as a real estate agent, but that I was posing as a *successful* real estate agent.

"I have a daughter your age," he said finally, almost with a sigh as if he knew he shouldn't trust me but was going to anyway. "It was lucky meeting you the other night. I found your card in my pocket this morning."

He pulled it out along with a few beat-up companions. One was keeping a wadded-up piece of gum. My fake one was pristine by comparison. Clifton put mine on the desk and shoved the others away. This appeared to be the best opening I was going to get, so I dove right in. "Such a shame about that customer. I confess I'm glad I missed the chaos, though. You must have been there for hours."

Clifton shrugged. "An hour, maybe. It's my go-to watering hole, so I didn't mind suffering a little inconvenience."

"I don't want to be nosy," I began, leaning forward in my nosiest position. "But what was it like? How did people react?"

"Oh, everyone was shocked, of course. Leah, the woman tending bar that night, she burst into tears when the police announced that the bar was a crime scene. But she's a sensitive little thing. Colt covered everyone's tabs and insisted they finish their drinks. The police didn't seem too happy about that, but since we weren't officially suspects, they couldn't make many demands of us. Two people tried to duck out the back, but they were stopped. They almost reached suspect status, I'd say."

"You'd think that everyone would want to help in a situation like that."

"They didn't look like typical Hamilton's customers. Blue jeans, sneakers."

I wondered why I hadn't noticed the pair. Casual clothes would definitely stand out, but they could have been in the back.

"A forensics team swarmed the basement, but the detective on duty didn't have much to go on. His questions were all pretty general: variations on whether we noticed anything or anyone suspicious."

I was willing to bet that Ellis's questions hadn't been general at all, but merely designed to seem innocuous.

"I know I didn't notice anything. It was pretty dead."

Mr. Clifton raised an eyebrow at my choice of words.

"I mean, well, my apologies. I didn't notice anything unusual, though."

"Nor did I. Let's not dwell on that misfortune." He clapped his hands together once as if to close that chapter of our conversation. "I relocated for work a year ago and am still renting an awful little two-bedroom. In desperate need of a gut renovation."

Clifton leaned back in his chair until the front legs came off the floor. If he was willing to trust me, I guess he was willing to trust the flimsy chair, too. I swallowed an impulse to reach out and grab his lapels before he tumbled to the ground. He managed to maintain his acrobatic act through my cautious response. I wanted more of his perspective on the evening, but was still hoping to get out of actually showing places.

"Well, it's as much of a buyer's market as you'll find in New York. What kind of work are you in? Co-op boards always want to know."

"After a few decades in litigation, I've gone into pharmaceuticals."

I could easily imagine his eccentric demeanor being memorable in a courtroom. I know from personal experience that "underestimated" has its own advantages.

"I'll miss the Upper East Side," he was saying, "but the building smells like formaldehyde. Formaldehyde and something else I can't quite put my finger on."

"You don't want to be close to any of your old neighborhood haunts," I fished.

Clifton waved a dismissive hand, and his chair snapped back down to the ground. "Let's see this Robert De Niro special."

My luck had run out. While I felt a pang of anxiety, I figured I could always pawn him off on a genuine real estate agent if he decided to make an offer somewhere. I set up an appointment with him for the next morning when, I hoped, I would have managed to drum up a few apartments to show. How hard could it be?

⟞⟝

Meeza looked as frazzled as I had ever seen her, haggling on the phone with a property manager about taking a look at a vacant Tribeca condo. She had not yet raised her voice, but her free hand was on her hip. I took that as a bad sign and closed my office door. I flopped down on the futon and tried to put the pieces together. The one person I really needed to talk to—the non-grieving widow Gloria Kramer—was off-limits. I wondered if Ellis would consider sharing information, but didn't count on it. In my experience, the NYPD wasn't much into quid pro quo. Even if they were, following a couple of stoners and finding out, oh, absolutely nothing wouldn't get me a very good exchange rate. It was worth a shot, though, and I flipped open my phone and dialed Ellis's number.

He picked up without saying hello and asked me if I had any more information on Leif.

"No, but I was wondering what you know about the widow."

"How long had you been working for her?"

"Just a couple of days. She made an appointment on Thursday, we met on Friday, and her husband was killed on Tuesday. I'd say it's been a busy week."

He paused long enough for me to know that he might spill something important. "On her own, she's worth about a million dollars. With Kramer's assets, about a hundred times that."

I made a choking noise that I hoped sounded surprised instead of jealous. I didn't really want Mrs. Kramer's marble floors and antique furniture. The view of the park would be nice, though. And not having to photograph people fornicating to pay rent. Unconsciously, I rubbed my neck in the spot where it ached from couch-sleeping. I really wanted a shower and was thinking about hot water when Ellis asked me if I was still there.

"Yep. That's a lot of motivation, but then why would she hire me to follow her husband?"

"Good question. Divorce would be neater than murder, and due cause—like an affair—would most likely make the settlement larger."

"That makes sense."

"But maybe she got impatient?"

"I work fast, but I didn't make a four-day guarantee. Listen, I really need to know who she suspects, who's on her radar. But I can't talk to her without her knowing that I'm still poking around."

Ellis didn't say anything, and I resisted an urge to say "please." He had always preferred directness. Some of my favorite memories involved our shared sophomore literature class when he would try and fail to read between the lines of *The Scarlet Letter* or an Emily Dickinson poem. It wasn't his failure that I enjoyed; it was his earnest attempt to apply his logical thinking skills. Professor Bronwell was impressed, too, and he received an A, while I settled for a B+. Of course, that was partly because I had a crush on three boys at once and was caught daydreaming on a near-daily basis. I was always wishing it was Friday night, so I could meet Mason or Dominic or Jules. Occasionally, I would blow off my crushes and spend the evening watching baseball with Ellis, but he had his fair share of liaisons as well. I didn't know about him, but my liaisons were a distant memory. Marco was the last man to see me naked, and it looked like he would keep that status indefinitely. I thought about what might have happened yesterday if Marco hadn't pulled an all-nighter and I hadn't been so pushy.

"I don't know how much I can share. Let me get clearance and stop by later," Ellis said, interrupting my fantasy.

"I'll be at my apartment." At least there I could indulge in a much tamer fantasy involving soap and shampoo. Out of habit, I hesitated before revealing my address. Could I still trust Ellis? I took a chance and recited the cross streets and apartment number. He hung up just as Meeza entered and plopped down beside me.

"Whoo. That was tough, baba, but you have a 10 A.M. appointment tomorrow. You'll have to show your credentials in the lobby. You have credentials, right?"

"You bet," I replied. Now there was something that I could handle.

———

Some dreams are more accessible than others. The water was so hot that it made my skin pink, and I was letting it run over my shoulders. I had already washed my hair and scrubbed my body, but wasn't quite ready to give up my favorite part of the day. Day? Who was I kidding—this was the highlight of my week. Eventually I stepped out of the shower, dried off, and slung my wet towel over the bar. I was examining my pink face in the mirror when the bathroom door swung open.

I screamed before I had time to recognize Ellis, gun drawn but pointed at the ground.

"Are you okay?" he asked.

"No! What are you doing? How did you get in here?"

Panic set in immediately, and I berated myself for handing out my address when I should have known better. Now I was completely defenseless. I snatched the towel and wrapped it around my body while Ellis turned around. He holstered his gun and looked back at me.

"Again, what are you doing?" I said, trying to cover more of my exposed skin by half-squatting.

"How long were you in the shower?" he asked. I wanted answers to my own questions first, but his tone was frighteningly serious.

"Ten minutes," I said, which caused a slight crease to appear between his brows. "Fine, twenty-five minutes. Maybe half an hour. I'm a terrible, water-wasting person. What's it to you?"

Ellis stepped back from the door and gestured for me to look past him. My Washington Heights rental was a decent-sized studio with a tiny separate kitchen. The main room fit a loveseat, coffee table, desk, and bed. Decorations were minimal, but the light was good, and all in all, I was happier there than anyplace else. Of course, at that moment, I wasn't very happy at all. The front door was wide open, and someone had ransacked the place. When I stepped out of the bathroom, I could see that my coffee table had been turned over, my drawers had been tossed, and my desk had clearly been searched. Black spots danced in my line of sight, and I sat down on the couch, pulling the towel tighter around me.

Had I gotten careless? Had the families of the men I'd put behind bars finally caught up with me? There was one particularly mean brother whom I never wanted to see again. I had a four-inch scar on my inner thigh as a reminder of his brutality. I let my hand wander to the puckered skin. After the trial, I had practiced blocking the memories, but every once in a while, they wouldn't be refused. Before I knew it, I was thinking about Signora Costa, and I knew exactly where she would lead me.

Signora Costa swore by chewing tobacco when cutting onions, and, superstition or not, her eyes remained perfectly dry. She wielded the paring knife like the best sous-chef in town, pausing only to spit strings of black liquid into a coffee mug. She took out her dentures for this ritual. "So that they dunna stain," she explained, pushing the open pouch toward me. I had grown fond of Signora Costa to say the least, but I respectfully declined. She shrugged as if to say "your loss." I had been living beside her for nearly a year, coming in and out with her daughter, La Zanna, whose real name was Agostina Maria Sofia Costa. The nickname stuck after she dug her nails into the face of a girl in her 7th grade class. She didn't improve on closer acquaintance, but she was my introduction to the Costas and, more importantly, beyond them. The Costas were small-time, but they had big-time connections. When I was with Zanna, no one paid much attention to me, which was the point.

I was snotting over the onions when several members of Signora Costa's family came storming through the front door. Her son Nino had a bloody nose, and Signora Costa crossed herself. *"Mio Dio, cosa ti è successo?"*

"It's nothing, Mamma. Just some punk who got what was coming to him."

At this, Signora Costa held up her hands to stop him and mumbled something about wanting no part in anything *malvagità*. She stayed out of the family business, never questioning the gifts—a new television or gold earrings—that appeared from time to time. She cooked, cleaned, and pretended her children worked in the restaurant industry if anyone asked after them at mass. She had told these lies for so long that she no longer bothered with them during confession. If she did any extra Hail Marys, no one knew about them.

"Mio Dio," she said to Nino. "Don't tell me."

Zanna was nowhere to be seen, but her other daughter Eva was pushing wads of toilet paper on her brother. Eva's fiancé Salvatore Magrelli stood by the door, stock-still and silent in his pressed suit. He wasn't around much, and I was sure that he and his brother Frank were near the top of the food chain. I had been digging into their pasts as discreetly as possible for about a month. I needed a deal, though, not general operations, and that required waiting and chopping onions in the Costas' tiny Bronx kitchen.

It didn't make much sense for the Magrellis to be involved with the Costas until you got a good, long look at the eldest daughter. Eva was named appropriately because it was hard to believe that other women like her existed, that she wasn't the first and only one. She was honey-colored from her hair to her tan, which you could see a lot of during the summer months. That day she was wearing cutoff jean shorts and a halter top. She had kicked off her heels as soon as she walked in the door, but if required to go out again, she would strap them back on like armor. Sometimes the men who hung around would argue about whether, if given the chance, they would come on her tits or ass first. Partly, these brags were just to piss off her brother. Nino was younger than a lot of the other neighborhood wannabes and took some hazing from time to time.

I wiped my nose and eyes on my sleeve and went into the living room to see what was really going on. Signora Costa started singing to herself, making sure that she wouldn't catch any snippets of our conversation. It was always the same song, something she'd picked up in her Venezuelan youth, I assumed, along with her recipes.

"What punk?" I asked, and Eva looked at Salvatore before turning toward me. Any time Eva looked at Salvatore before me, I felt a tightness in my chest wondering if they talked about me, speculating on whether I was a cop or not. Most likely, if they talked about me, it was just to call me a pain, but I couldn't be sure.

"This kid Nino knows from around here, says he knows what's going down on Saturday," Eva finally answered.

"Fuck," I said under my breath.

"You said it. Nino makes like he's going to take care of the problem himself right there and then like some sort of amateur." She pushed the tissue harder against his nose, and her brother winced. "We're not amateurs anymore, Nino, when are you going to listen to me?"

I glanced at Salvatore, who was analyzing the scene dispassionately. He made eye contact, and I looked away. Still I knew his "Come on, let's go" was directed at me. It couldn't mean anything good, but I rose slowly and followed him out the door.

"A couple of guys are on their way," Ellis said, easing down next to me on the couch. I'm not sure how long I had been sitting there, staring into space as I thought about my past life. Ellis put his arm awkwardly around my shoulder, then pulled me toward him. I forgot about trying to cover myself and pressed into his chest. After a few moments, the mood changed, and he began to run his fingers along my spine. I suddenly became aware that my towel had slid down considerably, and my bare breasts, though not visible, were pressed against him. "A couple of guys are on their way," he said again, more strained this time.

When he released me, you could see the imprint made by my wet hair on his gray shirt. I was staring at this criss-crossed impression when he suggested that I put some clothes on. I took underwear, jeans, and a T-shirt into the bathroom and told myself I could try to figure out if anything had just happened between us later. Much later.

I examined myself in the mirror again. I'm so used to being in disguise that my own face is a bit of a surprise sometimes. The pink had faded from my cheeks, and my normal tawny color was in its place. My gray eyes were a bit red from the water, and my hair had begun to dry around my ears. I couldn't see any resemblance between this woman and the happy-go-lucky girl I had been my first three years of college or the pretend-tough one I had been in the Costa den. I pulled on the clothes and went back out to survey the damage.

Ellis was examining the apartment without touching anything. "Is anything missing?" he asked.

My few electronic devices were all there, and the only other items of value were the wigs. I took a deep breath and opened the closet door, half-expecting a homemade bomb to go off. There was no explosion, but strands of hair fell to the floor. Kate and Kathy were safe at my office and Katya in my bag, but the remaining five wigs had been knifed. The mannequin heads looked gruesome, with slashes on their cheeks and gouges where their eyes should be. I reached out toward my favorite one, but Ellis grabbed my hand and tugged me back toward the loveseat, where I put my head in my hands. I could hear walkie-talkies in the distance, and in a minute, two police officers appeared at my door, hands resting on their flashlights. They didn't bother to knock, and Ellis greeted them with a head nod.

"Miss Stone? We'll need to get a statement."

I jerked at the use of my real last name. I glanced at Ellis, who didn't seem to think anything was odd. He must have told them my name when he called.

The older officer had spoken and was waiting for me to respond. I guessed his age to be about forty, and while he wasn't exactly abrupt, I could tell he didn't want to waste too much time on a B & E with little apparent damage. In return for his attitude, I told him as little as possible about my suspicions and stuck to the facts. I had no real reason to believe that my past had caught up with me. No reason except abject fear. A connection to the Kramer case was more likely.

The other officer dusted for prints, then they both turned to leave. They tried to close the front door, but it had been ripped off the hinges.

"Do you have someplace you can stay tonight?" the older one asked.

"Yes, I'm all set. Thanks, guys." They were already headed toward the stairs, so I'm not sure if they heard me. I was about to thank Ellis, too, when my cell phone rang, causing my heart to stop for a split second. It was only Meeza, telling me that she had checked my calendar and I had a nine o'clock appointment that night.

"With someone named Jimmy Cruz," Meeza said, waiting for me to confirm.

I decided against telling her about the break-in and just thanked her instead.

"You bet. I wish I could go with you, but I am being sent on a blind date with a friend of a cousin. Apparently he's a taxidermist, so maybe I'll bring you a moose head tomorrow."

"One can only hope." I hung up and told Ellis that I had an appointment. I can't say that I was excited about the prospect of meeting a new client, but since I had just sustained three thousand dollars worth of damage in wigs alone and didn't have renter's insurance, I couldn't be picky about time and place.

"At nine o'clock?" He sounded incredulous, but his expression was hard to read.

"A girl's gotta eat."

"Listen, is there any reason that someone connected to the Kramer case would want to scare you off? Did you see anything that night?"

Had I seen anything that night? It was entirely possible that I had seen the killer, but how was I supposed to know who was there for whiskey and who was there for blood? I shivered and wrapped my arms around my body. If someone had wanted to scare me, they had. My home address was as private as possible. I had all packages shipped to the office, and Ellis was the only person I'd ever told the address. I glanced at Ellis suspiciously as he waited for my answer. He looked as guileless as a lean, mean cop can look.

"Not that I can think of. Look, I really need to get out of this apartment, and work is as good an excuse as any."

Ellis offered to go with me, but I thought that would probably scare Mr. Cruz off. Clients liked me, or rather they liked Katya, because she was efficient but non-threatening.

"Rain check on the info swap?"

Ellis surveyed the apartment one last time, then rested his blue eyes on mine. His nod was almost imperceptible.

"You can stay with me if you want." His tone wasn't suggestive, but I felt a mixture of excitement and fear rise up in my throat. I shook my head, afraid to trust my voice.

"Be careful, then," he said and walked out.

I propped the door up against the frame and called my super, who promised to fix it right away. I was surprised that Tambo hadn't been lurking around, seeing why the cops had been called. On the other hand, I wasn't sure of Tambo's legal status, so I could understand his convenient absence.

I pulled on a suit and smoothed out the Katya wig from where it had been stuffed in my bag. I slipped it on in the bathroom and slicked down the flyaways with water. She looked more familiar than Kathleen Stone.

As I boarded the A train toward midtown, I tried not to think about how long my day had been. With any luck, my meeting with Jimmy Cruz would be short, and I could be curled up on my office couch by midnight. I was crossing my fingers that Clifton would provide some more on-the-scene information in the morning. I hated to admit that I was rattled, but I was. It didn't seem likely that the break-in was a coincidence, since nothing was stolen. Yet I was almost sure I didn't know anything that would point to a killer. Besides, if my former life were haunting me, well then, it would find me no matter where I went.

CHAPTER FIVE

Jimmy Cruz seemed to think his live-in girlfriend Seraphina Capra was having an affair with the drummer of their band, The Trash Kittens. It took about fifteen minutes to explain, even with the "ums" and "likes," so I was indeed back in my office by midnight. By 9 the next morning, I was laminating credentials, and by 10 I was presenting them to the property manager of a new Tribeca high-rise. The manager was obsequious, complimenting my shoes and asking about other apartments I might be showing my client.

"He likes this location, so I'm hoping to make a quick day of it and catch a movie."

The manager laughed for no apparent reason and placed her manicured hand against her chest to show off her gigantic diamond engagement ring.

"Wouldn't we all like that?"

Her overly helpful attitude changed when Clifton barreled through the revolving door. His suit wasn't exactly Armani, and it looked like it needed dry-cleaning, but when he flung his newspaper under his arm so that he could shake my hand with both of his, I smiled. If I were choosing teams between Ms. Prada Shoes and The Eccentric Lawyer, sign me up for Team B.

"New money," I mouthed at the now-icy woman by my side.

"I'll escort you," she said.

"That won't be necessary."

"I insist."

I was irritated by her attitude, not to mention that I wanted Clifton on my own. But what could I say? I let her escort us to the elevator bank, half-heartedly listening to her remarks about the Art Deco pattern on the marble floor. I thought perhaps I could involve her in the conversation I needed to have, particularly if I made it tantalizing enough.

"So, Mr. Clifton—any particular reason you want to get out of the Upper East Side?" I asked as we watched the floor numbers rise on the digital screen.

"Oh, I'm looking for something livelier. What did you say about downtown, Ms. Seasons? It's hot right now."

"Hamilton's is a nice spot when customers aren't being offed in the bathroom," I said instead of answering.

"I heard about that," Ms. Fancy Pants butted in. "Total scandal for that establishment."

"Right? I'm never tinkling in public again. Apparently the man was shot just after I left the ladies' room."

"No way!"

The door ding accented her exclamation, and we were greeted with an unnecessary blast of air conditioning. The hallway smelled of plaster mixed with fresh paint, and a drill buzzed behind one of the closed doors.

"How do you know?" Clifton asked me as we headed toward a door at the end of the hallway.

"I'm sorry?" I asked, as if I weren't thinking about the murder at all anymore. I ran my hand along the drywall, then examined the dust in the palm of my hand.

"How do you know you had just stepped away?"

"I ran into the owner yesterday when I stopped in for a drink. You know Colt, right?" I kept my attitude as casual as possible, leaving the latent threats entirely out of my explanation.

"Oh, yes, he makes his presence felt."

"You could say that."

Clifton barked out a loud laugh, which made our companion bring her hand to her heart. Once recovered from her third or so shock of the day, she gestured for us to go in first since the hallway was narrow. "Colt's a good businessman. I'm sure he isn't happy," Clifton added.

The manager moved around us to unlock the door, and we stepped into an enormous open room. The loft had floor-to-ceiling windows facing north and west. It was hard to decide where to look first. The midtown skyscrapers shone in the morning sun, but so did the Hudson River, as if man and nature were competing. A few sailboats were visible, enjoying the last possible days on the water. More practical boats like water taxis and freighters glided by, as well. Once I tore my eyes away from the view, I noticed the other advantages of the space, including top-of-the-line appliances and hardwood floors. A quick trip to the 200-square-foot bathroom, complete with double sinks and a Jacuzzi tub, and I didn't know about Clifton, but I was sold. I glanced at my fake client and couldn't read any emotion except for thoughtful. I made a game show-hostess gesture toward one of the spectacular views.

He nodded and stepped toward the Hudson side. "What do you think?" he asked. A pang in my chest made me wonder if he could really afford a place like this, and for a moment I was worried for him. It was an odd impulse, and I shook it off.

"If you're looking for something modern, this could be a great space for you."

The manager mentioned that we weren't the first ones to see the place and how she was certain offers would start coming in by the afternoon. Her tone implied we were riff-raff and should look elsewhere. Clifton thanked her for her time and suggested we grab a cappuccino to discuss the pros and cons. The manager sniffed at the word "cons." I must admit, I didn't see any either and was curious about what my client might put on that side of the list besides the price tag.

Down the street, we stepped into a café and ordered frothy drinks and pastries, which Mr. Clifton carried to the table for us. I had never questioned a witness openly and couldn't help but be envious of detectives who could take their witnesses into a windowless room and badger them. I really wanted to badger someone. Instead, I slid the scones toward Mr. Clifton and put on my most professional smile.

"I don't want to come across as pushy, but that is a great space. Do you think you'd want to live there? Or at least invest?"

"It has potential, but I'm concerned about the timetable. I'd like to move in right away." Ah, yes. There was a reasonable con. I must have been blinded by the bathroom tiles. "Perhaps you could look into the construction company for me. I'd like an assessment of their quality before proceeding. If you think it's up to par, though, I could make an offer."

My first reaction was panic at the thought of navigating an actual sale, but I swallowed that thought, knowing I could hand off my responsibilities if we got that far along.

"Of course," I replied.

Mr. Clifton leaned back in the wrought-iron café chair and bit into a scone, which crumbled onto his shirt. He brushed the bits away while sizing me up. I waited for the verdict.

"Can I be frank with you, Ms. Seasons?"

"Of course."

"I like your pluck, but I get the sense that you don't have as much experience as you implied when we met. Am I right?"

I hesitated, but not for long, before nodding. "I've recently switched careers. Like you."

"As I suspected. What did you do before?"

He seemed genuinely interested, and I fought back an unfamiliar urge to confide in this stranger. But I knew that wouldn't be safe for anyone.

"I worked for an uptown department store."

"And were you good at sales?"

"I was, yes. I also aced my real estate courses at NYU, Mr. Clifton. I can handle this."

I wanted him to trust me as much as I wanted to get the conversation back on track.

"You were lucky to meet me at Hamilton's," I said as a makeshift closing.

"That much, at least, is true. Leah said she had never seen you there before."

I pictured the pretty bartender and wondered if she had really not recognized me when I was there the second time. As myself, I make a habit of blending into the background, but my real estate alter ego didn't mind the spotlight. Then again, Leah and I hadn't swapped more than a few polite words.

"That's the young lady who waited on us?" I asked.

"Yes. She was upset, naturally. I don't think she even recognized me when I tried to calm her down."

He shook his head, and it suddenly dawned on me that it was no coincidence that his actions thus far had reminded me of my father. It wasn't just the age or one-puff cigarette habit; there seemed to be something genuinely paternal about the man.

"She must have been scared. Like someone being killed in your own home," I said gently. "I've been trying to forget what you said about those two guys sneaking out the back. It really bothered me. New Yorkers are known for coming together after a crisis. It's almost a disgrace."

"Well, they clearly didn't know the unspoken dress code, so maybe they were out-of-towners. Does that help?"

"Mr. Clifton, I think you're teasing me."

"Maybe just a little. It's true, though, they could have been tourists. They were young, around your age, I imagine."

That description wasn't particularly helpful, but I figured mid-thirties was a decent bet. They could have been Leif and his buddy, but they also could have been, oh, about a million other guys. Would Ellis have mentioned if he had detained Leif the night of the murder? I wasn't sure. I was lost in thought for a moment, and Clifton finished his cappuccino in the ensuing silence.

"I'm afraid I need to get back to the office. Please let me know when you complete your research. By the end of the weekend, if you don't mind. The property manager expects offers this afternoon." He stood, brushing the rest of the scone onto the floor.

"Yes, of course," I said. He had just given our acquaintance an expiration date. Until Sunday, I might be able to squeeze him for a bit more information, if I was clever. Then I would need to pass him along to a real broker, perhaps feign a failure of confidence.

After he left, I sipped my own sugary beverage and considered my options. I wanted to talk to some of the waitstaff, the bartender for sure, but that would require going back to Hamilton's. Most of my wigs were destroyed, and I couldn't afford to buy new ones until I used Mrs. Kramer's check. Somehow I didn't think Hamilton would welcome a repeat performance of Kathy Seasons. I could always go as Katya, but I only used her for client meetings. It was a rule I liked to keep. Kate was a possibility, but the blond bob left my face fully exposed, and I might be identified by anyone looking with more than usual interest. After last night, I was willing to bet that someone had more than usual interest in me, and I didn't mean romantically. I never went out as myself because I felt too exposed. I had lived in fear of exposure for years, and now that I had let myself think about the Costas and the Magrellis, I couldn't seem to stop.

———

I followed Salvatore Magrelli into the hallway as one person, and I returned as another. To this day, I'm still not sure why he took me with him instead of one of his hangers-on, an assortment of scarred and tattooed men in their twenties. When surrounded by this crew, Salvatore looked even more suave than usual. It was as if he wore cologne that made others sense power, but my suspicion that he and his brother were big-timers was more than a hunch. I would later unearth enough information to put them both on trial, something the District Attorney's office doesn't make a habit of doing unless they can win. That afternoon at the Costas, though, I wasn't feeling very confident about anything.

I mostly looked at my purple sneakers as I left the bloody-nosed Nino and his sister Eva and followed Salvatore down the carpeted steps. They were stained with unidentifiable substances—a winning combination of vomit and who-knows-what—but I wanted those stairs to go on forever. I didn't care if they were steps to nowhere, I was ready to cash in and call it quits. Instead, I shoved myself into the bright afternoon. When my eyes adjusted to the August light, I saw a handful of kids playing in a fire hydrant, running through the jet again and again. They hushed up a bit as Salvatore and I passed, then the shrieks resumed. At that point Salvatore hadn't even turned to look at me, but when we got to the corner, he stopped, and I sidled up beside him.

"Zanna's got some mouth on her."

I swallowed and nodded toward my sneakers.

"She thinks you've got, what word did she use? *Talent*." He paused here to let me know that he didn't like the word. Or, he didn't like its application to me. I could feel sweat running down my neck into my T-shirt. He adjusted his shirt cuffs, looking cool despite the ninety-degree temperature. "I said to Zanna, I said, we'll see," he finished.

With that, he crossed the street, and I followed. When we reached the brownstone, he spoke to someone over the intercom before being buzzed in. The building was in a similar condition to the Costas' building. The stairs may have been linoleum, but they were still stained and cracked. We took them to the third floor, where a boy no more than eleven opened the front door. Inside, a busted and bleeding teenager around Nino's age sat on the couch with a bag of peas pressed to his eyes.

When he saw Salvatore, he jumped up and retreated to the far corner of the room. First, he faced the wall, whimpering, then he turned to shout at his younger brother in Spanish, asking him why he had let in *el diablo*. I froze on the threshold, suddenly sure why I had been brought. I knew even before Salvatore pressed the handle of his Glock into my hand. Even before he released the safety and smiled at me.

I shook myself back to the present. Why was I letting myself fall into these memories? I drank the last of my cappuccino and decided on my next move. I had a few open cases that I could work on, including bandmates Jimmy Cruz and Seraphina Capra, but they all posed problems of one sort or another and wouldn't be easy to wrap up quickly. Plus, even combined, they wouldn't be as lucrative as Mrs. Kramer's payment. My hankering was to get ahold of the Hamilton's surveillance tape, but the police probably had that in their evidence bin. My thoughts swung back to the weepy bartender. I couldn't solve all my problems, but I had a pretty good idea where I could find a suitable disguise. Well, I wasn't sure about suitable, but definitely a disguise.

CHAPTER SIX

B ig Mamma's Burlesque Revue happened nightly at
the Pink Parrot, a midtown bar and club. The show
started at ten on weeknights, midnight on weekends,
and managed to draw a crowd every single time. Since it was
2 P.M. on a Friday, there were only a few people sipping daiquiris, and I was pretty sure they all worked there. Jeans and
tight T-shirts didn't imply much, but two of the men had false
eyelashes, and one was painting his toenails. I didn't think
the management would let a regular patron get away with
spreading noxious fumes all over the place, so I let myself
jump to some conclusions.

Up until that moment of my life, I had avoided a run-in
with the notorious owner of this hot spot, and I was half-
curious, half-scared to meet her. Lacy "Mamma" Burstyn was
a two-hundred-pound African-American woman who wore
expensive, tailored suits and crocodile boots when she wasn't
in sequined cocktail dresses introducing her stars. Her skin
was dark with a hint of cherry, and when she shook my hand,
I winced. If she didn't seem like the kind of woman who would

own a dozen successful restaurants and bars, she did seem like the kind to spit in the face of the mafia and refuse to pay for protection. That was big news in the late nineties. I told her I was pleased to meet her and, mostly, I meant it.

She had emerged almost as soon as I entered the bar, and I wondered aloud if she could smell someone who wasn't looking for a good time.

"We have security cameras," she deadpanned, clearly not impressed by my flippant tone. "What can I do for you?"

Mamma was utterly no-nonsense, and I explained that I was investigating the Hamilton's murder and needed some assistance from Dolly.

"Are you with the police?"

"I'm helping them." And I had done that one little errand, so it didn't seem like much of a lie.

"I don't want Dolly mixed up in anything that might jeopardize his career." Mamma looked me up and down, trying to determine how much trouble I could cause.

"He won't be. I just need a quick favor."

Mamma continued to evaluate me, not missing a detail from my patent-leather pumps to my unkempt eyebrows. What I really wanted to know was if she could tell that my hair was fake, but I decided to use my one question more judiciously.

"Ms. Burstyn, what do you know about Colt Hamilton?"

Mamma's eyes didn't betray anything, but her voice was even colder when she answered.

"I thought you said you weren't going to get Dolly mixed up with anything. Colt Hamilton is bad news, and I don't mean late-night public access programming."

"Would you care to elaborate?"

"No, I would not." She gestured toward an empty seat at the bar, and the men there snapped their heads back to their previous positions, trying to look nonchalant. The scent of nail polish was replaced with the scent of nail polish remover, and I guessed that it was difficult to eavesdrop and stay between the lines simultaneously. I sat down and smiled at them, but was ignored like a piece of lettuce in a rival's smile. Mamma left, and they didn't pay any attention to me until Dolly sashayed in wearing a green silk kimono and, I was almost certain, nothing else. I had never seen him sans wig before, and his crew cut surprised me. His face was scrubbed clean, and he looked both younger and somehow prettier. When he stooped to kiss my cheek, the men at the bar might have sighed.

"Well, Mamma doesn't like you one bit."

"She should get in line."

"Hmph. I should tell her that; she'd get a kick out of it."

Dolly pulled me up off the bar stool and turned my head from side to side.

"South American? Greek?"

"Mutt."

Like other Americans, I could rattle off the nationalities of my ancestors, but that type of identity never appealed to me. Identity emerges in a series of false starts, not origins. Stutter steps, not purposeful strides. One minute you're an invisible teenager, the next you're hunted by guilt, then—in the case of a few questionable career moves—criminals. Dolly didn't seem to mind my sourpuss attitude, though.

A daiquiri appeared in front of him, and he twirled the green umbrella between his fingers. I thought the bartender probably picked that decoration on purpose to match the kimono. What I couldn't decide was if Dolly would throw a fit over a pink umbrella or never even notice.

"I hoped that when you visited me, it would be during a show. I'm great, you know."

"I've heard."

Dolly smiled a little and squinted his eyes at me. "So, what sort of spy shit can I help you with today?"

I explained that my apartment had been ransacked, and Dolly expressed appropriate outrage that my wigs had been destroyed. He understood much more than the cops just how much of an investment I had lost. He was also willing to help me create a disguise for the evening. I followed him to his dressing room, an opulent space complete with the requisite vanity mirror, a claw-footed tub, and a daybed covered in gauzy sheets and satin pillows. Signed photographs lined the walls from actors, singers, and at least one recognizable Congressman.

"Is that—"

"You bet your sweet ass, and if he doesn't vote for the marriage equality bill, his wife might get an anonymous phone call."

I slipped on some of Dolly's costume jewelry and fantasized about a career change. This looked like serious fun.

"Big Mamma doesn't like Colt Hamilton much," I said, and Dolly didn't seem to mind the non-sequitur.

"True enough, not even one tiny little bit. Did you know they opened their respective bars the same month of the same year? Mamma had to deal with bricks through her front windows, visits from the goon squad, a couple of so-called 'electrical' fires. And what does Hamilton have to deal with? A running tab for a couple of local bosses."

"So she resents him."

"You got that right, sweetness."

I mulled that over while Dolly examined me. The first makeover attempt involved a sea-foam green wig, a pink tutu, and platform heels and while I really wanted to keep it, the outfit screamed "please look at me, I'm fabulous" rather than "inconspicuous." It did suit the daiquiris that arrived, and

I happily slurped mine while Dolly applied makeup. First, he took tweezers to my eyebrows even though I protested. Tweezed eyebrows would mean no Keith for a few weeks; but when I saw the result, it was a compromise I was willing to make. Suddenly, I had cheekbones, and I wasn't clear on what alchemy had made that possible.

"This is beyond Kitty. I don't have a name for this getup," I said.

"Kiki, obviously."

"Obviously."

"You know, you could perform tonight, and I could go chat with this waitress."

"Mamma said 'no trouble,' and I don't want to get on her bad side."

Dolly flopped down on his daybed, and I averted my eyes as his kimono split to his upper thigh.

"Honey, she only *has* a bad side."

"You're telling me that you're not on her good side? With the money you bring in to the Pink Parrot?"

Dolly grinned and rolled his head around to look at me.

"She says I'm lazy. Can you believe that? I work four days a week. I could work three at Pete's Paradise."

"Pete's Paradise is a shithole."

"True enough."

Dolly slipped off the daybed and surveyed me again.

"It's a shame to waste this work, but if you want boring, I can do boring."

⟻⟶

Dolly and I had conflicting definitions of "boring," but if I wiped off the cherry-red lipstick and swapped the cherry-red stilettos for my black pumps, I could pass for your average hussy looking for a sugardaddy or at least a real good time. I gave my strapless dress a good yank upwards before opening the front door to Hamilton's and letting the customers get an eyeful.

Some of the murder mystique had worn off, but there was a sizable crowd of after-work drinkers settling in for their Friday night binges. A woman wearing a low-cut leopard-print blouse and tight black pants gave me a finger wave in solidarity. *God help me*, I thought, and waved back. I sat down at the other end of the bar, assuming that the woman's friendliness extended only so far, and ordered a gin and tonic. I wasn't quite sure what Kiki liked to drink, but they probably didn't serve it here. Jägerbombs, maybe.

My tuxedoed bartender asked for a gin brand, then returned quickly with my beverage and glass coaster. I guessed his age to be about twenty-five, and I would have bet my handbag that he was an actor. He was ten pounds too skinny, but that only made his striking bone structure more pronounced. Blond hair, big smile—he looked like trouble disguised as a Golden Retriever, and I almost told him so. Something about my getup made me feel like a genuine cougar, even though I probably only had a year or two on him. The bouncer hadn't even carded me at the front door, which was lucky because I hadn't rustled up a Kiki driver's license yet.

"You been working here long?" I asked, crossing my legs and then uncrossing them. It wasn't meant to be a Sharon Stone imitation; I couldn't figure out which position covered the most flesh. His eyes didn't flick down, and I had to hand it to Hamilton's—their staff was certainly professional.

"A year or so. I mostly work on the weekends."

"So you weren't here when that poor man was—" I lowered my voice—"shot?" I sipped my drink to show how utterly dis-interested I was.

"No, ma'am." The waiter crossed the length of the bar to help some new customers who had entered, and I checked out my surroundings. I should have expected Ellis to be there, but he still took me by surprise. I had seen him in a suit once before, at graduation, and he had looked uncomfortable then too. Nonetheless, his wealthy parents had dragged him to a fair number of high-society galas before he had rebelled at eighteen. I would bet those gold cufflinks I could see peeking out from his sleeves were both real and his own. He had his hands wrapped around what I assumed was seltzer. When he felt me scrutinizing him, he sent a steely look my way, and I raised my glass to him. He nodded curtly, no apparent recognition, and I gave myself a point. If my one-time best friend didn't know who I was, Colt Hamilton didn't stand a chance.

Feeling more relaxed if not downright cocky, I left my barstool to check out the crime scene. The staircase was longer than I remembered, and I had to take a left at the bottom to reach the men's room. Meaning, the door was obscured from vision, even if someone were standing at the top of the stairs, peering down. Past the bathrooms was a third door with a padlock. I strained my memory to recall if the lock had been there on Tuesday, but I couldn't drum up the image. The room or closet would make an ideal hiding place for a murderer. For a split second, I wondered if I could pick the lock before anyone came down the stairs, but that seemed unlikely. I had bobby pins by the dozen, but no genuine lock-picking accessories with me.

I glanced at the stairs one last time before ducking into the men's room. It was how I remembered it: two stalls, two urinals, a sink, and that awful bitter smell of men's rooms the world over. Actually, the bitter smell was new because it had been masked on my previous visit by blood and excrement. I knew that the police had combed the site thoroughly, so I'm not sure what I hoped to find. In retrospect, snooping probably wasn't the brightest idea, which I figured out pretty quickly when I heard footsteps approaching. I rushed into the nearest stall and locked the door behind me. I slammed down the lid of the toilet and crouched on top just before the door opened. I could hear a zipper and then the release of urine, and I fought down panic and embarrassment. The guy must have already had a few drinks, because the stream went on and on. I worried that he was going to piss so long that more men would walk in, and I had a vision of myself squatting on that toilet until kingdom come. Finally, the stream faltered, then ended, and I heard the zipper one more time. When the sink water began, I said a silent prayer of thanks, but it was premature. The door to my stall was kicked open, and I stifled a shriek as I stared at Ellis's standard issue 9mm.

His eyes were even steelier than they had been at the bar, unimpressed, I suppose, by my exposed cotton underwear. I stuck my hands in the air.

"Out here," Ellis said.

I lowered a hand to yank my dress back into position, then put it right back up and did as I was told.

"Ellis, it's me," I said, but he already had me facing the wall, where he efficiently patted me down for weapons. "You can take longer, if you want." It was the wrong time to joke, but I figured I had lost all my points for the night anyway. When Ellis confiscated the Smith & Wesson from my purse, my sense of humor evaporated. He grabbed my wallet and studied my I.D. It was still my Kate one from yesterday's Mrs. Kramer surveillance, and Ellis heaved a deep sigh.

"You can't be serious. What the fuck do you think you're doing?"

I lowered my hands and clasped them in front of me without saying anything. I figured that was a rhetorical question. A man tried to enter the bathroom, but Ellis pushed the door closed and flipped the lock.

"Just a minute," he said in a not-so-polite tone. When he wheeled back around to face me, I could see him studying my face for Kathleen. When he found her, I couldn't tell if his anger increased or decreased, but he lowered his voice.

"Again, I ask you, what are you doing in here?"

"I thought maybe I could find something. You know, a clue."

"And you don't think that the NYPD has thoroughly examined this room for, you know, clues?" He planted a hand on either side of my head and leaned in, trapping me against the wall. He smelled like aftershave and dry-cleaning, and I could almost forget that we were in a men's room. Almost. And I almost told him that I thought I'd missed something the night of the murder, but I didn't think he knew that I had followed Mr. Kramer into the bathroom. Instead I made a noncommittal noise, a cross between "Beats me" and "Uh-huh." He studied me for another minute, then stepped even closer, so that our bodies were pressed against each other. I closed my eyes, and he sighed, pushing himself off the wall.

"Well, did you learn anything?"

I opened my eyes and tried to put my jumbled thoughts together. It helped that Ellis took his aftershave with him over to the sinks.

"I learned you like to relieve yourself before apprehending criminals."

"Yeah, but I didn't really wash my hands."

There was a hint of a smile present on his face, but only a hint.

"Gross. Listen, I want to know if that padlock was on the other door Tuesday night."

"The storage closet? Yes, it was. And that's all I'm telling you."

He gestured for me to leave the restroom, and when I did, two men were waiting impatiently. When they saw me, some of their irritation vanished, and one even high-fived Ellis. We reached the top of the steps to find Hamilton waiting.

"Everything okay?" he asked Ellis, eyeing me with a look of total indifference.

"Everything's fine. The young woman was just being friendly."

Hamilton's eyebrows raised a fraction of an inch, but he didn't smile. He turned and stalked back toward his office. I had half a mind to follow him, and my body language must have given me away because Ellis squeezed my arm and led me back to my stool. The actor-bartender was ready with a fresh drink, and I grinned at him.

"Some people can't take a joke."

He laughed and leaned forward conspiratorially after Ellis returned to his own perch. I watched the leopard-clad woman's eyes flit toward him appreciatively, and I stifled an impulse to hiss. With some effort, I returned my attention to the bartender.

"You don't know the half of it," he said.

"Really?"

He glanced around to make sure no one was within hearing distance, then answered, "He was in here last night. I think he might be F.B.I. or something."

I made my eyes widen in surprise and leaned forward a bit, too, so that our faces were inches apart. I could see the fine lines around his eyes, and I was betting he could count my fake eyelashes one by one. Maybe this dress isn't so bad after all, I thought.

"Because of the murder?"

"Yep, because of the murder. He only talks to men, and I don't think he's cruising them. I think he's, what's it called, profiling."

He put emphasis on "profiling," and I nodded earnestly even though I didn't think "man" qualified as a profile.

"He ever talk to you?"

"Only to order seltzers," he replied.

An elegant gray-haired woman needed her cigar lit, so the bartender bounded off. I was ready to call the night a bust. There was no sign of the murder-night bartender. I put down cash and picked up my bag. The on-duty bartender hurried to finish his job and came back to my side of the bar.

"Leaving already?"

"I thought I might hit up some livelier spots."

"Yeah, this place is kind of dead, right? Oh, sorry. No pun intended."

I turned to go, then turned back and leaned as close to him as possible.

"F.B.I. agents don't always look like they're supposed to. If you think of anything, you give me a call." I slipped him one of my blank business cards—just my cell number—and winked at him. So impersonating a federal agent could lead to a little prison time; I was sufficiently vague.

When I stepped out into the night, my skin prickled, and I shivered in the cold. The temperature had dipped considerably since I'd finished playing dress-up at the Pink Parrot.

"I would offer you my jacket, but I'm still mad at you."

I turned to face Ellis with my hands on my hips to show how impervious to the temperature I was, how little I needed his help.

"I can't talk to you here. Meet me at the police van on 75th," he said and slipped back inside.

I headed in that direction, walking briskly with the optimistic mindset that exercise would warm me up. Hamilton's is in a popular part of town, and in my five-minute walk, I passed the Starbucks where I had watched the crime scene earlier in the week as well as a few sports bars and a pet store helpfully still open at 9 P.M. You never know when you'll need a giraffe chew toy, I guess. The scenery distracted me from the cold, but when I got to the mobile command center, chill-bumps returned to my considerable amount of exposed flesh. I knocked on the metal door, but no one answered. I could see my breath in the air, which made me colder, but there was not much I could do except hop from foot to foot. Well, I could have gone home, and the thought had entered my mind when Ellis walked up with two cups of hot deli coffee.

"One of those better be for me," I said.

"I'm not sure you deserve one."

He knocked on the side of the van with his foot, and the door swung open to admit him. When I commented that his officer had ignored my knock, he goaded me: "No unsupervised civilians allowed. You know how it goes. We follow the rules."

I climbed up after him and eyed the young cop intently. He wasn't the same one from yesterday, but he could have been a carbon copy. Baby-faced and rail-thin. The kind that makes mothers shake their heads and wonder why we start wars in foreign countries or on our own streets.

"Did Detective Dekker put you up to this? Letting a lady stand out there in the cold?"

"Yes, ma'am," he answered, blushing and looking at my legs.

"Eyes on the screen," Ellis barked. In the poor lad's defense, he could simply have been wondering how my legs got their bluish tint.

Ellis handed me the extra cup of coffee and asked me if I had found out anything.

"Like I'd really tell you now." I slid into the only empty seat and kicked off my shoes. It wasn't exactly cozy, but it was the most relaxed I had been in several hours. I could feel the daiquiri and g & t conversing in my stomach. They didn't seem to like each other very much. I rubbed my feet and considered if I had learned anything. I knew the probable hiding place of the killer.

And I thought I might be able to get a bit more information from the actor-bartender. I couldn't quite understand why his behavior had become more flirtatious after I returned from the bathroom, but maybe that little trip was the tipping point for my reputation.

"The waiter seems a little shady," I finally offered.

"He seems like a typical bartender to me. Too good-looking for his own good."

"Yeah, probably."

"If you thought he was so shady, why'd you give him your card?"

I put one foot down and started to rub the other one, buying some time. I didn't think impersonating a federal agent would go over well at the moment. "I thought you were supposed to be looking for bad guys."

"You've always seemed to attract them."

I flushed at that, thinking back on Ellis's disapproval of my past associations. Despite everything I had systematically forgotten about my pre-undercover life, those particular memories wouldn't go away. Ellis was softer at the time, hadn't discovered sarcasm or free weights. He had a youthful sort of intensity, though, an unshakable belief that he was right and I was wrong. Scratch that, an unshakable belief that he was right and everyone else was wrong.

"He might remember something. A co-worker acting differently. Piles of money stashed in a trashcan. A severed hand."

The young officer laughed a little, but I got no response from Ellis.

"I think his pretty little brain's doing enough work memorizing monologues."

I made a tsking sound. "Condescension doesn't suit you." The solicitous Ellis from my apartment yesterday had vanished and been replaced by Detective Dekker. I wasn't the only one with multiple personalities.

"Who does Mrs. Kramer suspect, Ellis? Who were her husband's enemies?"

Ellis looked at me, and I could tell he wanted to deliver his line about needing clearance. Instead, he chose his words carefully.

"More than one, that's for sure. He's a bigwig at J & J Financial, but his family has money, too. He inherited South African diamond mines about a year ago."

"Nasty business, but who else but Mrs. Kramer would benefit from his death?"

"Well, his brother now owns all the mines, no sharesies, but we talked to him. He seems clean. What's a few extra million to someone who already has a bundle?"

I didn't balk at "sharesies" only because my mind was elsewhere. I asked, "What's this talk about gang connections in the papers?"

"As far as we can tell, there's no gang connection. Colt Hamilton does some mob palm-greasing, but that's hardly unusual."

"Could he be the target, though, instead of Mr. Kramer? Are we overlooking something obvious?"

Ellis posing as Detective Dekker gave me the steely eyes again. "We, and please note that the pronoun does not include you, are not overlooking anything."

I decided we were finished for the evening and held out my palm expectantly. Ellis slapped it.

"I can show you my permit to carry tomorrow," I said.

"Laminated and everything?"

"Of course."

Only the über-wealthy or über-famous were allowed to carry concealed weapons in New York City. That wasn't the official policy, but Ellis and I weren't fresh off the turnip truck. He was well aware that my legal status was fishy, and a quick run through the system would be grounds for arrest.

"I'm not under arrest." The statement, meant to sound authoritative, came out as more of a question.

Ellis removed his cuffs from his back pocket, and I held up my hands in protest.

"I'm going. Jeez, how's a girl supposed to protect herself in this big, bad city?"

"You'll think of something."

I was fuming, but deep down I knew Ellis couldn't return my Smith & Wesson without facing some serious scrutiny and maybe formal reprimands. Ironically, I had purchased the gun from a confiscated weapons sale in New Hampshire. Despite the bargain basement price tag, I was still feeling pretty sorry for myself. That was another wasted $300.

I slipped out of the police van and headed toward the subway. I knew that it would be safer to sleep at my office, but I wanted to make sure that my apartment door had been replaced. And yes, okay, I wanted another real shower. I wasn't cut out for eighteen-hour days anymore.

CHAPTER SEVEN

Reinforced steel would have been preferable to makeshift plywood, but when I went to retrieve my key, Tambo assured me that something better would be installed soon. Tambo's memory was questionable at best, but I figured if I reminded him enough, I could have something new by, say, my funeral. I could only hope that my ransacking buddies would be satisfied with destroying the fake me's for a little while and would leave the real one alone.

I checked the hallway before inserting my key. With a sudden chill that had nothing to do with temperature, I determined that the door was already unlocked and slipped my hand in my bag to pull out my gun, which was no longer in residence. My heart rate sped up, and I counted to ten to calm my nerves. I stood with my back flat against the wall and opened the door with an outstretched hand. When no round of bullets met me, I crouched down and peeked into my home. Marco was sitting on my couch, unimpressed.

"Shit, Marco! You scared me."

I stood up and pulled my temporary door closed behind me. With my forehead pressed against the plywood, I let my heartbeat return to normal before flipping the lock and turning around.

Marco waited until I recovered to respond: "No, what's shit is that door. A toddler could put his foot through it."

"Good thing I'm not being chased by a herd of three-year-olds."

"Yet." He grinned at his own joke, then shrugged. "It was unlocked."

I rolled my eyes at him, which I thought was a pretty good mask for the butterflies that had replaced the sheer terror in my stomach. Marco wasn't dressed in the casual attire that I had seen earlier in the week (baggy jeans, sweat-stained wife-beater). He had on gray slacks and a black sweater that fit tight across his chest. He had always been in shape, but now he looked dangerous, and I couldn't think of a single reason why he would be in my apartment. Actually, I couldn't think of a single reason why he would know this *was* my apartment, and said as much.

"V. P. gave me the address. He keeps me informed and said something about a break-in."

I should have known that V. P. would use the GPS systems in his vehicles to track down his clients' home addresses. I always paid my bills on time, but others might need some coercion. That left the little matter of how he knew my apartment number, but he probably guessed that the only unlabeled unit on the intercom system would belong to someone paranoid. Rightfully paranoid, I should point out.

"This city is getting too small." My voice was in that unflattering high range bordering on squeak, but I was too tired to care.

"First, you didn't think twice about dropping in on me. And second, eight million people should be plenty. Even for you."

There was a hint of an accusation in Marco's voice, but we both knew that I had never cheated on him when we had been together. When I was imagining Marco as my personal reset button, I never imagined falling for him, but I guess you never know what new game you're going to get. Before Marco was embedded with Los Guardias, we had tried to find a way to make it work. We had spent countless nights imagining our future, and I'll admit I was seduced by the romance of it. Marco could sneak away from his new "friends," we suggested; I could call in sick to work, we continued. Of course, we were too smart to attempt the fantasies. Even undercover cops who only specialize in small-time dealers still have erratic schedules and difficult domestic lives, if any. When Marco said good-bye on the morning of his assignment, it was a forever good-bye.

"Apparently not," I finally answered to him and myself.

Marco was surveying my apartment, but not with the same cop-face that Ellis had worn. Marco's face was detached. He doesn't spook easy. *And why was I talking to Ellis and Marco on the same day? What was this, ghosts of Christmas past?* My feet hurt, and I had a headache from too much alcohol.

"They wreck your dolls?" Marco asked. His face was still calm, but there was laughter in his voice.

I weighed several not-so-nice names for Marco before just saying yes and sinking down onto the couch beside him. I kept a few inches between us, but it didn't make any difference. My body still reacted in the same old ways.

"I like this one," he said and pulled at a blond curl, then slid his hand up and down the nape of my neck.

"It belongs to a drag queen who would be very mad if I mussed it up, so keep your hands to yourself." I closed my eyes and enjoyed the silence for a minute before continuing. "The police say the murder wasn't gang-related."

"I told you as much. I'm the police too, remember?"

I remembered, even if Marco still seemed partly in character. Or maybe he had become more callused with Los Guardias. Either way, I hated to admit that being around Marco and Ellis reminded me of how much more important I used to be. It was a good time to change the subject.

"Your neighbor Miguel didn't seem to like me."

"He isn't fond of kids."

Marco went back to fiddling with my blond curls absent-mindedly. He had never been particularly chatty, and I couldn't force him to talk about why he was really in my apartment. I doubted that he had come to check on the status of my wigs, though. My only choice was to wait and hope I didn't fall asleep while he was deciding to speak.

I had no idea where Marco's family was from, or if any members were still living, but I was pretty sure he was passing for Dominican these days. He used to have brown curls that would stick to his forehead when he was sweaty. His hair was short now, and when he pushed up the sleeves on his sweater, he revealed new tattoos that must have cost a fortune based on their size and details. A faint yellow circle under his left eye implied a fistfight two or three weeks ago. All in all, he looked like someone your mother would tell you to stay far, far away from.

"I might be coming up for air soon," he said.

That was definitely not what I was expecting him to say, and I opened my eyes, waiting for him to continue. Marco and I were anomalies in that we had chosen to run with the same crowd for long periods of time. Most undercover cops do buy-and-busts, important, but never getting to the root of the problem. We aimed for big fish, which meant no backup and no mistakes. One shot at most. I hoped this conversation meant that Marco was getting his shot, not that he was worried about being discovered.

"There's going to be a sting, and I'm going to disappear for a few months. I thought you might like to disappear with me."

I attempted a self-possessed response, but what finally came out in a sort of hushed whisper was "Holy shit."

"No, not holy shit."

Marco moved closer to me on the couch until my bare leg was touching his pants. He looked torn between caressing my thigh or the top of my breasts, but finally ran a finger along my temple. I could feel his breath on my neck as he watched my mind reel. Anyone else would have said something, "I've missed you" or "I want you," but Marco was finished talking.

I thought about how much I had ached when Marco disappeared. There was heartbreak, yes, and it was combined with a mess of other things. I realized that after my parents' deaths my senior year at John Jay, the undercover gig had been a kind of sedative. Without work and without Marco, I had to face the reality of being an orphan. I also knew that I had to reinvent myself in order to sleep at night without fear of being found. All of which is to say that I spent a lot of mornings thinking "what if Marco came back" before hauling myself out of bed. Then, day by day, it got a little easier. I was able to put a framed picture of Mom and Dad on my work desk without tearing up. I was able to laugh at my clients' hysterics. I was able to pay my rent and sometimes even forget that a few cruel people would like to see me dead. It wasn't an enviable life, but it was mine.

On good days, I can admit that I'd been lucky to get out of my assignment as early as I did. Undercover cops aren't exactly lifers, but short supply means reassignments are hard to come by. At any given time, there are only around a hundred officers working in organized-crime investigations. They're each given a detective's badge within eighteen months of accepting an assignment, but the promise of a quick transfer to a lower-risk position can be, well, let's call it negotiable. All cops face risks in the line of duty, but none so much as those living amongst the criminals. The year I graduated from John Jay, two of NYPD's finest were killed trying to buy illegal guns in Staten Island. It should have been a wake-up call, a reminder that I might be better off taking the detective's exam, but nothing could stir me from my slumber. Unaided by prescription drugs, my body had self-medicated, shut down essentially. The thought of death didn't make me shiver then. It does now, which should be a positive sign, but I'm ambivalent.

"Let me think about it," I finally responded, which sounded trite even to my ears. Marco's face got a little harder, and I resisted an impulse to explain how it had taken me too long to get over him. Instead, I met his gaze unflinchingly, and when he leaned even closer, I let him. He kissed me softly at first, then harder until he slipped his tongue in my mouth, and I reciprocated. It was only when he slid his hand under my dress that I reached down and stopped him.

"Who have you been seeing on the other side?" I asked.

He stood up and smoothed down his sweater without looking at me. He walked over to my closet and opened it, taking in the slashed costumes. I wasn't sure what the mutilated mannequin heads looked like to him, if they were as grotesque as they seemed to me. I would never know, either, because that was when he left.

The rest of the evening was spent sorting my stuff into two piles: salvageable and unsalvageable.

"We need a new office," Meeza said. "Something flashier, more spy-like."

"I'm not a spy" was my pithy response.

ERICA WRIGHT

I had officially hired her as my assistant, offering a commission on cases rather than an hourly wage, which I knew
would be too hard to guarantee. She seemed grateful for any
work more stimulating than staring at the clock all day and had
resigned from her secretarial duties. "It's a drag" was Meeza's
closing argument, and anyway I needed the help. I wanted
desperately to cash Mrs. Kramer's check, but I wasn't willing to
traffic in that kind of guilt. A little sexual perversion seemed
like nothing compared to turning my eyes away from a murderer. Meeza could help me with my open cases while I did a
little pro bono work to save myself from eternal damnation.

"But probably she didn't kill her husband, right?" Meeza
asked.

"I didn't think so at first, but she sure stands to gain a lot of
money from his death."

"Yeah, and she's got that PYT hanging around."

I thought about Leif's life of leisure and felt a pang of jealousy. "He probably wouldn't mind the money either."

I handed over a long-neglected case to Meeza, and she
flipped through the thin file. I had told Steve Stevenson multiple times that his wife wasn't having an affair, but he couldn't
seem to believe that anyone would be faithful to him. What
made the whole situation stranger was that Mr. Stevenson was
a catch, at least on paper. He was a veterinarian with a thriving
practice. He had health insurance and a way with animals that
would melt a lot of hearts. I had met him at his office, where
he was finishing up after everyone else had gone home. He was
maybe a little pudgy around the middle and was maybe going
a little bald, but he was decent-looking, especially when he tenderly checked the bandages of a hospitalized kitten. The only
thing that made him unattractive was his intense paranoia that
his wife was sleeping with someone else even after I followed
her around for weeks, chatted up her friends, and (in an act

of desperation that I am sorry for) planted a bug in her purse. No luck. She was squeaky clean, and I told Meeza as much.

The case seemed like a safe way to get Meeza started. I didn't want to take any more of Mr. Stevenson's money, but he insisted on keeping the case open. I was a bit afraid that he wanted lifelong surveillance of his wife, but a few more weeks wouldn't kill us.

"I ran Mrs. Kramer's cell phone and got a list of calls she's made in the past month," Meeza said, looking up from a wedding photo of the Stevensons.

"You can do that?"

"Sure. Can't you?" I could, but it had taken me weeks of trial and error and calling in favors. I had a system that worked most of the time now, but I was still amazed at Meeza's efficiency.

"Any names we recognize?" I asked.

Meeza pulled out some stapled papers and handed them to me.

"Well, you're at the top of the list as Katya Lincoln. And there are lots of calls to her husband. A few to the boy toy, Leif Nichols."

"How many to Leif after her husband's death?"

"One. On the day we saw him visit her place. Well, we think it was him at least. Is that suspicious? The call, I mean?"

"I don't know."

Meeza gave me a look that clearly said I wasn't trying hard enough. She was probably right. To be honest, though, I was a bit over my head. Undercover work doesn't involve a lot of detecting. No clues required, just open ears.

"Okay, okay. Let's think about what behavior qualifies as suspicious. Your husband is murdered, and not only are you not broken up about it, but you also aren't very scared. Now, why wouldn't you be scared that the murderer was after you?"

"Because *you* killed him or hired someone to do it."

"That's one possibility. What else?"

Meeza furrowed her brow as she speculated. "Because your husband protected you, didn't tell you everything he was involved in."

"Excellent. Now, let's say that in order to protect her from something, you act sort of suspicious. Coming home later than usual. Answering calls at odd hours."

"Avoiding questions."

"Exactly. Can you get me Mr. Kramer's phone records for the past month too?"

"Sure, but it will take me a little while. Can you wait fifteen minutes?"

Only Meeza's earnest expression kept me from laughing at her. "Yes, Meeza. I think I can wait that long."

Meeza picked up her phone and started speaking in rapid-fire Gujarati. When she laughed, I assumed the conversation was going well. After a few minutes, she hung up and grinned.

"Nothing to it."

"That seemed friendly."

"Yeah, I liked that one, but he turned out to be gay."

Before I could ask any follow-up questions, the fax machine whirred to life and three sheets of telephone numbers and names shot out.

"Impressive," I said.

Meeza glowed and slung her purse over her shoulder. "I'm going to go spy on the squeaky-clean lady. Do you think I need a disguise?"

I tried unsuccessfully to picture Meeza in one of my spare wigs. I decided her eyelashes would be a dead giveaway from every angle; it would be like trying to hide a cocker spaniel.

"Naw, you'll be okay," I replied.

I waved Meeza out the door and took the substantial list back to my office. Nothing jumped out at me, so I started at the top and Googled names. Most of the people were easy to check out: business associates, family members, dry cleaners. If I scratched all of those, I was left with three people whom Mr. Kramer had called more than once in the past month: Marvin Creeley, Bridget Barnaby, and Samantha Evans. I ran the names through my usual databases and didn't come up with anything too suspicious. Creeley had been arrested once about forty years ago for a public disturbance. It seemed to be connected to an anti-government protest during the Vietnam War. Barnaby was three times divorced and had an address in East Hampton. I suspected it was an upscale neighborhood that wouldn't take kindly to nosy P.I.s, but we would see. A search on Evans yielded an address and nothing else. The two women lived within thirty minutes of each other out on Long Island, and Marvin had a New York City address. That made him the temporary apple of my eye.

Persona Kate would have to do, and I unlocked my storage closet to retrieve the ash-blond wig and cardigan. I tugged my sneakers off and replaced them with ballet flats. I didn't have a plan exactly, but I figured questioning him directly wasn't an option. That left his place of business, a midtown hedge fund, open around the clock. Great, if there was anything I understood less than real estate, it was the exact nature of hedge funds. I wondered if throwing around terms like "selling high" and "bull market" would make me sound knowledge-able or insane. Either way, I made a three o'clock appointment, deciding to wing it as a representative from a small liberal arts college. I did not think that I could pass as "moneyed" myself, but "spends other people's moneys" seemed manageable. If Marvin doubted my sincerity, he didn't show it.

"May I offer you a coffee? Tea? Miss—"

"Miss Manning," I said, handing over my one and only Kate Manning, Alumni and Development card. I had invented the college's name, Rosebriar, and hoped no one ran a search before I exited the building. "And no, thank you." I didn't need to prolong my uninformed chat, since the only reason I wanted access to the offices was to get a glimpse at his appointment calendar. This item was in the possession of a ferocious-looking young man who sat at a desk directly in front of Marvin Creeley's office. By ferocious-looking, I mean that both his shirt and hair seemed starched into place. He wore a charcoal suit, complete with gold lapel pin that screamed "I make more money answering phones than you do doing, well, whatever it is you do."

My back was to the door, but I could picture this man nonetheless, guarding his computer like a well-dressed Cerebus guarding the entrance to the Underworld. I've never really understood why Hell's door needs to be watched, as if people are eager to slip into the world's longest-lasting rave, complete with rattling chains and fire pokers. To each his own, though, and I would wrestle that three-headed metrosexual if I had to. Just call me Hercules.

"Miss Manning?"

"Hmm?" I realized that I had been staring unresponsively out of Marvin Creeley's rather impressive windows for far too long. "Oh my, I am sorry. This city always overwhelms me. I mean, look at that building. It must be a hundred stories tall!"

"Oh, taller than that, Miss Manning. You've been to the city before, then?"

"Yes, a few times. The board isn't too pleased with our current financial situation, so I am, what's the term? Exploring my options."

Marvin looked undecided about that declaration, not quite certain whether Rosebriar College was an account worth his time. He was ever-polite, though, and handed me a stack of pamphlets and brochures that showed smiling, well-suited men and women shaking hands. Beats me what deals they were arranging, but they seemed mighty pleased with themselves. I slipped the glossy papers into my bag, thanking the man for his time and letting myself out. I made sure to close the door behind me as I surveyed my twelfth labor. Cerebus glanced up to give me a tight-lipped smile, then went back to licking his claws, I mean, typing.

"Excuse me, I'm so sorry to bother you," I began. The man lifted his head and raised his eyebrows. It was clearly the only response I could hope for, so I plowed on. "Marvin mentioned that I might be able to get a water on the way out. I wouldn't dream of bothering you, but I'm so parched from my flight." I shifted my bag to my other shoulder and stood in suspense.

There was a fifty-fifty chance that the man would send me on my own to the break room, but pandering to the boss won out over sheer exasperation, and he marched off into the distance. I slid into his still-warm seat and, after a few clicks, managed to locate the calendar. I flipped back to the week prior and scanned a jumbled list of names and notes that began at 7 A.M. and ended at 10 P.M. Whatever they did at hedge funds, it didn't seem worth that kind of schedule. I read as quickly as possible, looking for who-knows-what, but the only anomaly was a weekend away marked "Upstate. No calls." There were two appointments without names, one the Monday prior and one Tuesday. I had just double-clicked on the first one when the assistant returned, and I nearly jumped out of my skin.

"Excuse me, what exactly are you doing?"

He looked liked he might be ready to throw the water bottle at my head, and I instinctively slid backward. Unfortunately, I slid backward right into the wall connected to Marvin's office. It was too much to hope that he had missed the commotion.

"Sebastian, is everything all right?"

Sebastian and Marvin, it was a match made in heaven (or hell), and I wished that I had time to imagine the various shenanigans they could get into with commodities and tax shelters.

"Nothing," I said innocently. "I just wanted to sit down for a minute." I stood up huffily and grabbed the water before anyone could protest. I marched myself to the elevator bank and jabbed the button a few times. I could feel the two men staring at me, but neither said anything else. And when the doors pinged open, I could hear them discussing Marvin's next appointment. It was as if I had never been there.

CHAPTER EIGHT

I returned to the office, where Meeza was tapping her nails on the desk.

"Finally," she said by way of greeting.

"What's up?"

"What's up," she repeated and giggled. "Now *there* are some appropriate words. It turns out Mr. Paranoid Vet is paranoid because he's getting it up without Mrs. Paranoid Vet."

My jaw may have dropped; I had completely misread Steve Stevenson. After he was so sweet with that kitten, I put my blinders on. "That was fast, Meeza. Nice work."

"Well, I went to chat with Mr. Stevenson, tell him that I was taking over the case blah, blah, blah." Meeza waved her hand to emphasize her boredom with her own story. "When I get to the office, there's no one at the front desk. And do you know why there's no one at the front desk?"

I was pretty sure I did.

"You got it. The receptionist was helping Mr. Stevenson with a procedure." She put enough emphasis on "procedure" for me to know she wasn't talking about surgery.

"Now I get to help you with the big-time murder case, yes?"

Meeza handed me some photographs of a naked Steve Stevenson, and I clamped my eyes shut. It wasn't a professional response, but he was a man who looked better with his clothes on. He had also looked better when I thought he was one of the good guys.

"Send these to Mr. Stevenson and tell him his case is closed. Emphasize 'closed,' and bill him for this week."

Meeza nodded her head. "What a weasel," she said and looked at me expectantly.

"Yes, you can help. We're going to check out the others from Mr. Kramer's phone bill this afternoon." After Creeley, I was through with hemming and hawing. It was time to interrogate, a.k.a. badger, which I was going to deem "legalish."

I texted V. P. that I needed a ride A.S.A.P.

"Got it" was all I received in response, and I expected a two-hour wait. Instead, fifteen minutes later, I had an address a few blocks from the office. Meeza was still looking at me as if I might change my mind.

"Let's roll," I said, and she clapped her hands.

At Broadway, I could see my ride, and my heart gave a little flutter. It wasn't the Sentra, but my favorite: a Harley 250cc Cruiser. There was no way that V. P. had obtained this hunk of steel legally, and there was no way in which I gave two shits. This bike made me feel like a bona fide superhero. You didn't even have to try to go fast; you just thought "faster," and she accelerated. And then there were turns. On turns, you could be six inches from pavement and still know everything was going to turn out okay. I tried to stroll casually over to the bike since I was exponentially cooler now, but I couldn't resist turning to grin at Meeza.

She was stopped half a block away, arms crossed in front of her, shaking her head.

"No way, nohow am I climbing onto that death trap," she shouted.

She couldn't be talking about my baby, could she? I looked around, panicked, hoping to see a more dangerous-looking car, like a Miata. I've never trusted Miatas. Lined up by the curb was a series of sedans and SUVs.

"The Escalade?" I ventured.

Meeza snorted.

"That's not nice," I said, frowning.

"Not nice? It's not nice of you to try and kill me in the line of duty. *Sar Salamat, to Pagdi hazaar.*"

"What does that mean?"

"It means I'm not getting on that bike."

A few people turned to look at the beautiful woman shouting across the sidewalk. It might seem to the casual observer that we were having a lover's spat. I had a feeling that Meeza usually won those arguments, too. I could have just told Meeza to stay at the office, but that seemed petty. Besides, I was looking forward to having company on a ride outside of the city. I wasn't ready to cave yet, though. I blew out an exaggerated sigh of despair and began to plea-bargain. I offered additional commission, my favorite pair of heels, tickets to the show of her choice, and a home-cooked meal (though who knows what I would have made), to no avail. Finally, I texted V. P.: "Problem."

I wouldn't want to be listed as a reference for V. P., but anonymously I would recommend him to anyone. He called within thirty seconds, and I explained the situation. I expected him to complain, but he was understanding.

"Now, there is a sensible woman."

For most customers, the bike was the last choice. It left you exposed to everything from sun to gunfire. The only thing the bike was really good for was making a fast getaway, and V. P. didn't take kindly to people stealing from him. V. P. charged me extra for the bike because I liked it so much. It wasn't fair, but I understood the dynamics of supply and demand.

V. P. said that he would swap the bike for a car, but that I had to come to him. He gave me the address, and Meeza said that she would meet me there. I watched her hail a cab as I kick-started my ride and tried not to have an orgasm in the middle of the street. The ride to the address V. P. provided was an hour too short for my taste. I arrived in about twenty minutes and idled outside a chain-link fence. It looked like it might house a few criminals and Rottweilers. Glass bottles were duct-taped to the top to deter visitors, and a few were broken in the gravel for good measure. It didn't seem like the best idea to drive cars in and out over glass, but I wasn't the expert. A man dressed in torn jeans, a leather jacket, and dark sunglasses approached the entrance and unlocked it. He waved me in just as a yellow taxicab slid into view, and Meeza hopped out. I could see the guy reach for his gun, and I cut the engine as quickly as possible.

"She's with me," I shouted, losing all pretense of looking cool. I flapped my arms in my best mother-hen impression to get his attention and convey "harmless." He said something into his walkie-talkie, then put his gun away. Meeza was busy paying her driver and didn't notice anything out of the usual. When she saw the guard, she gave him a smile and a little wave. I held my breath, but the guard looked downright bashful. He ran his hand through his hair and nodded us through. We walked past him and were greeted by about a dozen cars in various states of disrepair. There was my nondescript Sentra, a few Lincoln Town Cars, a couple of makes I didn't recognize, and a Porsche 911 with the paint stripped. A plywood building sat at the edge of the lot with "Office" spray-painted on the side. I figured that was our destination.

I knocked on the door and then entered without waiting for a reply. V. P. sat behind a desk with his Caterpillar boots propped up. I had only met him a couple of times, but he was memorable. I would guess his age around thirty, but it was hard to tell. He had dark, smooth skin and a lop-sided grin that seemed innocent. I imagined it helped keep him out of jail from time to time, though I was sure he had spent his fair share of days behind bars. He had an ugly tattoo on his forearm that I could never decipher. It looked like a fish with a woman's face, but it could also have been a boat or a refrigerator.

"Ah, you must be Miss Meeza," V. P. said, ignoring me completely and fixating on my assistant, who was standing with her back against the door.

"Meeza, this is V. P.," I said, gesturing toward him. He rose to his feet and walked around his desk. He kissed Meeza's hand, and I threw up a little in my mouth.

"Vincent Patel," he said, and Meeza giggled.

I turned to make sure this was the same woman who had once smacked a man with a stapler when he wouldn't leave her desk. She looked the same, although there might have been a little pink on her temples. Feverish, I concluded, that was the only explanation.

"You own all this?" she asked.

All this? Good grief, I thought. *What is the world coming to?*

V. P. had jumped at this introduction and was filling Meeza's head with information about his growing business and future prospects.

"Would you like to see my inventory?"

"You mean cars, right?" I asked, which prompted V. P. to glare at me. He didn't slow down, though, and Meeza and I followed him out of the office toward the lot. My precious 250cc was already parked, and now I only hoped for something with both fenders. V. P. walked briskly past the assembled pack, though, toward a second gated fence. When he unlocked a padlock and led us toward a garage, I knew that I had been bamboozled.

"Hey, what is this?" I asked.

"This is for our VIP clients; you have been upgraded."

V. P. used a remote to open the doors, revealing four mint-condition luxury cars: a Porsche 911 Turbo (paint still on); a BMW X5; a Jaguar XF; and a Lexus LS.

"We'll take the Lexus," Meeza said without hesitation.

"You're my kind of woman," V. P. replied, which garnered more giggles in response.

———

Ten minutes later and I was behind the wheel of the most luxurious car I had ever driven: leather interior, seat heaters, GPS, satellite radio. The dashboard looked like a spaceship, and I accidentally turned on everything from the help hotline to the windshield wipers. The experience put me in a good mood despite worrying that Meeza's mother might kill me when she found out that her only daughter had a date with a glorified car thief.

"He is an entrepreneur," was Meeza's defensive response. I rolled my eyes at her, and she stuck her tongue out at me. "Well, at least he's not a taxidermist. Seriously, would you let someone who's had his hands in raccoon guts put his hands on you? I don't think so. And Vincent's Indian. What can my mother say? All I ever hear is 'Meeza, why can't you find a nice Indian boy and settle down?'"

"I think you missed the 'nice' qualification. Plus, you didn't give that taxidermist a shot. Maybe he only does trout."

Meeza stuck her tongue out at me again and turned up the radio. Arcade Fire was wailing about the suburbs as we drove toward the suburbs. It was really too bad that we were investigating a murder instead of cruising to Atlantic City. Meeza seemed like the lucky type, and I could have napped in the sand for an hour. But, hey, there were beaches in the Hamptons, too. Maybe we could steal a few minutes for non-investigatory activities. It was the last optimistic thought I had all day.

⟼

To say that I knew Bridget Barnaby was going to be belligerent as soon as I pulled up to her security gate would imply a psychic ability that I do not possess. So I'll only claim a gut feeling that the interview was not going to go well as soon as the cussing over the intercom started. I was impressed, however, by how crystal-clear the words were. This was no McDonald's drive-thru.

"I want all of you fucking dumbasses to leave me the fuck alone."

Meeza clucked disapprovingly from the seat beside me. "Such language."

As politely as I could, I explained who I was. Maybe I fudged the truth again a little, but I was working with the police tangentially. And Meeza didn't cluck, so I figured my little fib couldn't be all that bad on the morality scale.

After a bit more creative cussing, the gate purred open, and I swung the Lexus around the marble fountain and parked in front of the entrance. I half-expected valet men to scoot out, but no one appeared, so I assumed they were on their lunch break. Meeza and I rang the doorbell, then let ourselves in.

Themes are usually reserved for restaurants, bachelorette parties, and amusement parks, but Ms. Barnaby's house deserved a catchy name like Oceans Away or Sea Sick. The walls were painted with underwater panoramas, complete with whales, starfishes, and dolphins. Mermaids lounged on sandbanks with their nipples covered by snails. The snails had red puffed-up lips, and the whole effect made me shudder. The undulating lights didn't help, and I wouldn't recommend the place to an epileptic. I looked away from the walls to take in the fountain on the staircase landing. It featured a merman blowing into a conch shell, leaving his considerable natural parts open to the breeze. A steady flow of water poured through the shell and made me have to pee.

Ms. Barnaby's heels announced her welcome. She came into view wearing a red bikini with a transparent red sarong wrapped around the bottom half. Her tan could only be described as crispy, and I was pretty sure we had interrupted her work toward extra crispy. The overall effect was grotesque, but she smelled like fresh pineapple, and I considered conducting our interview with my eyes closed. I held out my hand, but she brushed it away.

"Five minutes. I spent all fucking yesterday talking to you pigs."

Up close, I could see that the sequins on her bikini top spelled "Hot Stuff." I was wondering if she had made Mr. Kramer's bed a little bit hotter before his untimely end.

"We're sorry about that, Ms. Barnaby," Meeza said.

Ms. Barnaby lowered her big sunglasses to get a better look at my assistant. She frowned and slid the sunglasses back on. Despite the dancing lights, it still had to be pretty dark behind those lenses. I couldn't decide if she was hiding eyes bloodshot from tears or booze.

"You don't look like a cop," she said to Meeza. "You, maybe," she said to me, and I flinched. Those were words I had lived in fear of hearing for two whole years. I was still wearing my Kate wig, but had added a baseball cap. I blamed the Red Sox logo and tried not to get sidetracked.

"We'd like to know about your relationship with Stephen Kramer," I said.

"There was no fucking relationship to speak of."

"Then why did he call you six times this month?"

Her eyes were invisible behind the shades, which made it more difficult to read her reactions. She was quick to respond, I gave her that much.

"I was helping him plan a surprise party for his wife."

It was a decent story, if it checked out. The answer sounded rehearsed, but she had probably answered these exact questions before. I could overlook a little rehearsal.

"How nice," I replied after a pause. "Where's it being held?"

"The Great Oaks Country Club. It's around the corner from their beach home. Or *her* fucking beach home now, I should say."

It's not that difficult to prove that someone is having an affair in the present. Sometimes it takes a little patience, but eventually the cheating spouse leads you to the lover. I had never tried to prove that someone had been having an affair in the past and, more importantly, didn't know where to start. If the Great Oaks Country Club really was booked, I would feel a lot better about Ms. Barnaby and her social planning skills. I would also be nearly convinced that Kramer hadn't been guilty of an affair.

I asked her where she had been the night of the murder, and she flipped me off.

"You can let yourselves out," she said and left us standing in the foyer. I accidentally looked at the mermaids' snail pasties and shuddered again.

"Bridget Barnaby should be called by a different 'b' name," Meeza said as we got back into the Lexus. Then she appeared to forget all about the unpleasant interview and changed the subject. "This car is like a zen garden. The temperature control makes me feel at peace."

"But on the bike, you feel like you could kick in some heads. You feel alive."

"Until you crash and feel really, really dead."

I mulled that over as I punched Samantha Evans's address into our GPS system. We drove from a rich-and-famous neighborhood to a comfortable one and pulled up in front of a white colonial. The shutters were painted a cheerful yellow, and all was quiet on the street. On another day I might have thought things were looking up, but I didn't trust that day one bit.

"Maybe I'll stay in the car on this one," Meeza said, adjusting the temperature control from seventy-five to seventy-four. She seemed to be humming with contentment, and I thought that perhaps she could achieve a state of enlightenment in the car. I wasn't sure if that would help us or not, but I left her and headed toward the house.

No one answered the bell, and the door was locked when I tried the handle. I peered into the window and saw a television screen displaying an infomercial for knives that could cut through pennies. I knocked in case the bell was broken, but no one came to the door. Around the back, the house had a small deck with a smoking grill. No one was around, but there was a plate of raw hamburgers on the railing alongside ketchup and a pitcher of lemonade. The scene had all the makings of a last-of-the-season barbecue. I knocked on the back door, then tried the handle. The door swung open, and I called out "hello," expecting to see someone washing lettuce or stacking plates. The kitchen was empty, though, so I crept toward the living room where the television screen now showed someone cutting tomatoes into roses.

When I walked around the couch, I froze. A woman was slumped forward, a line of blood dripping from her forehead onto the beige carpet, where it turned instantly brown. I backed up against the wall and forced myself not to scream or make any sudden movements. It was obvious that the woman had only just been killed, and there was a possibility that her attacker was lurking nearby or had already spotted me. I reached into my bag for my Smith & Wesson and came up empty-handed.

CHAPTER NINE

I didn't have time to curse Ellis for confiscating my firearm, so as quietly as possible I retraced my steps back through the kitchen and sprinted back around the house to the Lexus. I ripped open the door and flung myself inside.

The car accelerated even better than the motorcycle, but I didn't enjoy it. Meeza was gripping the armrest tight enough to leave crescent-moon imprints with her fingernails. I drove a few blocks away and parked on the busiest street I could find. There were a few kids playing basketball, and a man watering his yard looked up and waved at us. Meeza unhooked her nails from the leather and waved back, polite even in a crisis. She should add that to her resume. I choked out the basics to her, then dialed 9-1-1 and reported the murder. I called Ellis, too, who arrived as I was giving my statement.

When he approached the officers huddled around me, my stomach began to churn with some emotional cocktail that didn't have an exact name, so I decided to ignore it. I had taken the Kate wig off in the car and was feeling exposed. It took an effort to uncross my arms and shove my hands into the back pockets of my jeans to look less vulnerable.

Ellis nodded at me, then talked privately with a couple of the milling officers. They probably weren't happy about having a big-city cop on their turf, but the catchword was "cooperation." They all shook hands in a show of camaraderie, and Ellis circled back to where I was standing. He stared down at me for a few beats without blinking, mumbled something about "interfering with an investigation," and then crossed his arms in front of his chest. "Ha," I thought, but it wasn't much of a victory. Ellis didn't look vulnerable so much as held-back. It seemed as if he wanted to yell at me, but was resisting out of a sense of decorum or shared history. I appreciated the effort, but the silence bothered me. I broke it by asking him when he had spoken to Samantha Evans.

"We interviewed her yesterday. She said she was friendly with Kramer, but was vague about where they had met. Said they went way back, but there is a good twenty-year age difference. They weren't grade school buddies."

"Did Mrs. Kramer mention her at all?"

There was a loaded pause before he answered. "I know we asked for your help with the boy, but it would be better for all parties if you stayed out of this."

"I'm freelancing. It's allowed."

Ellis hesitated for a second, deciding whether to share information, I assumed. That seemed to be the game we were playing these days. When he responded, I hoped it was because he thought I might be useful, but it could have just been because he hoped I would go away.

"No, she didn't mention Samantha Evans."

"What about Bridget Barnaby?"

Ellis closed his eyes and for a brief moment looked amused.

"What did you like best, the pissing statue or the topless mermaids?" he asked.

I said I was partial to Ms. "Hot Stuff" Barnaby herself.

Ellis uncrossed his arms, and the chaos in my stomach eased. "No, Mrs. Kramer didn't say anything about the sea lady, but her story checked out. There's a room reserved at the country club, and Mrs. Kramer and Ms. Barnaby play tennis together sometimes."

"She leaves her pool?"

"Hey, if she plays in one of those little dresses, she can still work on her tan."

Ellis was as loose as he was going to get around me. I wanted a list of Mrs. Kramer's suspects, but decided to start with the big money request first in case a negotiation followed. I didn't know anything about hedge funds, but gambling, I could fake. Start high, go low.

"I'd really like to take a look at the Hamilton's surveillance footage. Do you think you could make that happen?"

Something complicated flitted into Ellis's blue eyes. His response wasn't at all what I expected. "What surveillance?" he asked.

He glanced around to see if anyone was listening to us, and I glanced around too, out of habit.

"Hamilton mentioned the surveillance tapes when I sort of ran into him at the bar," I said.

"When was this?"

"Wednesday."

Ellis walked back to his car abruptly. I started to follow, but he held up his hand to stop me. He barked some orders into the CB radio, then returned to where I was standing. He leaned close, and his breath warmed my ear.

"How'd you like to watch me question Colt Hamilton about some missing surveillance tapes?"

My stomach began to churn again, and I didn't bother to analyze my emotions beyond "excited."

Meeza was more than happy to return the rental car to V. P., so I climbed into Ellis's cruiser. It was an hour drive back to the city where his precinct was holding Hamilton. I had a feeling that the entrepreneur wouldn't much like having to wait, but I couldn't say that I cared. There was a time when the lack of conversation between Ellis and me would have gone unnoticed, but we hadn't spent any considerable time together since we were officially hired by the NYPD. Training lasted for a few months, then I disappeared into the bowels of the city. I bore witness to cancered intestines moving money, guns, and drugs unbeknownst or unacknowledged by the visible parts of the city's body. My outlook on life changed as easily as my accent, and I was still trying to shake off the melancholy that had settled in as soon as I turned in my badge. When I filed reports on drug lords or, more often, underlords and underlings, I felt nauseous panic but also hope that something was being done to stop the spread of the disease.

All of the other undercover cops I knew had taken brief hiatuses and then returned to the streets or, if they were really done in, quiet desks. With a rank of detective, they had more responsibility and more prestige. That seemed to be what Marco was proposing for himself, but I didn't want to think about his proposal right now. Even a week alone with him would break down my resolve to learn to like this new life away from beatings and killings. I must have laughed at myself when I had that last thought, because Ellis asked me what was funny.

"I was congratulating myself on leaving behind my life of violence."

"Well, two dead people in a week isn't so bad," he said, but he was kidding.

"Did you check out Marvin Creeley too?"

"Yeah, he seems clean. Hamilton has some investments with him, but the figures are normal. And his calendar is so packed that he has an alibi for every crime committed in the past ten years. And every appointment is boringly legit. He's making gobs of money the old-fashioned way."

I wondered if Ellis was thinking about his own parents' meteoric rise to money in the seventies. Probably not. He had never seemed very impressed with their lifestyle. Once, he mentioned that he was grateful not to have any student debt. I had just told him the amount of my parents' life insurance policies, and I'm pretty sure he was giving me a hint. Intended or not, I took the advice, and I became debt-free too.

Ellis had rolled up his sleeves to drive, and I could monitor his mood by the veins on his exposed forearm. Right at that moment, he was relaxed, and the veins were barely visible, like rows of freshly planted beans. If he gripped tighter, they would balloon out into mole tunnels. I wanted to avoid that, so I didn't tell him that he would see me on the tape if he ever got his hands on it. Well, not that he would see me; he would expect that, since he knew I'd been following Kramer around town. But he wouldn't expect to see me descend to the bathroom minutes after Kramer did.

Between imagining myself on a suspect list and finding Samantha Evans dead, my nerves were on edge. It was difficult to block out the unwanted memories. I tried not to, but I thought about the sound of Salvatore Magrelli's Glock being fired into the forehead of a teenager. I had shoved the gun back at him before sprinting for the stairs. I stumbled down a few, slamming my shin into the linoleum, but I wasn't fast enough to miss the main event. There was a shot, followed by the hysterical screams of the kid's younger brother. I expected to hear a second shot but it never came. I learned later that Salvatore had recruited the kid, and he was out selling pot before he turned twelve.

At that moment on the stairs, though, all I was thinking about was myself. I was thinking about running all the way back to the precinct. When I wrenched open the building's front door and was greeted by the humid summer afternoon, I knew I was in a hell as real as any afterlife. I even knew what the devil looked like and who shined his shoes. If I could have caught my breath, I would have heard him coming for me, one evenly paced step after another.

Salvatore holstered his gun before following me into the afternoon. I sputtered an apology, but he shook it off.

"It's nothing," he said, and relief flooded my system. It was premature. When we got back to the Costas' building, he stopped me before entering the apartment. He shoved me against a wall, covered my mouth with his hand, and held up a single finger to his lips. With my head held back, I never saw the knife coming. He sliced my thigh with such speed that it didn't even hurt at first, and then I was bleeding all over that damned ugly carpet. He knocked on the front door, and I crawled into the Costas' apartment.

Someone took me to the emergency room, but I don't remember who. Maybe Zanna. I remember telling the doctors about an accident with a paring knife. I mumbled something incoherent about how I should have chewed tobacco because the onions made me cry. I couldn't see what I was doing, I said.

—✦—

There were a couple of familiar faces at the precinct, and they gave me a hard time about finding a dead body.

"Life not interesting enough for ya?" asked Sammy Carter. Sammy had scraped by at John Jay, barely graduating, but scoring high enough on his officer exam to be admitted. By the looks of his bloodshot eyes and two-day beard growth, I would say he was scraping by here as well. Of course, I'd heard he'd gotten married and spawned some little Carters, so maybe they were tiring him out.

"Totally dull without you," I replied as Ellis led me past the duty desk.

I was taken to an observation room and told to keep my hands to myself. I wasn't sure exactly what I would steal, but I supposed the precinct took some pride in its collection of assorted coffee mugs. The Garfield one with a lasagna joke was nice.

When Ellis left me, I watched Hamilton and his lawyer sit quietly. Hamilton had on what I imagined was his casual weekend attire: pressed-but-not-starched khaki pants, buttoned-but-not-all-the-way-to-the-top collared shirt, and a dry-cleaned-but-not-new tweed jacket. He reeked of respectability, as did his starched, buttoned, and dry-cleaned attorney. They murmured a few words to each other, but mostly they checked their watches and tapped their feet impatiently. By the time Ellis entered the room, I was getting impatient as well and really wanted to do the questioning myself. It seemed like an ideal opportunity for some badgering, and I hadn't satisfied that urge completely with Ms. Barnaby.

"It's nice to see you again, Detective Dekker, even if I'd much rather this conversation happened in the comfort of my office."

"I didn't like your office much. Needs a window."

"True. What can I do for you?"

Ellis took his time sitting down across from his suspect. He slid his chair away from the table, settled in, and leaned back without saying anything. I'm pretty sure he took longer than necessary just to piss me off. I let out a strangled noise of frustration that no one could hear, but Ellis could imagine if he thought back far enough. He had been taking his time with me for a while.

"I've been thinking," Ellis finally began. "A fine establishment like Hamilton's should have video cameras. They might prevent some unfortunate events."

"We've never had any unfortunate events before last Tuesday, Detective."

"Really? Because I thought I heard you were missing a little money last year. $100,000, if I remember correctly."

"What," I said aloud to no one. I wanted an explanation immediately and doubted I would get one ever.

Hamilton's lawyer leaned over and whispered something to his client, who nodded once.

"Yes, one of our staff was embezzling via the company credit card."

"And why isn't that person in jail, Mr. Hamilton?"

"We handled the problem in-house."

"I see." Ellis leaned back farther, letting the front two legs come off the ground. It was a schoolboy move, relaxed and unassuming. "Where are the tapes, Mr. Hamilton?"

"I wish I could help you, Detective, but we don't have cameras. Important people come to relax at my place. Our clientele values privacy above all else, you understand."

"Above safety?"

"We can provide both."

"You like to handle problems in-house. I can respect that. Threatening a customer with fake tapes isn't respectable, though, which leads me to believe—you being a respectable man and all—that the tapes are real."

Ellis kept up his casual façade, barely glancing at Hamilton to see how he took this revelation. I was watching more intently and still didn't notice any discernible reaction. I got the feeling that Hamilton had been through an interrogation process before, maybe several times, and itched to get my hands on his file.

"If you are arresting my client for something, I suggest you do so now," said the lawyer. "Otherwise, I think you've taken up enough of his valuable time."

Ellis rocked back again and nodded. The lawyer and Hamilton stood up and walked past Ellis, who remained sitting and staring out into space. After a moment alone, he looked toward the two-way glass. "You know if you signed back up for the force, you could do the questioning," he said to the empty room. I was almost sure it was a compliment.

CHAPTER TEN

I woke up to good news and bad news, both delivered via my cell phone. The good news was that the Hamilton's actor-bartender had called and said he remembered something unusual about the night before Kramer's death. The bad news was two-fold. First, Clifton wanted to make an offer on the Tribeca apartment, and I hadn't a clue how to go about doing that. Second, Meeza had accepted a dinner invitation on my behalf with her parents and V. P., and I was expected at their Queens home at 7 P.M. sharp.

I tried to cancel the dinner plans, but when I called Meeza at 9 A.M., her mother had already started cooking. I could hear her whistling happily in the background.

"She's making *pani puri*, which you'll love."

Even without informative whistling, I could deduce that Meeza was also happy. There was a different inflection in her words, an affectionate bounce on "you" and "love." Instead of begging out of the meal, I thanked Meeza for the invitation and made a mental note to pick up flowers. I wrote down the address and turned my attention to the other problem, how to navigate the New York City real estate market without a degree.

I meant a real estate certification, but frankly, you need a bioengineering PhD to understand all the nuances of property laws, application procedures, and maintenance fees in this city. And forget about the interview process. Even if I could figure out how to put in an offer on the co-op loft, I was pretty sure that the property manager wouldn't put in a good word for Clifton. He would need to be prepped, and I wasn't the woman for the job. Well, okay, who better than me to show someone how to blend, but I didn't relish the thought of playing Henry Higgins to James Clifton's Eliza Doolittle. I could have blown him off completely, but there was the possibility that I would need that alibi after all. Disappearing wouldn't be particularly confidence-inspiring.

I was late by the time I climbed out of the Canal Street station and hustled toward the coffee shop where I was meeting Clifton. He was standing outside talking to a smoker, but not indulging himself. Enjoying the secondhand effects, I assumed. He didn't seem disappointed by my arrival, though, and launched into an explanation as we waited for the barista to steam milk.

"Well, I returned home after we saw the co-op, and I swear the building had added wet dog to its usual formaldehyde perfume. It was enough incentive for me."

I wondered briefly what he would think of my run-down walk-up, but decided the smell of laundry and empanadas beats dissected dog any day.

"I was there for maybe five minutes before I left a voicemail for my personal assistant to find out more about the construction. Then I walked back over to our favorite rendezvous point to drink my way to smelling less. Will I be seeing you at Hamilton's before I leave that part of town?"

"Let's not get ahead of ourselves. You haven't even made an offer. Plus, this is the first place you looked at, and there's a lot on the market right now."

"Wet dog, Ms. Seasons. Like living at a vet's office."

The barista handed me my drink, and I dropped a dollar in her tip jar. Clifton repeated after me, then we settled into a corner table beside an absinthe poster featuring an older gentleman and a younger woman. I noticed the coincidence despite my sudden nervousness. I glanced at my napkin, wondering if I would feel more relaxed tearing it into shapes.

"As you know, this is my first major sale. I don't want to make a mistake," I finally said.

I went ahead and started to tear the napkin, just to see what happened. I didn't feel calmer, but it probably added to the illusion that I was beginning to doubt myself.

"I understand, but you seem capable to me."

His assessment gave me a perverse desire to see the sell through. Even as the thought entered my mind, I knew it was impossible. Instead, I excused myself and told him I needed to check with my associates. I stepped outside, weighing my options. The easiest one would be to say the apartment had already sold, but that felt too shady. The man needed a place to live. I flipped through my phone until I located the real estate broker who had found me my office space. After leaving a sufficiently vague message about referring a friend, I felt somewhat relieved.

By the time I returned to our table, Clifton had finished his drink and built a miniature tower out of my napkin pieces. I was pretty sure he was teasing me again. When I sat down, the pieces tumbled down to the Formica.

"Well," he said. "Do I get the place?"

"I'm afraid the process takes a bit longer than that. I called a friend of mine who specializes in high-rise condos. He's going to walk you through the process. Think of him as a consultant." A consultant who does all the work and gets all the commission.

"If you insist, Ms. Seasons."

There was a distinct skip in his step as he hailed a taxi. I would be excited, too, if I could wake up to a view of sailboats on the Hudson. I, on the other hand, was feeling deflated. Besides buttering up my possible alibi, the meeting had been a waste of time. I sipped my warmish cappuccino and planned out the rest of my day. It was surprisingly full for a Sunday and included a borrowed wig, a family dinner, and a clandestine rendezvous. Okay, so returning to Hamilton's for a chat with the bartender wasn't exactly a rendezvous, but I needed some motivation.

⟴

Mamma was expecting me. I decided she must have security cameras trained down the street, because by the time I moseyed through the front door of the Pink Parrot, she was waiting for me, arms akimbo and a playful smile on her lips. She wiggled her eyebrows and seemed to be an entirely different person than she had been on my last visit. Gone was the no-nonsense businesswoman, replaced by a free-loving bon vivant. It didn't take long for her to reveal the source of her joy, either.

"You, young lady," she began, "are exactly the sleuth I want to see. Sit down and let me buy you a drink. Hauling Colt Hamilton's sorry ass in for questioning? Now, that deserves a reward."

Mamma laughed and swung her substantial self up onto a bar stool. She patted the one next to her, and I gamely obliged. When one of those umbrella fruit concoctions appeared before me, I took a compliant sip.

"Now tell me everything you know," she said.

I wanted to tell her exactly nothing, but I also wanted to stay on Mamma's good side. Plus, I liked her. It's easy to like someone who not only defies the laws of gender discrimination but also makes a mean strawberry daiquiri. Or, even better, makes them appear as if by magic. I took another pull from my straw and thought, *now this is the life.*

"Mr. Hamilton wasn't exactly forthcoming about his security measures," I explained.

"That figures. Wouldn't want to embarrass his girlfriend."

I froze with my lips around the straw, and the sweet liquid slid back down into the glass.

"Girlfriend?" My tone was far from light, and I was afraid of scaring Mamma off. I shouldn't have been; she was game for a little gossip.

"Everyone knows he was banging a waitress who managed to skim a hundred grand from the till. Can you imagine? If one of these boneheads stole even $100 from me, I would cut off his dick, bronze the thing, and keep it as a paperweight. But what does Hamilton do? He covers for her. Says she has a problem and checks her into a rehab facility. Now, isn't that about the craziest thing you've ever heard?"

"Just about. $100,000? Hamilton doesn't seem real sentimental."

"You're right there. If I were her, I'd be watching my back."

"So she's out of rehab?"

"That's the word on the street, but no one was sure exactly which girl was responsible. There are a lot of pretty ones, and they come and go. Actresses, students, nannies. They don't last long. Not like here. You can make a career at the Pink Parrot."

When she said "you," she didn't mean me. As if on cue, the door to the dressing rooms was thrown back, and Dolly strolled in dressed for his first performance. His sleek blond hair was tucked behind one ear, presumably to show off the cascading rhinestones. He wore a black and white floor-length dress, reminiscent of Julia Roberts's Oscar-winning frock, with platform heels that brought him to just under six feet tall. Damn, but he was lovely. Even the way he walked was feminine, as if his hips were marbles rolling around in someone's palm. He winked at me, and I felt outclassed and outmanned. A whistle came to my lips unbidden.

"I like yours, too," said Dolly, close enough to finger the tips of my red hair. "Better than that sorry brown bun. Big Mamma, you wouldn't believe what this girl goes around looking like. You would flat-out die."

"She can look however she wants, if she keeps putting scum like Colt Hamilton behind bars."

"I don't think he's going to be charged with anything," I said.

"Oh, that doesn't matter much. He's embarrassed now and like to do something stupid. You wait."

"Yes, ma'am," I said. It seemed like the only response at the time. I took the loaner wig from my bag. "I'm afraid I need to keep this one more day."

"And how did Kiki perform?" Dolly asked.

How did Kiki perform? Well, Marco seemed to like her, but he was waiting in my apartment before he saw her. In fact, the previous time Marco had seen me, I had been outfitted like a teenage boy and now that I thought about it, his interest in me was a little pervy. Okay, so not quite, but it was an excuse if I needed one.

"She did okay," I finally replied.

Dolly made a disgruntled noise in response.

"Okay, okay, she was a hit. Tongues lolled, tails wagged, are you happy?"

"Why yes, as a matter of fact. Yes, I am. And I'm not taking it back, not ever. Think of it as your secret weapon, more subtle than a .22."

Out of the two, I would have preferred my Smith & Wesson, but a lady has to use her available resources.

⟶

The *naan* was fresh out of the oven and filled the Dasgupta home with its tempting aroma. There were chutneys on the table, as promised, and enough *hara chana masala, mailai kofta,* and *bhindi bhaji* to feed a circus troupe, including the elephants. Helpfully, Mrs. Dasgupta had written the names of the dishes on seating cards and, as if that wasn't endearing enough, drawn stars to indicate spiciness. One star meant mild; five stars meant hold on to your hat. V. P. was chatting amiably with Meeza's father, who nodded delightedly. "His own car dealership. How about that?" I heard him say at one point, as if talking to his family's ghosts.

I was trying to help in the kitchen, but kept being rebuffed. Meeza's mother was barely five feet tall, but her presence was commanding even in her relaxed clothing, a *salwar* and *kameez*, which she named for me when I complimented her on the colors. She seemed pleased when I parroted them back to her correctly. Meeza was dressed in jeans and a V-neck sweater. The effect was casual, but I could tell that my assistant had made an extra effort. Her hair was even straighter and shinier than usual, and her cheeks were swiped with blush. Or, she was in a perpetual state of excitement. I couldn't imagine V. P. warranting such a reaction, but I would give him credit for trying. His shoes were shined and went well with his suit. The result was a little mob-audition for my taste, but maybe Meeza saw leading-man potential. And maybe if I lived with my parents, even solicitous ones like the Dasguptas, I would be willing to overlook a little hair pomade.

It was hardly surprising that my parents were at the fore-front of my mind as I watched mother and daughter spar affectionately.

"Wait, *ladli beetiya*," Mrs. Dasgupta said as Meeza swiped a small baked item from the tray freshly removed from the oven. She slapped her hand lightly, then handed her a napkin.

My own parents had died shortly after my twenty-first birthday. They were caught in a building fire while I was at a dance club downtown. I arrived home hiccupping, makeup sweated off, heels in hand. My first reaction to the fire trucks and police cars was a giggle and a remote fear that I might be arrested for disorderly conduct if I kept asking what was going on in a loud, slurred voice. When I finally processed the infor-mation, I was definitely disorderly, but I was also excused.

"Kathy, tell me again what you do."

My eyes focused on Mrs. Dasgupta, and I watched her turn expectantly toward me. The gold bangles on her wrist shuffled musically against each other.

"She's in real estate, Ma, I told you," Meeza answered.

"Ma? Who is this Ma?" Mrs. Dasgupta sighed, then patted her daughter on the cheek. If I hadn't already guessed that Meeza was an only child, that moment of indulgence would have given it away.

When dinner was ready, we moved to the table, and V. P. was sandwiched between his date and me. I leaned close and whispered out of earshot that he should learn to keep a secret.

"You didn't want to see Marco?" he asked, masking his face in feigned concern. I shrugged noncommittally. His hair smelled like fresh coconut and made me think of pineapple-flavored Bridget Barnaby who, despite her eccentricities, didn't seem to have much to do with the murder of Stephen Kramer or Samantha Evans.

"I'm saying I value my privacy."

"As do I." He locked eyes with me, and I knew he was warning me against revealing his real occupation. He needn't have. I can keep a secret with the best of them, and I understand that what's good for the goose is good for the gander.

Nonetheless, I could feel my blood pressure rise as he challenged me. I was civilized enough to avoid a scene and placated my anger with the array of delicious foods in front of me. It worked, and I was glad that I had worn a dress, so that my stomach could expand at leisure. In contrast, Meeza nibbled delicately and kept up the flow of conversation. I was out of my league when the topic turned to Indian states, but Mrs. Dasgupta described Gujarat with such tender attention to detail that I could imagine it clearly. Marble temples, bustling markets, cricket players. She spoke of the ancient port of Lothal where 4,000-year-old wells, staircases, and carvings can still be observed. And she caricatured her relations, every uncle and aunt lovingly mocked.

"My mother was a storyteller too," V. P. said, breaking up a lull that had fallen as each of us meditated on parts of Mrs. Dasgupta's vision. I was picturing the carts spilling over with local vegetables, wondering if animals or children were the first to snatch up the fallen goods.

Meeza lightly touched V. P.'s outstretched arm and while I couldn't see his face, I could imagine him enraptured. I excused myself on official real estate business.

CHAPTER ELEVEN

P hase three of my day was the most exciting, but I was in a food coma and carrying leftovers by the time I approached Hamilton's at 10 P.M. I slipped into the Kiki wig, applied red lipstick, and tried to sashay. My legs didn't feel like sashaying, though; they wanted to waddle. So I waddled my way to the bar and ordered a seltzer from a pretty young bartender—one of several on staff, I now understood, and not one I had seen before. It didn't seem likely that I would run into the one who had worked the night of the murder again. I looked around for the previous night's server but didn't see him, or hardly anyone for that matter. The place was unusually deserted even for a Sunday. What really lifted my skirt, though, was that the door to the back offices had been left unwatched and ajar. How could I resist?

Moving at a pace slightly faster than a waddle, I slipped through without drawing attention to myself. The offices seemed deserted as well, but I took my heels off and slipped them into my purse—I wasn't ecstatic about announcing my presence. It was doubtful that Hamilton would be in a particularly good mood after his visit to the pokey. Only one door was closed, and consequently, that was the one that drew my attention. With a little wish for luck, I turned the knob, and the door swung open into pitch blackness. I felt along the wall for a switch, but didn't find one. A whooshing sound came from my mouth, and I guessed it to be a sign of fear. Undeterred, I placed my right hand on the wall, made my way into the space, and shut the door behind me. I dug around in my purse until I located my cell phone to use as a makeshift light. It didn't illuminate much, but I kept it pointed ahead of me.

After a few steps, it became apparent that I was in a hallway, not a room. I crept forward until my stockinged foot slid off into nothingness. At least, that was my first impression. After the blood started pumping through my veins again, I shined the phone down and found a step. With one hand now pressed against a wall, I made my way down the staircase, counting as I descended into colder air. After twelve steps, the wall on my left disappeared. I maneuvered my phone until I could see that I was on a sort of landing, with a hallway to my left and more steps in front of me. I paused, listening for boogeymen from either direction. When no one came tearing after me, I continued down the second set of steps. The room at the bottom was perceptibly colder, and I felt sure somehow that I had reached the cellar.

I looked around until I found a dimmer switch, which I lifted slightly until the room hummed and glowed. I glanced back up the steps to see if any light would escape at the top, but I felt reasonably safe in the low lighting. The orange hue made the place look like something out of a cheap sci-fi film, as did the steel tables and walk-in humidor. There was also a smell of nail polish remover, stronger than it had been at the Pink Parrot. It made me glance around nervously, but there was no one else in the cellar. Perhaps one of the waitresses had been doing a touch-up.

I approached the humidor with, I'm embarrassed to say, a bit of awe. I'd never seen such a beautiful piece of furniture. If this had been my bar and my humidor, I wouldn't have kept it in the basement, that's for sure. The wood, which looked like oak, was carved into delicate patterns. Even the shelves had details noticeable under the boxes, tiny ivy leaves and acorns. The glass above the door was etched with the Hamilton's logo. I wanted to take a closer look, but the handle wouldn't budge. I knew that if I tampered with the lock, Hamilton would report it to the ever-lurking police, so I gave up on that idea as quickly as it occurred to me.

The rest of the room was uninspired by comparison. I did wonder why several boxes of cigars were left on top of tables, but perhaps those were the cheap ones. There were a few racks of wine and a dozen or so kegs, but nothing else that really jumped out at me. I turned the lights off and retreated back up the stairs. My plan was to go directly to the bar, but curiosity got the better of me. I stopped at the midway landing and turned down the hallway I had ignored before. When one of my shins bumped into something hard, I stifled a yelp and looked down to see that I had run into a box of wine glasses. I moved my phone around, illuminating shelves stacked with tumblers, pint glasses, jars of maraschino cherries, paper towels, and toilet paper rolls. There was that faint scent of nail polish remover again, but this time the source was clear: a gallon of acetone was tucked into a corner, and there must have been a spill. The darkness may have disoriented me, but I knew that I had walked into the supply closet adjacent to the bathrooms. I also knew the murderer's escape route. With access to this closet, he or she could flee up the stairs where I was betting there was a back entrance. There would be no need to reenter the actual bar.

My throat tightened in anticipation, the way it used to when I overheard specific details of a cocaine shipment. I wanted to discuss the discovery and was afraid that I wouldn't live to do so. I studied the room, trying to memorize as many details as possible. The room housed all the banal products that keep a bar running smoothly and cleanly. There wasn't much of a reason to keep it locked, but then again, even cherries have a price tag. I wouldn't want them stolen either. As if reading my mind, keys jangled from the other side of the door.

I looked around in panic for a place to hide. Everything was out in the open, so I tucked my phone into my purse and backed out into the dark toward the staircase. I pressed myself against the wall and hoped that Hamilton's had filled up in my five-minute absence and that the server was in a hurry for more glasses. The padlock slid off the door, and my heart began to pound. Any moment, and the light would be switched on. Except it wasn't. I could hear a body moving toward me in the dark, and I wasn't sure how to react. I couldn't move back up the stairs because I would be heard. And I certainly didn't want to move toward my visitor. After what seemed like a minute, but must have been ten seconds or less, a big, muscular body brushed up next to mine and froze. "I'm really lost—" I began, but before I could make any excuses, the man pushed me into the wall and tried to get his hands around my neck. My attacker couldn't see very well either, though, and I twisted out of the way. As I prepared for a second blow, the man changed his mind and sprinted up the stairs. The shock wore off quickly, and he couldn't have had more than a three-second head start. I took off after him, stumbling and then scrambling up.

I could see his frame silhouetted in the light when he pulled the door open and slammed it behind him. I reached it seconds later and yanked it back open. My eyes immediately filled with hot pink spots, but I kept moving forward. I doubted that the man would escape through the bar, so I sprinted in the other direction, running down the hallway, out a metal door, and finally into an alleyway. I heard the door automatically lock behind me before my attacker grabbed me by the front of my dress and slammed me down against the pavement. I heard the material rip and felt my skin sting at the scrapes. I was caught off-guard as much by the blow as by recognizing the man as the actor-bartender. His blond hair was less perfectly coifed and stuck to his forehead in clumps. Not so much golden retriever as Rottweiler now, he slammed me against the ground a second time, and I whimpered.

He loosened his grip and wiped his brow, a momentary lapse in judgment. While I had received sophisticated hand-to-hand combat training at the academy, I'd found the weekend self-defense class my parents insisted I take as a high school senior to be more helpful. The mantra was "every tough guy knocked down," which meant aim for the eyes, throat, groin, or knees to take an attacker down. I glanced to see what was available and kneed the man in the groin. He rolled off of me, and I sprung to my feet. He was trying to rise when I kicked him in the throat. After that, he lay down obediently and gasped for air. I knelt on top of him, keeping weight on his windpipe. I punched in Ellis's number with steady hands that I knew wouldn't remain so for long. The adrenaline was already leaving my body. Ellis hung up before I had even finished telling him my story, and moments later I could hear sirens in the distance. The bartender tried to stand, but I pressed my knee down harder. It was his turn to whimper.

"We've got about one minute before cops get here and do what they do best, which is fuck with punks like you. What were you doing in that storage room?"

"Storing something."

He gasped once as I increased the pressure on his throat, then let out a single, painful laugh.

"Cute. What were you storing?"

He shook his head, and the sirens got louder. I eased my knee back enough to open his jacket and check the pockets. I pulled out his wallet and a memory flash drive. Without a doubt, I knew I had struck gold because he tried to grab the drive from me. I slipped it into my bag before two armed officers turned the corner and asked us to freeze. I raised my hands and stood up slowly, eager to show that I knew the drill.

"You Kathleen Stone?" one of them asked.

"Yeah, but you can call me Kiki." I may have winked, but I'm not telling.

I was drinking coffee at the nearest precinct when Ellis careered through the door. "Are you hurt?"

He leaned down so close that I could see a tiny scratch on his glasses. I was wondering how he got it when he grabbed me by the shoulders and I winced. His apology was mumbled, and I'm not sure I accepted it. He stepped back and turned around, running his hands over his head in a ritual that I assumed helped to calm him down. I thought it best not to say anything until the ritual was completed, so I took another sip of my coffee. When he stuck his hands in his pockets and sighed heavily, I decided it was my turn to speak.

"The guy called me this morning and arranged a meeting, said he had information that might help me with my investigation."

"*My* investigation."

I shrugged, but that stung and made me wince again. I mouthed "ow" and closed my eyes for a beat.

"Do you need to see a doctor?"

"No. Maybe a trainer. I nearly hurled up some excellent Indian food trying to get up those stairs."

Ellis sat my coffee down and turned me around to examine my back. He lowered the collar of my dress gently and let out a small whistle. It was hard to concentrate on my story with his breath on my neck, but after a few seconds he took a step back.

"I think you're going to have some nasty bruises. A few scrapes and cuts, but you're right, you don't need a doctor. Well, not an M.D. You should really think about seeing a shrink."

I knew better than to shrug again, so I just ignored this comment and continued. "Anyway, the bar was empty, so I decided to do a little spelunking downstairs. There's a passageway that leads from the supply closet directly to Colt Hamilton's office."

"Also, directly to the alley, as you know firsthand."

I wanted to throw a first-class tantrum, but I opted to tap my foot instead.

"Are you going to let me finish?"

Ellis raised his eyebrows and gestured that I had the floor.

"He was surprised to find me in the closet—"

"I bet."

"Hey!"

"Keep going."

"I'm just saying, why make an appointment with someone and then attempt to knock her senseless?"

"Because you startled him?"

"But why wasn't he upstairs in the first place? It was after ten."

Ellis went back to the head-rubbing thing, but this time I decided it meant he was considering my unspoken speculation that the bartender was in cahoots with his boss.

"Have you run the financials for the bar?"

"In the red."

My little celebration dance didn't last long because of the stinging. I was still elated, though, knowing we were getting closer. There was something fishy about a bar that operated in the red and sent its embezzling waitresses to rehab.

"You look ridiculous in that wig."

This deflated my glee some, especially since Ellis couldn't have looked any better in his dark jeans and baseball tee. His hair was young Robert Redford-tussled like he had been lying down, and I hoped he had been alone. Not that the hope was fair, mind you, since I was currently weighing a romantic offer from someone not named Ellis, but I made the wish all the same.

Ellis suggested that I go home while he talked to the bartender who, according to his confiscated wallet, was Brad Messer. Part of me wanted to object to being shuffled off, but most of me wanted to see what was on the flash drive tucked safely in my purse. My only real regret of the evening was that my delicious leftovers were probably still sitting by my barstool.

<hr>

I went through the warzone motions when I got to my apartment, making sure the main room and bathroom were both clear. In lieu of a gun, I had picked up a bottle of wasp spray to keep by the front door. Not exactly deadly, but it did have a range of twenty feet. When I was sure the coast was clear, I flipped open my laptop. If there had been popcorn, I would have made some, but my cupboards were pathetically bare. I had read once that the contents of your refrigerator are a reflection of how you feel about yourself. In my case, I felt like expired yogurt and condiments in takeout packets. Past my prime but still efficient?

A typical surveillance shot appeared on my screen when I opened the file. The camera was stationed in a corner behind the bar and looked down at the barstools and open floor space. The front door was barely visible, but anyone who entered would be caught as he or she approached. The white date in the corner was from one month earlier, so I fast-forwarded to the night of the murder. I would be lying if I said I knew what I was looking for, but at least one man did not want me to have this footage. *Maybe more than one*, I thought, glancing at my violated closet.

I watched Mr. Kramer enter and make a beeline for the bar. A waitress with a blond ponytail poured him a drink before he even asked for one. He waved off her selection of cigars and turned his attention to the broadcast ballgame. During the three or four days I shadowed Kramer, this was the first bar he had ever entered. Nonetheless, it was apparent that he was a regular at Hamilton's. I'm no body-language expert, but he didn't look like he was planning on getting shot in the head. He looked like he'd stopped in for an after-work drink and would soon be moseying home to the missus. He didn't even look like an adulterer, though the philandering veterinarian had knocked my confidence on that one. Maybe I couldn't tell an adulterer from a mailbox. I would have to rethink my position on kittens, too, with their deceptively innocent eyes and noses.

I watched myself enter the bar as Kathy Seasons—shoulders back, briefcase clutched, head tilted as if curious about everyone there. It was a bit like watching a game tape, and I decided the tilted head was overkill. A woman who had been showing apartments in heels all day would be less approachable. I also should have taken off the scarf like a man loosens his tie. But the hair was perfect—I missed that original wig. The new red hair was nice, but not as elegant as the first incarnation.

I knew what I had done next, so I turned my attention back to Mr. Kramer who sat, undisturbed, watching Mariano Rivera work his magic in the seventh. When Rivera pitched another no-hit inning, Mr. Kramer slid off his barstool toward the staircase. *This is it*, I thought.

I glanced at myself to see if I was watching my target, but I appeared to be engrossed in conversation with Clifton. Mr. Kramer descended the stairs and I watched to see who followed. Only one person did, and she was wearing a fetching red wig. Well, it was too much to hope it would be that easy. Thanks to my evening adventure, I now knew that the Hamilton's alley door locked automatically and didn't have a handle for reentry. So I was looking for someone descending the bar stairs or going through the door to the offices. People who disappeared through those exits and never reappeared were automatic suspects.

I watched for half an hour standing at my desk before I decided to get more comfortable. I slipped the Kiki wig onto an empty mannequin head in the closet and tried not to look at the wrecked ones. The head I used only had a tiny nick on the right temple. If I pulled the hair forward, the injury was barely noticeable. I dropped my dress into the hamper, pulled on sweatpants and a John Jay T-shirt, and settled down in bed for a Sunday Night Movie.

CHAPTER TWELVE

I awoke with my laptop on my stomach, staring at my retro flying toasters screensaver. The post-fight adrenaline must have left my body and been replaced by fatigue. I had no idea when I had fallen asleep, so I would have to start at the beginning. Also, it was 9 A.M., and Meeza was calling me.

"Where are you? We have cases to solve."

"We don't solve cases. We stalk adulterers." I closed the laptop and moved it into a safer position on my bed.

"I have taken a case. I'll see you in an hour."

Meeza sounded chipper, and I hoped it was caused by her mother's delicious mango chutney, not a sleepover with my car dealer. On the plus side, she might smell like his coconut pomade.

As soon as the shower water hit my scrapes, I wished I had cleaned them the night before. I scrubbed myself quickly, then doctored everything I could reach with antibiotic ointment. The bruises had blossomed overnight and now were full-blown violets. *Stupid wannabe actor. May he bartend for the rest of his life.* Unless, of course, he had shot Mr. Kramer in the head, in which case I would wish on him an even worse fate.

I chose basic dark jeans and a button-down shirt, so that I wouldn't have to pull anything over my head. I looked a little like a server myself, but didn't much care. The majority of my day was planned around watching surveillance video and didn't require anything glamorous.

When I called Ellis to ask about the previous night's inter-rogation, he picked up on the first ring.

"How are you feeling this morning?" he asked.

"Like I went skydiving without a parachute."

"That bad?"

"Fine. Like I wrestled with an alligator."

"Oh, then that's okay. Listen, I want to tell you about Brad Messer, but I can't get away until tonight. Dinner?"

There must have been some leftover adrenaline in my system because my pulse sped up and beads of sweat popped out on my forehead. He suggested an Italian restaurant that we both had liked in college. On the one hand, the genre suggested romance; on the other hand, the familiarity suggested friend-ship. Just in case, I slipped a pair of red heels in my bag before rushing out the door. With any luck, I would only be an hour late for work.

⎯⎯⎯⎯⎯⎯

"Her name is Hamsa Malik, and her husband Naaif is a real skirt-chaser."

Meeza's accent was rarely apparent, conditioned out of her in the fifteen years since she and her family moved to New York from Gandhinagar. The cadence of "skirt-chaser" was just a bit off, though, and I suspected that she had never used the term before. Perhaps she had just learned it in her conversation with Mrs. Malik. The good news was that she didn't smell of coconut, implying that V. P. had been a gentleman after dinner.

Or that he had been scared away by her father. Either scenario was fine by me.

"How do you know her husband is a skirt-chaser?"

"Oh, everyone knows. He's never been caught, but now his card is up."

"Time is up."

"What?"

"Nothing. Listen, Meeza, it's not the best idea to take on friends as clients. Sometimes they don't actually want to know that their husbands or wives are cheating. They want you to discover the opposite, that their lives are happier than they thought. That it's okay to take out a mortgage on a new house or splurge on a vacation because their assets are safely joined. Do you know what I mean?"

The energy seemed to leak out of Meeza's body as I watched. For some reason it made me think of my father's only magic trick, which he would perform when my elementary school classmates came over for slumber parties. He would put a piece of clear tape on the side of a balloon, then puncture it with a sewing needle. Amazingly, the balloon wouldn't pop. I would always find it the next day, though, deflated and forgotten in a corner. What were the names of those girls? I couldn't remember.

"You've never helped out a friend before? Professionally, I mean," she asked.

I thought about how to answer that without making Meeza's doe eyes widen in pity. The truth was, I hadn't spoken to anyone I would consider a friend in years, until one week ago when Ellis popped onto the scene. In fact, Dolly and Meeza were the closest I had to friends even though I knew they both had real sets of people that they hung out with on the weekends.

"Never," I finally answered, honest while not exactly forthcoming.

Meeza gnawed a little on her lower lip, trying to decide on the best course of action.

"I'd really like to make a go at this. I hated being a receptionist," she finally said.

I nodded. What could I say? I would have hated that boring job, too. Meeza decided my nod was approval enough and perked back up. She was no balloon, that's for sure.

"Do you need me for anything today?"

"Nope. I've got a few things to work on here, then I'm going to give Seraphina Capra another shot."

"That's the rock-star girl, right? Garbage Monkeys?"

"Trash Kittens."

When I had met Jimmy Cruz the night of the break-in, I wasn't in top form. I spent half the time glancing over my shoulder to see if anyone looked suspicious at the coffee shop. Jimmy was younger than my typical client, mid-twenties and skinny as a piece of wet laundry. "I know she's having an affair," he had said of Seraphina, pushing his bangs momentarily out of his eyes. "I don't know who the guy is, though, and I think what I want is to beat him to a pulp." On the one hand, I should probably have excused myself when my client threatened violence. Another dead target, and I would definitely find myself in a holding cell. On the other hand, his biceps were smaller than mine, and I couldn't imagine a guy wussy enough to be overpowered by Jimmy Cruz.

Meeza swept her long black hair into a serious investigator bun and slid on dark sunglasses. She was dressed in black jeans, black T-shirt, black blazer, and black sneakers and looked like an extra on *Alias*. She bounced out the door, presumably to spy on Mr. Malik. Meeza hadn't yet asked me for any advice, so I figured she had some sort of plan. I thought I probably needed to fill her in on how to get officially licensed as a private investigator soon. If anything happened, though, I would claim her as my assistant even though I certainly wasn't going to take any money gained from a case that she acquired.

Temptation got the best of me, and instead of cruising Seraphina Capra first thing, I popped the flash drive into my laptop. In fast-forward, men in suits and women in pearls chugged their martinis and smoked cigars down to nubs. They cackled over jokes, then turned serious to talk mergers and franchises. At least, that was the soundtrack I imagined over the silent images. A few old friends slapped each other on the backs, and one young man found the only other young woman in the place and skedaddled. After an hour of viewing, everyone who had descended the stairs had also ascended them, and I was rethinking Meeza's receptionist job. At least I could file my nails.

"Excuse me?"

I jumped and looked up to find James Clifton staring into my office. My immediate reaction was guilt since, if I glanced down, I would see him nursing a whiskey on my computer screen.

"I'm looking for Kathy Seasons, and there's no receptionist at the front desk."

He stepped back away from the doorframe. I prayed that my face hadn't shown any sign of recognition even though, to be honest, I wasn't all that worried about him recognizing me. I know it sounds odd, but sans makeup and wig, I really do look like a different person. Not so far removed from the performers at the Pink Parrot, actually. Just to be safe, I slipped on a slight French accent and told him that I remembered him from the last time he was here. Closing the lid on my laptop, I offered to take a message. I started to rummage through my top drawer to keep from making direct eye contact.

He smiled and pretended to doff a hat in my direction. It was both a ridiculous and an endearing gesture, but I was too keyed up to be charmed.

"No, I'll leave one myself. Her door's open," he said.

Because there's nothing to steal in that empty space. He waved a crumbled ball of paper and a pen at me, then disappeared. I got up quickly and shut the door, leaning against it until my panic subsided. What would he think if Kathy never replied to his message? If Clifton knew I had been playing him this entire time, he might go straight to the police. Who wouldn't suspect me then? When my heartbeat had returned to normal, I dialed my own real estate broker again, and this time he answered in that friendly, practiced voice that people who earn commissions perfect.

"Yes, Ms. Lincoln, of course I remember you. Is everything working out with your office? Do you perhaps want to upgrade to a larger space?"

I explained to Henry "you can call me Hank because we're buddies" Stonebrook that I had been apartment-hunting with a friend and had seen a beautiful loft down in Tribeca through the building manager. My friend had decided spontaneously to make an offer, but needed someone to navigate the sale.

"I'd be more than happy to help," he said, and I could picture dollar signs rolling over his eyeballs.

"Oh, you're a lifesaver. Can you tell him that Kathy Seasons asked you to call?"

There was a moment of silence while Hank processed the possibility that something suspect was going on, but his avarice won out over his curiosity, and he answered with an affable "You bet" and hung up, no questions asked. I tried not to draw any parallels, but I couldn't help thinking of myself folding Gloria Kramer's enormous check into my pocket. Well, at least James Clifton was out of the picture. No more faux father-daughter dates for us.

After another hour of scrutinizing the footage, there seemed to be three people who had gone downstairs or through the office door and never reappeared or appeared only after the murder. That was two more than I would have liked, but it certainly narrowed the playing field. The first was, as expected, Colt Hamilton, but he could have been doing work in his office. The second was a female server, young and blonde, whom I didn't think I had seen before. She could have exited out the back after her shift. Finally, there was a thirty-something man with sideburns and a receding hairline. The quality of the tape wasn't great, so when I zoomed in, he became blurrier, not clearer. He needed to be run through the system, which meant that I had a teeny confession involving evidence theft to make to Ellis over meatballs. Normally, the thought of Lucello's pasta made my stomach growl in anticipation; that afternoon, my stomach did a little flip and settled into a gloomy disposition.

I had already tailed Seraphina Capra twice without observing any suspicious behavior. I was nearly ready to give up and tell Jimmy Cruz he could pick out a ring, but it was hours until my scheduled dinner with Ellis. Which is to say, I needed something to get my mind off of my inevitable confession. Somehow, "stealing evidence" didn't exactly roll off the tongue. The roof tar on the building adjacent to Seraphina's had permanently stained my jeans by the time the wannabe rocker flipped her lights on. I had been staked out for twenty minutes so that I could be there when she got home from work. I must admit, I wasn't expecting the show I got.

Most of the time, photographing men and women engaged in sex acts feels textbook seedy, a violation of the agreed-upon moral code. Not quite incest or cannibalism level, but on par with selling crack to kids or leaving a puppy unattended in a hot car. Sometimes, though, and I wouldn't admit this except under duress, the events are stimulating. Sometimes, I stay a bit longer than required, and that afternoon, as I watched Seraphina Capra's lover undress, I couldn't take my eyes off his tan, smooth chest. He was Jimmy Cruz's opposite with six-pack abs and python-esque biceps. He looked like he could crush the little emo singer. To a certain extent, I was required to watch for longer because Seraphina remained clothed as the man surveyed his prey. Then he struck and held her against the living room wall. I zoomed in and snapped off a few shots as he unbuttoned her blouse and yanked her jeans to the floor. When he pressed his head between her legs, I took one final shot, fanned myself in exaggerated fashion, and took off.

I assuaged my guilt with an all-business trip to the office, where I printed the photographs and dropped them into a manila envelope. I left a note for Meeza with instructions on how to bill Jimmy. In movies, the P.I. always hands over the photographs in person and watches stoically as the husband or wife cries, but I've never been up to that. I trust the U.S.P.S. men and women just fine, and I've never once had to call in a bill collector. Sometimes a tearful client will show up at my office, but I discourage this behavior. Most of the time, I avoid telling clients the office address and meet elsewhere, and my reasons are not solely about privacy. I also keep a stack of business cards for a therapist who works on the third floor. I've never actually met her, but she's sent me bright yellow roses on two occasions. See? I give back to the community.

I opened my office closet and surveyed the contents: one cheap blond wig bought before discovering the superior skills of Vondya; a box of now-useless ammunition for my Smith & Wesson; a gray suit; and a pack of drug-store brand underwear because you never know. I pulled out the date heels from my bag and slipped them on. It was a slight improvement, but nothing to really impress someone. I tried lipstick and tousled my hair, hoping for faux Melanie Griffith circa *Something Wild*; the result was more frazzled housewife on a girls' night out. When I daydream, I look like Halle Berry, but even I know that's a stretch and a half. The tar stains on my jeans were a nice touch, but didn't scream "sexpot" or even "normal human being." I decided on desperate measures, dialed a number on my cell, and waited impatiently.

CHAPTER THIRTEEN

When Dolly arrived, he was wheeling a carry-on suitcase and wearing a skeptical face. "How do you work out of this place?" was his opening gambit.

I glanced around at the nondescript office, which I never paid much attention to: dirty window facing the back alley, gray metal filing cabinet, faded couch, desk, and chair. It sufficed, and it didn't have that cheesy frosted glass on the door with "Private Eye" in black laminate letters. That would be hitting rock bottom, I had decided when I rented the place, when I had, for all intents and purposes, hit rock bottom.

"Those damn plants are the only classy things in here," he continued. I followed Dolly's eyes to my African violet and Boston fern and silently agreed. I needed to buy Meeza some sort of thank-you gift because I couldn't remember the last time I'd given them so much as a glass of water, much less a good pruning.

I let Dolly finish his assessment. "You need some curtains, throw pillows for that piece-of-shit futon, and a photograph or two wouldn't hurt anyone."

"I'm not here that much," I said defensively. *Only seven days a week and some evenings.* "And I bet your apartment looks a lot better. Has paintings on the wall and chandeliers in the kitchen? Uh-huh, I thought not."

Dolly gingerly sat down on the couch and crossed his calfskin riding boots at the ankles. He had tucked tailored gray slacks into them and topped the outfit with a navy V-neck sweater. Basically, he looked way too chic for my office. I was surprised he felt confident enough to sit on the couch. Seeing it through Dolly's eyes made me think it looked like bedbug central.

"I'll work on it. At the moment, I'd just like to work on me."

Dolly clapped his hands together, but the gesture wasn't from excitement. It seemed more like the beginning of a pep talk. What a little league coach might do as he watched his shortstop pick a dandelion and his first baseman pick his nose. The clap was meant to convey "We can do this!" without giving away the "In an hour, I can have a drink" interior monologue.

"No Kiki?" Dolly asked.

"No Kiki. I'd like to look like me, only better."

"Ain't that the holy grail of beauticians worldwide. But we'll work with what we have."

Like Meeza, I had been an only child, so swapping clothes was unfamiliar to me. John Jay College was a commuter school, and I had lived with my parents up until their deaths my senior year. Then I proudly lived in a rat-infested studio in Bushwick, funded by what remained of their life insurance policies after I paid back my student loans. My classmates thought the place was cool, and who was I to argue? Looking at Dolly, though, who couldn't be any cooler, I was reconsidering my social standing. It was probably a lot lower than most of Dolly's acquaintances. Maybe I would count as community service. He could write me off on his taxes or something.

I undressed to my cotton skivvies and slipped into an emerald green cashmere dress and almost instantly regretted my decision to borrow clothes. What if I spilled something on it that a dry cleaner couldn't remove? On the other hand, I wanted to run my hands over my own body, and that had to be a step toward attractive. I added dangling earrings and my own heels. I was ready to see the effect, but Dolly shook his head. When he brandished a pair of barber scissors, I instinctively backed into a defensive position.

Dolly persisted. "Nuh-uh. Your hair is cut like a boy's. If you don't let me give you some girl bangs, you can't wear the dress."

"Are you going to wrestle me out of it?"

Dolly put his free hand on his hip and gave me his best "don't tempt me" look. Chastened, I sat down on the edge of the couch and closed my eyes tight. I could feel the tiny snippets of hair as they fell across the bridge of my nose. When I cut my hair short after leaving the police force, the experience had been wholly negative, a safety measure. This was the only time in the past three years that a professional had tackled my hair. I had done the necessary touch-ups to my look over the bathroom sink. While trusting Dolly, I realized how many things I had let slide with no one to hold me accountable. No family, no friends, no boyfriends, no bosses. It was perhaps time for me to come out of my self-imposed shell. Even turtles poked their heads out from time to time. To give myself credit, I was making steps in the right direction. I had let Meeza in on my big bad secrets. Well, maybe not my biggest and baddest, but secrets nonetheless. Hanging out with Dolly could easily become a habit, and I had a date tonight. Okay, so it was probably a business meeting, but I didn't let myself dwell on that teensy detail.

Dolly finished the makeover with lipstick, eyeliner, and mascara. He tied a scarf around my neck, which covered most of the bruises. The result was better than I had hoped for. I hugged Dolly spontaneously and told him that I could never thank him enough.

"You know what you can do for me? You can get rid of that ugly brown bun wig."

And to prove how grateful I was, I said I would think about it.

———

I arrived first at Lucello's, dashing my hopes for a dramatic entrance. Instead, I sat and fidgeted with the ends of my borrowed scarf. When Kathy or Kat or Katya eats alone, it's no big deal. When Kathleen Stone eats alone, she feels a little like a loser. *But I'm not eating alone, that's the whole point,* I reminded myself. A waiter appeared, soliciting my drink selection.

"Your house red will be fine," I said because I know a Mom and Pop joint from Cipriani's when I see one. Even if I've never seen the inside of Cipriani's.

The waiter bowed slightly, approving my choice, and a second person stopped by to fill up my water glass. I was thanking him when Ellis walked through the front door, jangling the bells. The maitre d' approached, then retreated when Ellis's eyes stopped at my table. I could see the sweat stains acquired in a hard day's work, but Ellis still looked good in his khakis and blue collared shirt. I stood as he approached, my napkin tumbling to the floor so that I had to squat to retrieve it. His eyes flicked down to me, and his face softened a bit as mine reddened.

"Nice dress," he said, dropping his bag on the floor and sliding into his chair.

The waiter rushed over with a new napkin, and I sat back down, chagrined and trying to think of a reasonable excuse for standing in the first place. It wasn't as if Ellis would miss me in the tiny restaurant. There were only eight tables, and they were crowded intimately together. The waiter must have been rooting for me, because he addressed Ellis before I was forced to defend myself.

"Signore? What would you like to drink?"

Ellis ordered a beer and popped an olive in his mouth.

"Really nice dress."

One compliment made me feel good; two compliments made me feel like overkill incarnate. I took a sip of my wine and leaned back a little to show how relaxed I was. When that didn't seem to work, I took a gulp of wine and asked after his family.

To be perfectly honest, the Dekkers scared the bejeesus out of me. They were Ivy League and smelled it, the mother like she bathed in Chanel Number Five and the father like he shaved with truffle oil. To say that they were disappointed in Ellis's career choice was a bit of an understatement. They locked their youngest son out of their Long Island estate when he rejected Columbia's offer of admission. You'd think they would have appreciated the money he was saving them by enrolling in one of the city university schools, but all they saw were wasted golf lessons and SAT classes. Somewhere during his senior year, when he was up for valedictorian and featured in the school newspaper, they had offered an olive branch with the caveat that he make a monthly pilgrimage home. I had accompanied him on one of these pilgrimages and, to a certain extent, the experience had started my disappearing act.

I had asked Ellis not to tell them about my parents' recent deaths, and I spent the weekend pretending to be another rebellious trust fund kid, an ideal Ellis playmate. Not that I lied exactly, but I wore the right kitten heels and tailored trousers. It was a friendly favor to Ellis, to get his parents off his back for a few days, but it was the best weekend I'd spent in months.

"Do they still ask about me?" I teased.

"I'm afraid not. They don't know it was you who put that stuffed fox on a float in the middle of the pool."

"Thanks for taking the blame for that one."

Ellis chuckled. "I think Dad liked the joke, actually. And there was no damage to the pelt, most importantly. That little vixen's a family heirloom, you know."

He imitated his father's timbre, and while it sounded nothing like I remembered, I laughed at the effort. By the time the spaghetti and meatballs arrived, I was on my second glass of wine and had stopped worrying about getting a piece of bread stuck in my teeth. We were reminiscing about our favorite undergrad moments, including the time we graffitied a tunnel in Riverside Park.

"That could have been the end of our distinguished law enforcement careers," I said.

"No way. That wasn't graffiti; it was street art."

"Black spray paint by bored punk kids doesn't impress the gallery crowd. We didn't even bother to buy cool colors. Neons or something."

Ellis started cutting up his pasta into bite-sized pieces as I rolled mine onto my spoon. His tidy approach had some appeal, but I liked the instant gratification. Plus, it was less memorable. Someone might remember a customer who cut up her pasta like a seven-year-old. Of course, my instincts were at odds that night—dressed to impress but acting, per usual, to be invisible.

I brought up the time he locked his roommate out of the apartment so that he could watch the Super Bowl uninterrupted. "You know, for most people, the Super Bowl is social. It's about chili and making fun of the commercials."

"Exactly, it's bullshit. The most important game of the season, and everyone's thinking about potato salad."

The conversation swung naturally between college pranks, professors, and bad dates before turning inevitably—unfortunately, I should say—to work. About halfway through our meal, Ellis brought up Brad Messer, and I put my fork down to lean closer as he filled me in on his interrogation.

"Messer said that he was going downstairs to get some extra towels when he sensed someone in the corridor."

"And the roughing-up in the hallway? Did he have anything to say about that?"

"Yeah, he said you did your fair share of roughing." Ellis's eyes were professionally vacant but still blue enough to lose your resolve in.

"And you believe him?"

"No reason not to. He has neck bruises to corroborate his story." The pale eyes flicked over my expression, and it was clear he knew that I was withholding information. He put his own fork down and waited. It was a standoff, and I caved because it was the honorable thing to do. I also needed information, hopefully an I.D. for the mystery man on the tape.

"Messer called me and said he had information," I began by way of defense.

"He wanted—," here Ellis paused but found his footing soon enough. "He wanted a date. He didn't have any information."

I considered this theory but didn't fully buy it. Ellis didn't buy that I had told him everything. "What aren't you telling me?" he asked.

I paused, taking one last breath before incriminating myself. "Something might have fallen into my possession."

A hint of anger flickered onto Ellis's face, then extinguished. He nodded for me to continue.

"Surveillance tape."

This time the anger stayed. He held out his hand, and I removed the flash drive from my purse. As soon as I dropped it into his palm, he shook his head. He reached down to unzip his bag, and instead of dropping the drive into it, he pulled something out. It was a clear plastic evidence bag with a familiar red wig inside. He held it up for me to see, then tucked it back out of sight.

"We have your briefcase, too, from the trashcan down the street. It's covered in fingerprints."

I nodded while I processed the idea that I was a suspect and had been for at least a few days. On some level, I suppose I already knew. That was why Ellis kept popping back into my life. Both Hamilton's cigars and my shifty eyes were under close watch. So much for the green dress, I might as well have worn my pajamas. The flannel ones with the saggy bottom. I was nothing more than a job for him. A job with history, maybe, but still a job. I felt my throat constrict with tears, but knew that as long as I didn't say anything for a couple of seconds, no one would be able to tell.

"This," Ellis said, holding up the surveillance tape, "looks really bad."

I wanted him to say that he could never suspect me, and when he didn't, I knew that he was right. This was really bad. Nonetheless, I wasn't entirely out to sea.

"I have an alibi," I began, feeling relieved. "I was sitting with a man named James Clifton. I have his number right here."

I fumbled to open my cell phone, but Ellis put his hand over mine to stop me.

"We talked to Mr. Clifton. He speaks very highly of you, but says you left the bar for a few minutes."

I stared at Ellis until tiny black dots began to obscure my vision. I shook my head to clear them. He stood up, and while I wanted to follow, I was afraid of his reaction. And after he watched the tape, I would be afraid of being arrested. He didn't leave immediately, though, and after a moment I felt his knuckles caressing my cheek.

"I waited for you to call me," he said quietly. "I read about the Frank Salvatore trial in the newspaper and thought, she'll call me any day now. She'll have missed me as much as I missed her."

I flushed because I knew he was disappointed in me. I flushed because while he had been waiting for me, I had been in bed with Marco Medina. I swallowed hard before responding.

"You never said anything."

Ellis took his hand away, but I still didn't look up. When I was sure he was gone, I asked for the check and a doggie bag. The doggie bag was provided, but the check was not.

"The gentleman took care of it earlier."

Rats, I thought. As if I could feel any worse. The waiter shook his head sadly, providing unnecessary confirmation—he had been rooting for me, and I had let him down. *Well, he should get in line.*

CHAPTER FOURTEEN

T he next morning, the most optimistic thought that I could rustle up was *at least I wasn't told to stay in the country*. It wasn't much, but I was able to drag myself out of bed and into the shower, which was a start. At the office, Meeza still didn't smell like coconut, and I added that to the list of positives in my life. She had set up a makeshift workspace on my couch, and I glanced over her shoulder to see a photograph of a middle-aged Indian man. He had his arm slung around a woman to his right, but she had been cropped clean out of the picture.

"Mr. Malik?"

"Yes, I already know what he looks like, but there's other information here about work and hobbies."

"Hobbies?"

"Yes, apparently he likes to visit those Turkish baths and play chess in Washington Square Park."

"Both sure-fire ways to meet ladies."

I took another look at the photograph and noted his unruly black hair and innocent smile. I had to bite my tongue not to point out the resemblance to her new romantic interest. Like it or not, I had to give V. P. a fair shot. Meeza already knew the worst about him—I hoped—and she was a grownup.

Meeza closed the Malik file as I handed her Jimmy Cruz's manila envelope with billing instructions. I was glad to be done with Jimmy and Seraphina, my first and hopefully last wannabe rock stars. Jimmy's payment would be appreciated, but I didn't need his melancholy; I had enough of my own. Before I could stop her, Meeza opened the flap and dumped out the photographs. The first one showed the shirtless, muscled other man sucking on one of Seraphina's nipples.

"*Aare bhagvaan!*" Meeza flipped through the images and giggled. "The taxidermist did not look like that, or I never would have left him at the Applebee's." She slipped the photographs back and turned to her laptop to type up the invoice. For a split second, I felt guilty about her working conditions, then told myself she could take over my desk as soon as I left town. And yes, I was having a harder and harder time thinking of a reason not to run away with Marco. That is, provided I wasn't in the slammer soon.

Marco and I were made of the same mettle. We could disappear into crowds and reinvent ourselves by the time we emerged on the other side. Drug dealer on Monday, upstanding citizen by Friday. And there was no doubt about our attraction. Perhaps I had been drawn to Marco originally out of some desperate need to forget about my life, but it would be wrong to say that was all there was to it. Maybe I should have called Ellis after the trial, but it was too late for that now. Marco had been the one to walk into the room. And Ellis didn't call me either, come to think about it. He could have tracked me down with a little effort, couldn't he have? Well, maybe not. I had made a point of being hard to track. I had swum through rivers like any fox worth her salt knows to do.

There was no way to reach Marco via phone, which I knew to be permanently tapped by the NYPD. That made a personal visit mandatory. With my new haircut and eyebrows, Keith would be hard to pull off, but it was my only feasible option. I went home to change, wondering why I'd bothered to make the office trip in the first place. I could say the same of Meeza, who called me in a hushed whisper to say that she was at the gym, watching Mr. Malik use the free weights.

"And that means that he is cheating on his wife, the no-good cheater."

I wanted to scoff at Meeza's conclusion, but she was probably right. Most fifty-five-year-old men do not begin spontaneously working out without motivation. A new special friend was motivation.

"You know, I am not sure that I want to date anyone after all, if men can so easily rove their eyes elsewhere."

"There are good guys, too," I ventured to suggest. "Somewhere."

While I wanted her to run far away from the shady car dealer, I didn't want my bright assistant to reject relationships altogether. She seemed like an ideal candidate for love. Not to mention that Mrs. Dasgupta would have my head if Meeza swore off men because of her new job. Of course, Mrs. Dasgupta might also have my head when she learned a little more about her daughter's current suitor. Maybe I would be long gone before either of those beheadings became necessary.

I couldn't get my new, hipper bangs to stick in skaterly fashion to my forehead, so I tucked them and the rest of my hair under a flat-billed Mets hat, complete with stickers. The ripped jeans and T-shirt were thrown on, and my disguise was as good as it was going to get. A safer bet would be not to get caught this time. I didn't want a repeat performance with trigger-happy neighbor Miguel.

Despite my shoddy costume, no one gave me a second look on the train, which was a good sign. Still, I wasn't taking any chances, and I found an alleyway across from Marco's building to do some preliminary surveillance. It was six o'clock, a busy time for most buildings, and this one was no exception. After watching the working poor shuffle home, rubbing their necks as they unlocked their front doors, the gang members, or wannabes, stood out. They walked faster, more confidently, as if they belonged somewhere better. I recognized a front when I saw one. The only other place they would end up was prison. Even the most successful criminals would stay close to their home neighborhood, would need mothers, aunts, cousins to give them alibis. The senior members of these gangs were wealthy, sure, but they weren't moving to the suburbs and putting in swimming pools. And the higher up in the organization, the more they needed to watch their backs.

I glanced behind my own just in case, but there was nothing in the alley except for a razor-wired fence and bags of trash. I was crouched behind a plastic bin, watching for signs of Marco or for signs that the coast was clear. I wanted to sit, but the crouch made me less vulnerable. I could leap up if necessary. Where I would leap was another question entirely. From time to time, I shifted my weight to keep my blood circulating, and let me tell you, the whole operation was very romantic. I knew that if I ever did get to talk to Marco, I would smell like day-old garbage—a particularly unique perfume of rotting vegetables, dirty diapers, and rat feces. My nose became immune to the combination pretty quickly, but I knew what to expect from nestling in an alley.

At 6:30, Marco sauntered toward his building. His pants were hanging even lower than the last time I'd seen him here, and he held them up with his left hand as he high-fived someone he passed on the sidewalk. The man said something in Spanish that I couldn't make out, and Marco nodded, an agreement to something that probably wasn't weekend volleyball. Another string of Spanish was directed at Marco, and since the woman spoke at a volume to raise the dead, I could make it out: "*Me estás poniendo muy caliente.*"

In my desire to get a closer look at the flirt, I knocked a few empty beer cans that clanged as they hit the ground. I flattened myself against the wall and waited for someone to appear, machetes or fists drawn. After a minute of silence, I risked a look. I shouldn't have worried about being discovered; Marco and the mystery woman couldn't have been less aware of their surroundings. Her back was to me, and his hands were grabbing her ass and pulling her body against his. Even from across the street, it was obvious that their tongues were heavily involved.

I swallowed the nausea and leaned back against the brick building. Womanly intuition had never been my strong suit, but I should have guessed that he was seeing someone, especially after his moody reaction when I asked him about undercover involvements. This "should have" didn't make me feel any better. To make matters worse, I could now detect a whiff of wet dog hair among the array of odors, and that one is hard to scrub off. I counted off the minutes until I reached five and looked back out. Marco and his woman were nowhere in sight—presumably upstairs and in bed by now—so I stood and flexed my legs until my knees didn't ache. Everyone stayed a respectful distance away from me on the trip back home. I considered adding Garbage Lady to my rotation of disguises.

⟡

With back scratches and break-in paranoia, showering had lost some of its appeal; nonetheless, it had to be done. I locked the door, then soaped up and washed off as quickly as possible. When I emerged to a perfectly ordinary-looking apartment, I exhaled and sank down on the couch to feel sorry for myself.

In one corner of my mind, I knew I couldn't blame Marco for having a lover or lovers on the other side. Being taken seriously by a group like Los Guardias required certain behaviors, and sex should have been the least of my concerns about Marco's dealings. And to be honest, Marco should have been the least of my concerns, period. There was a fair chance that someone somewhere was currently considering whether to arrest me on two counts of homicide. Maybe many someones in many somewheres.

Before I could mosey too far along this mental path, my cell phone lit up with a text message from Ellis: "i.d. from tape."

My survival instincts must have kicked my self-pity instincts in the nuts, because I decided the message meant that at least one important person didn't suspect me. His vote of confidence didn't mean I was off the hook, but maybe it meant I could do something to help myself. I dropped my towel into the hamper and dressed quickly in jeans and a sweatshirt. With no one to impress or deceive, getting ready was a lot easier. I was at the precinct in half an hour, and if Sammy Carter looked surprised to see me, it was hard to tell.

"Are you here to turn yourself in, or give Ellis a hard time?"

"What would you do?"

Sammy buzzed me past the duty desk without saying anything. He was undecided about me, but I would take that over open hostility. No one else bothered me, though a few might have stared a second longer than necessary. I walked into the observation room and watched Ellis interview the man I recognized from the surveillance footage: mid-thirties, built, dark-haired. On the tape, he had been wearing a crisp beige suit that looked as expensive as a suit can look on grainy footage. In person, his clothing was worn-out and not exactly Hamilton's-appropriate. Three photographs were splayed on the table, but the man was shaking his head.

"I got nothing to do with this. I've never seen this girl."

"Her name's Samantha Evans. Does that ring any bells?"

"Nuh-uh, I told you everything I know. You can't prove shit."

Every visible muscle on Ellis was tense. He looked like a mountain lion, motionless but poised to strike. His interrogatee didn't look particularly prey-like, though. He looked relaxed, and I would have bet a box of doughnuts that he had a criminal record that would wear out a printer.

Ellis moved, and I jumped. His movements only took him to the door, though, where he disappeared, then reappeared in the observation room. We stood side by side, peering through the two-way glass. While his mind was surely on the investigation, I couldn't help mine from wandering toward our dinner conversation.

"I knew you were here," he said. He was avoiding eye contact, but at least he was speaking to me.

"Liar," I mumbled.

"I have instincts."

"What do your instincts tell you about this guy?"

Ellis handed over a thick file, which I flipped open and scanned while he talked.

"I don't need instincts. This guy is a professional, even if he's never been officially convicted for it. Most recently, he did eight months for involuntary manslaughter at Green Haven, which I think we might as well start calling 'basic training.' I want him locked up, but I also want to know who hired him. He says he doesn't know; that the person used a voice distorter. Doesn't even know gender."

Ellis's eyes flicked at me on "gender," then he looked away.

"Those distorter things might as well come standard on phones these days," I said. "A murder charge dropped to involuntary? That must have been some plea-bargaining."

"He gave up the person who arranged the contract. I'm surprised he's still working, actually. I guess word never made it back to the streets."

Ellis turned his back to me, and I watched our killer through the two-way glass. He was digging something out from under his thumbnail as if he were watching a football game in front of his television at home, not under arrest for murder one.

"Is that even possible? No leak?" I asked.

"It happens."

"Or maybe his contractor wasn't much liked. Who was he?"

Ellis took another step away from me before he answered, and I felt my neck prickle. My instincts were working, too.

"Salvatore Magrelli."

Otherwise known as The Brother Who Got Away.

When I went to court to testify, there were three names: Salvatore Magrelli, Frank Magrelli, and Darío de Luca. Three weeks into the proceedings, Salvatore Magrelli's name was dropped from prosecution. It was described away by "lack of evidence," and I was too tired to think about the consequences. Months of living in a rundown motel, unable to cross the street without an escort, had left me twitchy and impatient. I should have protested. I should have wanted the thing done right, but fatigue is no friend to principles. And anyway, even if I had stood by my principles, it was clear that a more powerful hand than mine was pulling the strings.

I always hated that metaphor. It made me picture political puppeteers dancing their killers through the city, or, in this case, out the courthouse front door. My own name was withheld during all the proceedings. I was Witness A. I had been taken to a safe house as soon as my cover was blown, but three months after I disappeared from the Costas' lives, the Magrellis were arrested for the first time ever. Which is to say, the math would point to me. The only thing I had going for me was that no one would recognize me now. It wasn't enough to calm my nerves.

"Magrelli had my apartment ransacked. As a warning."

I was surprised to hear my own voice. I hadn't meant to speak exactly.

Ellis nodded. "That's one theory."

I tried to puzzle out another one, but just stared blankly at the back of Ellis's head.

"Come with me."

Ellis led me out of the observation room, handing off files to a new recruit who had clearly been eavesdropping on our conversation. The tips of his ears turned red when I glared at him. He opened a file and started flipping through pages for something to do. I made a tsking sound as I passed, but the noise caught in my throat. We were passing into the bullpen, and it had been years since I'd been inside the cubicle hell that was the headquarters of a precinct. I didn't recognize any faces, but conversations about wives and little league games stopped as I passed. A few furtive glances told me that my identity was common knowledge.

Ellis steered me toward a whiteboard in the corner. Had he decided to share information after all? I glanced at him, but he gestured toward the board with Stephen Kramer written in small print at the top. Our victim's name was eclipsed by the information scribbled and stuck around him. There was Mrs. Kramer's net worth circled in red. Meeza's snapshot of the possible Leif. A map of the Upper East Side with escape routes highlighted in yellow. Then a photo of me as Kathy Seasons taped across the "Salva" of "Salvatore Magrelli." I whirled to face Ellis, and a few officers snickered. They weren't newbies, though, and didn't blush when I glared at them.

"Out of all the people swirling around this big fucking mess of a case, who had opportunity, know-how, and motive?" Ellis asked.

I shook my head as his meaning sank in. I wasn't just a suspect with the NYPD in general: I was a suspect with my former best friend. "No way," I said. "I'll cop to opportunity and know-how, but motive? What possible motive could I have?"

And what possible motive could Ellis have for making me face an audience of officers and detectives? Was I going to be sacrificed as a warning to bad cops everywhere? Was he trying to shame me into a confession?

"Pick a number, Kathleen." My name came out in a hushed slur, and Ellis held up a fist to enumerate my shortcomings. "One," he said, unfolding his thumb. "A payment from the deceased's wife. Two, a preexisting tie to drug lord Salvatore Magrelli—"

"My preexisting tie is not a happy one," I said, thinking about the thirty-two stitches that my thigh had required.

I was shaking now, trying to control myself. I wasn't sure if I was more afraid of being arrested or being Salvatore's next target. Knowing Salvatore, it would be quick, at least. He was efficient, if nothing else. And maybe he did just want to scare me off like he'd tried to do that afternoon at the Costas. He could have killed me, and except for Zanna no one would have shed any tears. Her mother would have taken chewing tobacco with her to the funeral. Who am I kidding? I would have had a cop funeral. If Signora Costa came at all, it would have been to spit on my grave. Most of the guys at my old precinct would have said something along the lines of "Damn" or "Tough break," but they wouldn't have mourned me. Ellis didn't strike me as a weeper. He continued with his theories, ignoring my clenched jaw.

"Salvatore Magrelli's the only one who walks? That suggests favors, but I'm not done yet. This is the one I like the best.

Three, intimidation. You scratch his back, and he doesn't set his hounds on you."

Ellis shook his three fingers in my face, and I batted them away.

"If he's involved in any way, I need to be on a bus or plane right now. I need to be far from here."

I could just make out the smiling face of an officer over Ellis's left shoulder. The woman looked like she could have used a soda and some jujubes.

Ellis put his hand down. "You can't run away, because that would look even more suspicious."

I wanted to beg him to believe me, believe that I had nothing to do with Stephen Kramer or Samantha Evans, but instead I waited for his verdict. This demonstration seemed like a trial with Ellis as jury and judge. I hoped he wouldn't be the executioner too. When he turned away from me, I could see the outline of cuffs in his back pocket, and I rubbed my wrists unconsciously. There was a time when Ellis would have dismissed everything as coincidence, but many years existed between then and now. For the past week, I had been the primary suspect in a double homicide.

"There's something about the Evans murder I didn't tell you."

I stared at Ellis's back and waited again.

"There were multiple wounds to the face. It wasn't a single shot like you reported." Finally, Ellis turned around and faced me. At first I wasn't sure what he was saying. Was he implying that I had lied on purpose?

He continued: "It won't hold up in court, but I know you wouldn't have needed more than one shot. For that matter, neither would that punk sitting in the interrogation room."

I nodded, because I couldn't think of anything else to do or say. This had clearly been a show of solidarity, not a trial. He wanted everyone in the room to know that he was on my side, even if that meant putting his own reputation, and maybe even his detective rank, on the line. I was relieved, but I wasn't sure how long Ellis could keep the others in the precinct away from me.

Finding the real perpetrator fast was the best solution to both our problems. If that person had escalated from arranging a killing to physically killing, then we were dealing with someone volatile. This new discovery also put the widow back into the spotlight, especially with her dual monetary and romantic motives.

Ellis and I were on the same page for the first time in days. "We need to step up recon on the boy toy," he said after he was sure I had processed everything.

As the conversation had escalated, we had crept away from each other. I was standing beside the whiteboard, and he was now at least five feet away. My throat had constricted as soon as I was sure I wasn't going to be arrested, at least not yet. I tried to swallow the tears of relief but couldn't hold back any longer and let a few trickle down my face. I was glad Ellis believed me, but I wasn't sure I could forgive him for embarrassing me like this.

The woman with the movie-theater smile was looking down at her desk now, and I knew she was thinking that I had betrayed some sort of female code. I wanted to shout at her, *I'm not a cop anymore, lady! I can cry if I want to.*

Instead I asked, "Step it up from what," wiping snot from my nose with the sleeve of my sweatshirt.

"From nothing."

I weighed the pros and cons of what Ellis was offering though not stating. I knew he didn't have the authority to offer me work in an official capacity, considering my suspect status. Instead, his offer was a sort of dare to anyone who wanted to see me arrested. It stopped the tears.

Ellis continued: "Leif Nichols doesn't have a criminal record of any kind, so the information we have is akin to hearsay. He has a Pennsylvania driver's license, which doesn't help us. Mostly what we have, we got off the Play or Stay website. 31, 5'11", works in advertising."

Ellis was still five feet away, as if afraid to be too close. That was fine by me. There was a possibility that I would lash out at him. There was also a possibility that instead of affection, I would see disgust or disappointment in his face. Maybe he didn't suspect me, but he couldn't be happy about the mess I'd gotten us into.

"Works in advertising and is free in the afternoon," I parroted back. "I don't think so. Also, the man we suspect is Leif doesn't reach 5'11". 5'8" tops."

"Scrap all that, then. Just find out what you can."

Ellis stalked across the bullpen back toward the interrogation room. I stood facing a sea of unfriendly faces. And by sea, I mean a dozen or so men and women talking shop and answering phones. I waded in, dodging jellyfish frowns and shark snickers. *Scram*, they all seemed to be thinking simultaneously. And I did.

CHAPTER FIFTEEN

The only thing I knew for sure about our supposed Leif Nichols was that he liked older, rich women. I couldn't pull off millionaire, but Kathy Seasons was comfortable. I lamented the prettier red wig—probably being called "evidence item C" by now—then donned some fake diamond studs and an old Chanel purse that I hoped read "vintage" instead of "used." Not that Leif had struck me as someone who would know the difference, but thoroughness never hurt anyone. With nowhere to start except outside Mrs. Kramer's building, I texted V. P. for a vehicle.

"I'm in luv," he replied.

"I still need a car," I typed. "No bike. No hoopties."

I didn't hear back from him, but when I walked out of my apartment building an hour later, there was a familiar Lexus at the curb. I was feeling quite classy until I remembered that I still had to peel the key off from the undercarriage. A woman watched the proceedings skeptically, then her dog relieved his bowels on the sidewalk and she turned her attention to getting all of it into a plastic baggie. I had the key in the ignition before she finished. Mrs. Kramer's aversion to dogs made a little more sense all of a sudden.

At the office, Meeza was scanning Craigslist ads for possible clients. I peeked over her shoulder and noticed that most of the ads were private investigators looking for cases, not the other way around. That sounded about right, based on my experience.

"What do you think would be a more attention-grabbing heading? 'Discreet but Cheap' or 'We Find the Truth'?" Meeza formed her fingers into a gun and pulled the imaginary trigger. Then she laughed at herself and went back to scrolling. "I would consider this one: 'Honest Surveillance at Your Service.'"

"If they have to say they're honest, they're probably not honest."

"Good point."

I dropped my fancy purse onto the couch and rummaged through the mostly empty metal filing cabinet. If I had to stake out Mrs. Kramer's place again, I was determined to multitask. There were two open cases that I could research while waiting for the lady to finish her afternoon delight.

"I don't know if I'd put up an ad there," I said, glancing at Meeza's intense face.

"How do you normally get clients?"

"Mostly referrals."

Meeza looked dejected, and I knew she was thinking about how long it would take to build a reputation as a first-rate sleuth. Mr. Malik had flown overseas for business, leaving Meeza no other option than to wait for his return.

"And who knows who he'll be entertaining in Hong Kong," she said, putting the emphasis on "entertaining." I wondered if there was some sort of euphemism cheat-sheet that Meeza was studying at night.

"You can help me with my other cases, if you want."

This seemed to appease her, especially since she could do preliminary work while joining me on the stakeout, a.k.a. sitting in the Lexus. She dropped the case files, her laptop, and a portable Wi-Fi device in her oversized purse and beat me to our ride. Maybe her ad could say "Faster Than Lightning When Luxury Cars Are in the Picture." We were on our way within minutes.

"How does the air-conditioning smell so fresh? Like pure oxygen."

"I'm pretty sure that's just recycled air, Meeza. And anyway, it's September, we don't need to turn the A/C on."

"Maybe you don't need it on your side, but I need it on mine."

She set her temperature knob to seventy-two and leaned back into the lumbar-cushioned leather seat. I wasn't sure how the car would handle our different temperature preferences, but since I was pretty sure it could transform into a plane, if necessary, I didn't worry too much. I drove the ten blocks and found a parking space catty-corner from Mrs. Kramer's front door. It was 9 A.M.—too early for social calls—but I wanted to be in place.

Even with tinted windows, the Lexus didn't look suspicious on the Upper East Side, so I felt confident that we could stay for several hours. I took one of the case files from Meeza and glanced through the materials. It was one that I was cowardly avoiding because the client was a newlywed. There was nothing more depressing than those cases, with their fresh shock of disillusionment. I grimaced as Meeza pulled up their wedding photos from a photographer's website. The one in the center showed the tuxedoed groom kissing the top of the bride's head. Her eyes were closed and her hands splayed across his chest. I needed a break; I needed for this particular case to lead nowhere. It had been too long since I could file something under "Misinformed," if you didn't count Steve Stevenson, and I didn't.

"It says that they live in Brooklyn on Pineapple Street. How could anything go wrong on a street named after a fruit?"

I smiled at Meeza and hoped she was right. She gave me additional information about the bride—her work schedule and weekly yoga classes—which I mentally stored away. I decided the case could wait a few more days and flipped open the second one. It was unusual. A mother wanted to make sure that her son in college was attending classes and not partying with his friends day in and day out. With the cost of tuition these days, I didn't blame her. The main challenge wasn't passing as an undergrad, though nineteen would take a little emergency eye cream, but getting into New York University buildings. The security was tighter than you find on non-urban campuses, and every building required a student I.D. to be swiped for entry. Then there was the issue of befriending the kid so I could hang around long enough for the information I needed. At minimum, it was a four-day operation, but could take much longer, especially with my current, well, distractions.

I looked toward Mrs. Kramer's building, but except for the doorman wiping a smudge from the front door, there was no action whatsoever. I started Googling what the kids were wearing these days, letting Meeza enjoy the ambience.

Two hours and two bottles of water later, Meeza was bouncing in her seat. Her cheerful disposition was being called into question, and I suggested that she go in search of a bathroom. It didn't take much encouragement, and I was left watching the quiet apartment building by myself. The situation felt familiar except that the new car smelled better than the Sentra. I knew that someone from Ellis's team was conducting auditory surveillance a few blocks away, but that was none of my concern. The name of the game was "delegation" or "teamwork" or something, and I was going to play by the rules this time.

I closed my computer screen, which was displaying college-appropriate skinny jeans from Forever Twenty-One, and pulled my prop newspaper from the back seat. There were more uprisings in the Middle East, and the cover photo showed a young woman bleeding from a head wound. She held one hand on the gauze and the other over her face to shield her identity, presumably, from the cameraman. I pitied both of them, the woman fighting for her rights, and the unseen person trying to document it. The image felt invasive, but also necessary. It was meant to shake us out of our own apathy, an easy emotion if I've ever met one. I was reading about homemade bombs when Possible Leif sauntered into view. It wasn't a fair reaction, but something in my gut heaved when I saw him. *What a little punk,* I thought.

Ten minutes later, Ellis called to make sure that I had seen him enter the building. He had his own ways of verifying, and I wondered about the young officer whose job description now included listening to sex tapes. Had he anticipated such tawdriness when he took his entrance exam? I also hoped my own assistant would pop back up soon, because I figured Leif's visit wouldn't take more than an hour and could be much quicker.

But when someone tapped on the driver's side window, it was Ellis, not Meeza. I pressed a button, and the glass rolled soundlessly down.

"I'm just picking my brat up from ballet. You know how it goes," I said.

"V. P. must have upgraded your status."

"That's one way to look at it. My new ride has more to do with Meeza than me, though."

Ellis placed his hands on the open window and leaned down. "She's cute and all, but V. P.'s got his priorities wrong."

I snorted, and Ellis changed the subject.

"I have some information on the second victim, Samantha Evans. I want to check it out myself," he said.

"Okay, I can drop by tonight. Will you be at the precinct?"

He nodded and pushed off the car. I started to roll up my window, and he put his hand on top of it, causing a sensor to react and stop the operation.

"Be careful with this one. We don't know anything about him."

"You bet," I said. There was a time when I would have balked at such instructions, determined to take care of myself. That day, I wasn't complaining. With a landscape of violence on both local and national levels, asking me to take care of myself seemed appropriate.

Meeza opened the car door and slid in.

"What did I miss?"

"Our goose is in the nest."

Meeza giggled as I knew she would, and I settled back in my seat. T-minus thirty minutes, tops.

⸺⁕⸺

It was another two hours before Leif emerged from the apartment building, looking no worse for the wear. He set off toward Madison Avenue on foot, so I told Meeza that she could either wait there or take the car back to the office. From the gleam in her eyes when I handed her the keys, I figured she would be gone by the time I followed Leif around the corner.

Leif was surprisingly predictable for someone defying stereotypes by getting it on with a woman old enough to be his mother. He journeyed on foot to the nearby Chipotle and ordered an enormous burrito. I eyed it enviously but didn't want to get too close to him, so I window-shopped until he finished. There was an array of furnishings and clothing that I would never be able to afford, plenty to keep me busy while my suspect gobbled his lunch. His path from the fast food joint was exactly the same as our previous one, and I was soon watching him nap on his towel on what must have been chilly grass in Central Park. I decided against sitting in the brisk air and instead walked around the perimeter of Sheep Meadow, keeping my target in sight.

It was hard not to get distracted by the early fall patrons, a ragtag assortment of families kicking soccer balls, stoners sprawling under trees, and a few teenagers skipping class to scream and flirt at each other. The ubiquitous pigeons paid no mind to any of these and paraded in front of the lone hotdog vendor, who was reading a battered paperback. If I wasn't trying to hunt down a murderer, it would have been a pleasant stroll, and I promised myself that I would spend more time outside if I wasn't serving time next week.

I willed Leif Nichols to do something suspicious. He might have snored in response, but he didn't wave a gun around or shout bomb threats. The teenage boys looked more dangerous as they slung their girlfriends onto their backs and raced across the field. I bought a hotdog in consolation and asked the man what he was reading.

"Slaughterhouse Five."

It was a bold choice. I expressed my approval by ordering a Coke as well.

In the ensuing ten minutes, I managed not to spill mustard or soda on my suit, which was a step in the right direction. I tried to remember how long I had watched Leif nap the previous time, but I had been more focused then, less distracted by Marco-induced heartache and possible murder convictions. I repeated my go-to mantra in such situations, "rent, rent, rent," then tried out "no prison, no prison, no prison" and watched Leif roll over onto his side. His sleek physique showed the hint of a gut in that unflattering position, but I didn't think that fact was worth reporting.

I was on the lookout for the friend who had met him previously. No one resembling the Dumbo-eared man who wouldn't give Kate the time of day approached, but someone else did. A fortyish woman with a rambunctious pug headed in Leif's direction. When she got about twenty feet from him, she let the pug off its leash, and the dog bounded toward its target. Leif heard it in time to sit up and push the beast away from his head. The thing gladly jumped into his lap instead.

"Samson," the lady called, and the pug sauntered toward her. Samson couldn't make up his mind, though, and headed back to Leif, who was scrambling to his feet. The woman walked leisurely over and kissed Leif on each cheek. She said something, and I tried to move closer without being obvious. Not that either person was engaged in particularly paranoid behavior. They didn't glance over their shoulders or even seem to notice their park neighbors. I slipped off one of my shoes and pretended to dig for a pebble.

"No, that's too late," the woman was saying. "I take Samson for his walk around eight, then take a bath."

"How about five, then?"

The woman looked thoughtful, then nodded. She scooped up her dog, who squirmed to get free and was successful, dropping a couple of feet to the ground. He grunted once, then started rooting around in the grass for buried dog treats.

When she walked away, Leif tried to dust off what I assumed was a charming combination of dog hair and slobber. Then he plopped back down on the grass and closed his eyes. I dug out the imaginary stone from my shoe and continued past him until I got to a park bench. I wanted to sit closer, but it seemed unlikely that Kathy would risk getting her suit and purse dirty by picnicking on the grass. Never mind that she probably wouldn't eat a hotdog either. I was pretty sure that Leif hadn't noticed me in the two minutes it took to wolf down my snack.

I wrapped my scarf tighter around my neck to stay warm, slid my sunglasses on, and pretended the fresh autumn air was just what the doctor ordered. I was really trying to figure out what the hell was going on with Leif Nichols.

I had seen jealous lovers—red-faced and fist-clenched—and Leif was no jealous lover. He didn't linger outside Mrs. Kramer's apartment building, interrogating every man under sixty. He didn't wander aimlessly and downtrodden under the linden trees. Then there was this new lady who, I supposed, could be an aunt, but wouldn't an aunt place a friendly phone call instead of setting up a dinner in person? I took note of her appearance: 5'7", 150 or 160 pounds, expensive blond high-lights. Finally, and most importantly, how did Leif support himself, lazing about all day?

I waited to see if anyone else drew near before I wandered over to the suspect's area. I stood in front of him and stretched, letting him see how relaxed I was going to be about the whole thing. Then I turned and smiled at him.

"I saw what that nasty beast did to you," I said.

Leif leaned up on two elbows and looked me over.

"I'm sorry?"

"That little yappy thing. A pug, right? Stupid-looking dogs with all those wrinkles. We don't want them on our faces; why would we want them on our dogs?"

It was Leif's turn to smile, and it was clear that he was no big fan of Samson, regardless of what the owner was paying him. And if I was right, the owner was paying him handsomely for services rendered. It took a while to get to specifics, though. Leif offered me a spot on his towel, and I accepted, slipping my heels off and wiggling my red, pedicured toes. I fiddled with my fake diamond studs and all in all threw signs of my well-offness in the man's face. The only thing I didn't emphasize was my own face, not for fear of recognition, but for fear that he would know I was more or less his age. Finally, he asked me to dinner, and I said I would treat him.

"You know," I added, "I keep a maid on staff who does an excellent lasagna. Maybe you should come over. You can be discreet, right?"

"I'm a consummate professional."

"As I suspected."

I pulled out a pen and piece of scrap paper from my purse and handed it to him expectantly. He knew what to do and immediately scribbled down his number and name, Leif Nichols. This was our guy after all. Below his name, he wrote a price that made me rethink my current profession. I stopped myself from fantasizing about how I'd spend my hourly wages, but that Tribeca loft popped into my head before I could stop it. The views were impressive.

"My name's Kathleen Stone," I finally said. "I'm working with the NYPD."

Leif tried to get to his feet, but I grabbed his arm and yanked him back down.

"That was entrapment," he said. "I know my rights."

"I'm not interested in your career. Well, actually I am, but I need to talk to you about your relationship with Gloria Kramer." Leif tried again to get up, and I tightened my grip. "Please," I added because I figured it couldn't hurt.

"What do you want to know?" Leif lay down, and if I had to describe his attitude, I would call it sullen and downright toddler-like.

"Does she pay you in cash?"

He nodded and crossed his arms over his chest.

"What's your real name?"

"Leif Nichols."

"Really? You have a 'Stay or Play' profile using your real name?"

"That's not how I usually meet clients. It's just for fun, you know? But when Gloria decided to play with me, I recognized her photo from the paper. She and whatshisname donated ten million dollars to the hospital. Ten million dollars, you know? She was my kind of woman."

"Did you know that whatshisname is dead?"

"Yeah, Gloria mentioned it."

"Did you know that he was shot in the head?"

Leif uncrossed his arms and sat up. He suddenly looked pale and frightened, which was the right response. He was moving lower down my suspect list.

"Shit. No way. Please tell me it was suicide, that he's involved in some sort of Ponzi scheme and it's about to hit the papers."

I shook my head.

"Murdered? And you think I did it?" Leif's voice rose with the questions.

"We're just trying to gather as much information as possible. If you were a prime suspect, the police would have arrested you, right?"

Right? Unless I wasn't the only one getting special treatment. I shook that thought away.

"Yeah, that makes sense."

"Where were you last Saturday night about six o'clock?"

"With a client."

"Would you mind telling me the client's name?"

"Yes, I would."

I slid my sunglasses off and rubbed my head. You try to reason with children, and they want to pour flour in the toilet.

"Okay, would you like to be arrested?"

I'm not sure what makes a sigh petulant, but Leif's definitely was. He snatched the slip of paper from my fingers and wrote down a name under his hourly rate. I dropped it into my purse, stood up, and crammed my protesting feet back into the Kathy Seasons heels.

"I gave you the lowest rate, just so you know," Leif said. It was probably the best compliment I was going to get that day, so I took it.

As I walked toward the train, I dialed Ellis to report my findings. He said he would check on the alibi, but he also agreed with my gut feeling: Leif Nichols wasn't our man.

"I've got a big discovery to share too." Ellis paused to make sure I was on the edge of my seat. I was. "Our second victim, Samantha Evans? She used to work at Hamilton's. And her mortgage was new. Do you want to guess the down-payment amount?"

"One hundred thousand dollars?"

"Bingo."

"Do I get a prize?"

Ellis ignored me and kept talking, filling me in on Samantha's background check. There was no way to link the down-payment money to the missing bar money, but it was certainly something to think about. Was Hamilton the mystery guest who had never showed up to eat hamburgers and drink lemonade? Or had he shown up, but with an entirely different agenda? Maybe it was time to check out the victim's rehab facility.

"How do you feel about a little undercover work?" I asked, betting Ellis wouldn't be able to resist. He didn't.

CHAPTER SIXTEEN

Whilshire Farm wasn't actually a farm at all, but did encompass one hundred private acres for a variety of well-to-do sex addicts and overeaters. Midday, they mingled like they were on a yacht—martinis swirling and laughter rising. It seemed like the only people not invited to the A-list party were actual addicts. Mostly, the guests were substituting rehab for court-mandated community service, and hey, they were paying a staff, right? Some of those janitors and groundskeepers could have been illegal, making their charity work even more admirable. I felt torn between vomiting and giggling and, instead, clung to my faux-husband's arm while trying to look simultaneously contrite and better than everyone else.

Ellis had gone over the top for his role as the concerned tycoon. He had pomade in his hair, which gave it an ever-wet 1930s style, and wore a pinstriped three-piece suit, his own most likely. If he looked more Halloween than authentic, the staff didn't bat an eye. He had been referred to them as a big spender with a big problem: the missus, the ball and chain, little ol' me. Apparently Mrs. Vanders had a wee problem with hitting maids and needed a few months to recover from the traumatic experiences.

"Of course, Mrs. Vanders, you've been under a lot of stress," said the director, Delores Dawson. She struggled against Botox injections to show appropriate signs of concern. When that failed, she pushed a glossy brochure in my direction, and I nodded at the smiling images of cocktail hours, white-gloved dinners, and king-sized beds. I doubted I would even have to recite the serenity prayer if I didn't want to.

"I'll do it," I said, nodding enthusiastically, and frankly, the enthusiasm wasn't all fake. I was thinking about the on-site masseuse and how much tension my maid-disciplining had caused my neck and shoulders. I must have tensed up before I swung. Yes, there was that niggling nausea caused by the ethics of the place, but I thought I could choke down some lobster in the line of duty.

Mr. Vanders walked me outside to say a dry-eyed good-bye while someone brought my Louis Vuitton (knock-off) luggage to my suite. He embraced me, and I could smell aftershave and sweat, a combination that made me run my hands along his chest. It was all part of the act, so why not enjoy it? He leaned his mouth next to my ear and whispered, "The department won't stand for this long. Twenty-four hours, got it? See what you can dig up."

"You look like a cartoon character."

"I look like my Uncle Alfred."

"All right, Bruce Wayne."

I hadn't met an Uncle Alfred on my Dekker weekend visit, so I couldn't tell if Ellis was yanking my chain.

"I'll miss you, too," I said in a loud voice and took a step away from him. I finger-waved to two of my fellow inmates, an ascoted investment banker with a predilection for role-playing prostitutes and his codeine-happy "but I don't have a problem" wife. Hey, I needed someone to sit with during dinner. They were going in to change, and I did the same, hoping that the simple black dress I'd packed fit the bill of money-without-trying. I tucked a minuscule bug into my bra and tested it out. "Apples, bananas, and carrots." There was no earpiece, so I could only transmit, not receive. A little green light appeared when I spoke, though, which confirmed that something was happening.

Whilshire Farm prided itself on exclusivity—no more than one hundred guests at a time. The dining room fit the group comfortably, and I sat down by the parking-lot couple and reminded them that we had met earlier in the day.

"Of course, dear, the maid-beater." The wife, a Mrs. Lawrence Cavere, threw out the term offhandedly, so I responded with an equally offhanded nod and change of subject.

"How long have you two been here?"

"This time? What is it now, honey?"

Mr. Cavere looked up from his bisque, puzzlement furrowing his brow. "They all run together, don't they? We come at least once a year."

"You voluntarily come to rehab?"

The word "rehab" got a much more visceral reaction than "maid-beater," and I had a sudden urge to drop "cannibalism" into the mix, just to get a sense of the scale we were working with. Would "incest" raise an eyebrow?

"Well, the first time, no. Larry was having dinner with a young lady who turned out to be a whore. You know how it goes." Mrs. Cavere put the word "whore" in quotation marks, and I wasn't sure if that meant the lady wasn't a prostitute, or if Mrs. Cavere didn't know what quotation marks implied. The scale of off-limits language for the Caveres wasn't coming across too clearly. I tried to push those thoughts aside, though, because—as fun as Guess the Taboo was—it was possible that this charming couple had met the victim.

"Oh, I know. My girlfriend Samantha was here recently and raved about this place. Said if I ever need a break from reality, come here."

"That is exactly it. A break from reality."

Mrs. Cavere dipped her spoon into the bisque and sipped contentedly. I thought her codeine problem could be manufactured, but I wasn't sure about Mr. Cavere's "whores."

"Samantha said she met a lot of nice people here. She just raved about an enchanting couple from the city. It couldn't have been you two, could it?"

Mr. Cavere straightened his ascot and leaned closer to me. "Could have been. What did you say the girl's name was?"

"Samantha Evans. Pretty blonde in her late twenties." I had to stop myself before I gave them the full stats: blonde, blue eyes, 5'5", 125 lbs.

"No, that doesn't ring a bell, and I remember the young ones." Mr. Cavere winked, and I managed not to wrinkle my nose. The bisque helped, as did the medium-rare steak, fingerling potatoes, julienned greens, and chocolate mousse. The coma-inducing meal made for an early evening, and I was swimming on top of a feather mattress by 10 P.M. At 3 A.M., my cell phone vibrated, and I squinted at the number even though I knew who was calling.

"I was already up," I whispered.

"We could hear you snoring," Ellis replied and hung up.

I dug around in my bra until I unearthed the bug and put my lips close to amplify the sound: "I do not snore." I slipped the device back into the underwire and tugged on black sweatpants and a black tank top. If I ran into anyone, my excuse would be insomnia, and someone would probably offer to rub my feet or supply Ambien. I cracked the door and looked up and down the hallway. All I could see were fake candles dimmed to a comforting romantic hue, so I tiptoed out onto the carpet. I knew the patient files had to be kept somewhere in the office, and I had a decent sense of the building layout. I would have to make my way through the dining room, across the lobby, and into the administrative wing.

The candles stopped at the dining-room door, and when I opened it, pitch black greeted me. I had a flashback to descending into Hamilton's basement and stepped into the room quickly before I chickened out. It was necessary to close the door behind me in case someone else was prowling around and prone to suspicion. At the moment, I was less worried about nosy Nellies than murderous ones waiting in the dark to pounce on unsuspecting private investigators, but I couldn't use my cell-phone flashlight and risk unwanted attention.

The round tables created a first-rate obstacle course, which I took at a snail's pace, hoping to avoid noises and bruises. I felt in the dark for tablecloths and used them as guides, inching my hands around one until I needed a new one. Before long, I had made it to a wall, except that it wasn't the wall I wanted; it was the doorless east side of the room. Changing tactics, I followed the wall until the coffee and tea table blocked my way, then I waded back out into the black. Finally, five or so minutes later, I had silently made it to the other door: locked.

And here's where I would like to point out that I am a professional. I didn't throw a tantrum; I didn't even curse under my breath. Instead, I pulled out the lock-picking kit that I had brought along for the office door and removed the first metal piece I touched. My opponent was a knob lock—not exactly Fort Knox—and I didn't worry about using exactly the right tool. My biggest concern was leaving telltale scratches behind, so I felt with my left fingertips for the opening before sliding my pick into it. Gently, I manipulated the cylinders, wiggling from side to side until something popped and the handle turned freely. Fake candlelight greeted me, and I checked the knob for evidence of tampering. It looked clean to me, so I stepped into the building's lobby.

Unlike the windowless dining room, the lobby was mostly glass, and I could see the driveway and surrounding woods. Hopefully, my twenty-four-hour stay would not involve bonding exercises in trees. I didn't want to walk across a tight-rope or trust-fall from a stump. Whilshire Farm didn't seem like that sort of place, but you never know about treatment facilities, even luxury ones. Terms like "unity" and "commu-nication" are important to boards of directors.

The administration office had security on a par with the door I had just jimmied, and within two minutes I was crouched by one of four filing cabinets, flipping through the "E" folders. Samantha Evans's report was easy enough to find, despite being wisp thin. It consisted of a single sheet with name, address, and two signatures—one for admittance and one for discharge—in the same black inky scrawl. I couldn't make out the loopy name, but I took a photo of the page in case Ellis might have better luck.

My only real job was to read the file on Samantha, but I'm nothing if not industrious. I put the file up and started opening others. The Caveres' files were much more interesting. Mrs. C. had at least a dozen pages of therapist notes, complete with diagnosis ("histrionic") and cure ("relaxation"). The following sheet of paper listed her relaxation sessions, including daily massages, sauna visits, and horseback riding. I couldn't quite picture Mrs. C. bouncing on top of a mare, but what happens one hundred miles north of Manhattan has always been a mystery to me. Mr. C.'s file was equally packed and mentioned a particular prostitute by name ("Candy") and cure ("relax-ation"). I flipped the files shut and crammed them back into their places. My own file was a boring slip of paper, so I began opening others at random. Some were twenty or more pages full, while others looked like mine and Samantha's. I wondered if perhaps some client information was more confidential, if Mr. Hamilton had paid extra to have his sweetheart's remain hush-hush. Maybe he wasn't as forthcoming as the Caveres, who didn't seem to mind advertising their dysfunctions.

My curiosity sated, I pulled the office door shut behind me, then tried to jump back through it when headlights swam across the wall. Unfortunately, the door handle had locked behind me as, I now suspected, had the dining-room door. The bare-bones lobby left much to be desired in the way of camouflage, so I went for the giant pot. I crouched down behind what seemed to be a fake ficus. The management had stuck an air freshener under the bottom branch, and I could only think *classy*. I held my breath until the car parked and killed its lights. When I peeked out, I could see two silhouettes in the parking lot. Men, probably, but I couldn't be sure. It seemed like an odd time to be conducting business, but if a celebrity showed up in our midst tomorrow at breakfast, there would be a reasonable explanation.

After about five minutes, the car drove off, and the other person walked into the woods. I got goosebumps on my arms, but was probably overreacting. I straightened up, causing the plastic leaves to rustle.

Unlocking the front door, I stepped out into the night. It was at least ten degrees cooler in the country, and my goosebumps turned to the chilled variety. I whispered into my cleavage that I had seen a suspicious person disappear into the woods and that I was following up. I really meant "following," but since the transmitter was only one-way, there was no one to squabble with me.

The pebbled driveway crunched loudly, and I sprinted across it to get away from the noise and the moonlight. My first step into the woods took care of that problem. It was if someone had turned on a horror movie soundtrack, and above my thudding heartbeat, I could hear twigs snapping, coyotes crying, and amorous cicadas buzzing away. Deep breathing seemed to help, and I reminded myself that I had once had nerves of steel. I could lie straight-faced to dope dealers and take a punch to the stomach with grace. My present-day nerves of rubber said they didn't care about all that, and what was that shadow over there? I ducked behind a pine tree, but when the shadow didn't move, I inched closer and found a tree trunk covered with motivational phrases and long lengths of nylon rope. Just as I suspected: team-building claptrap.

Since I was weaponless and couldn't think of a reason not to, I gathered up one of the ropes used for, I assume, lassoing couples together and making them maneuver an obstacle course, and continued in what I guessed was the direction of the suspicious character. Of course, if anyone saw me, "suspicious" would probably spring to mind, too. I looked like a deranged strangler on the prowl. My nighttime insomnia excuse wouldn't carry much mileage in the middle of a forest.

Twenty minutes or so later, I leaned down toward my cleavage again and whispered, "lost in the woods now. Over and out." My one consolation was that it had to be four o'clock in the morning by now, and Ellis would be kept up, listening to my progress. I stopped and listened again, this time making out the sounds of, I swear, wolves and bears and maybe lions. You know, escaped from the zoo or something. God help me, I didn't want to get eaten. I longed for pavement, streetlights, and twenty-four-hour diners. And in my longing, I made a light appear. Well, probably not, but there was definitely a glimmer of light in the distance. I walked toward it with a new fear of being shot, but decided, between the two, I preferred bullets to razor-sharp teeth.

A cabin loomed in front of me with Tudor-style siding and shingled awnings. It looked straight out of a fairytale, but that was no comfort considering the staggering number of decapitations, poisons, and general blood loss in those stories. I crept close to the window and looked inside. A man I had never seen before was sitting at a round table, punching numbers into a calculator. The scene was not exactly sinister, and I waited for something more interesting to happen. Not that I had wanted to find a witch testing a kiddie stew, but I wouldn't have minded something a bit more titillating than an accountant. Still, I had nearly been eaten by a lion to get this far, and I didn't want to waste the opportunity. I dropped the rope, walked around the house, and knocked on the front door, wishing I could see the man's reaction, but settling for a conversation.

He opened the door cautiously and peered down at me. "Yes?"

"Wonderful! I've been wandering around for hours in that God-forsaken wilderness." I pushed past him into the small interior space and looked around with my best impression of disdain. "I thought I was going to freeze to death. Haven't you heard of placards? Guideposts? Street signs, for heaven's sake!"

"Dr. Goldman." The man stuck out his hand, and I shook it waspishly.

"Kennedy S. Vanders. Do you, by any chance, have gin?"

<hr/>

While the cabin didn't have a roaring fire, it did have central heat and air and, yes, gin. It was quite cozy, to be perfectly honest, and I struggled to keep up my hoity-toity airs. I wanted to wrap my hands around my glass, close my eyes, and nap.

Instead, I sat straight up, occasionally took a dainty sip, and commented on the cobwebs. The cabin was clearly used on a regular basis. It was well stocked and moderately clean, but the corners were neglected.

Dr. Goldman had been an employee of Whilshire Farm for ten years and had been hired by the founder, Delores Dawson, herself. He was what you might call a wealth of information. The facility was intended to give "a delicate clientele more choices than AA." When I pointed out that there weren't many drug or alcohol addicts in our midst, Dr. Goldman complimented my acuity and explained how the facility had evolved into its niche market (niche problems). There was already a glut of upscale facilities; this would cater to a different need. *At these prices, it better,* I thought.

"You have all this land," I said, gesturing dismissively toward the window. "Why not expand?"

"We don't want any patient to get lost in the shuffle."

"So, everyone gets personal attention."

"Of course."

I trod carefully and didn't ask about Samantha. Instead, I talked about the general services rendered and guessed the staff to be around twenty-five. I tried to do that math in my head. Three thousand dollars a week times one hundred customers minus salaries and upkeep. I didn't come up with an exact number, but the place was obviously doing okay.

"You work late hours, Dr. Goldman. I hope they're paying you well."

Dr. Goldman chuckled and spun his gold wedding band. He glanced at a cardboard box filled to the brim with papers.

"Not late, Mrs. Vanders. Early. My day starts at 3:30 with some calisthenics, then I come here to work quietly until my appointments begin at 9. Between you and me, I'm working on a memoir."

It wasn't exactly a confidence-inspiring confession, but he was trying, so I nodded condescendingly. Oh Mrs. Vanders, you're not an easy one to impress, are you?

When the sky turned from navy to soupy gray, Dr. Goldman walked me back to the main facility. He didn't tell me to watch out for man-eating beasts, so I figured we were more or less safe. And when he didn't ask me how I'd managed to get out of the building, I assumed he was oblivious, discreet, or knowledgeable about a back entrance for the patients. They would hardly lock us in at night, would they?

I crashed into my bed, not even bothering to update New York's Finest on my whereabouts. I figured they could deduce the situation from my snores.

CHAPTER SEVENTEEN

The psychologist's office was Pepto-Bismol cheery and, despite the nicer furnishings, reminded me of my NYPD-assigned psychologist's office where I had reported twice a week for a month after my undercover assignment. One session of trauma debriefing followed by what felt like countless sessions of evaluation decidedly did not equal a cure. At least not for me. But I had been recertified after fully recounting every nightmarish twist and turn of my life undercover. The psychologist had been particularly interested in my scar story and had made me tell it three times.

"And you didn't think Mr.—I'm sorry, what was his name again?"

"Salvatore Magrelli."

"Right, you didn't think Mr. Magrelli was going to hurt you when you disobeyed him?"

I balked at the polite address of "Mister," wasn't crazy about "disobeyed," and, come to think of it, didn't much like anything that came out of my psychologist's mouth. He could have blown bubbles in the air and their iridescence would have irritated me. Did I mention he made me repeat the story three times? I couldn't tell whether he was a sicko and enjoyed that sort of thing or if he was listening for discrepancies. Either way, he concluded that if I could talk about it, I wasn't suffering from it. Many people were impressed by how quickly I had been cleared. They were less impressed by my resignation a month later.

I wasn't looking forward to the inevitable memories and poured my concentration into being Mrs. Vanders, housewife and philanthropist (except when it came to the personal staff). What trauma would she have to recount? Exactly. None.

"Why are you here, Mrs. Vanders?" Dr. Goldman asked.

"Because my friend Samantha Evans recommended Whilshire Farm highly."

Dr. Goldman opened my file, which I knew to be empty, and seemed to study it. I was pretty sure by his concerned expression that he was thinking about the next chapter of his memoir and how best to make himself appear like a wunderkind. He released an almost imperceptible sigh, then took out a clean legal pad and made a note on it. I guessed at what it might be: "Make my first wife a supermodel?" "Turn my private high school into a violence-filled nightmare?"

"Very logical, Mrs. Vanders, but let's talk about before. What made you ask your friend, Mrs. Evans, you say? What made you ask her for a recommendation?"

"Oh, I didn't ask her for a recommendation. And it's 'Miss.' Young, pretty, you surely remember her."

Dr. Goldman furrowed his brow, and I wondered if the early morning gin was clouding his synapses. While he had been hammering away at his keyboard, I had been snoozing. We weren't exactly on an even playing field. That was okay by me; I was more interested in winning than playing fair.

"I'm not at liberty to discuss other patients," Dr. Goldman finally said. "Whenever you're ready, tell me about Miss Gonzales."

I was prepared for the question and raised my eyebrows slightly at the name, just as I had rehearsed with Ellis.

"*Consuela* is lazy. I find her napping during the day, as if I'm running a hotel. Wouldn't that make you angry?"

"And you hit her with a hairbrush."

"Grazed her. I threw it to get her attention. Then, two days later, I'm in civil court with a team of lawyers. This is what happens when service employees unionize."

It was a gauntlet, and I was keen to know how Whilshire Farm treated their patients' indiscretions. It was as I had imagined all along—Dr. Goldman said he sympathized.

After an hour of sympathizing, I slipped into the dining room to grab a bottled water before my spa appointment. I mean, physical therapy session. I didn't like what I saw; there were maintenance workers replacing the lobby-side doorknob. I froze, but decided it could be coincidental. It seemed unlikely that anyone would inspect the locks daily. Sure, there were some high-dollar prescription medications in this place—some of which Dr. Goldman graciously offered me at the end of our hour—but they were kept in the nursing wing. There wasn't anything to steal in the dining room except sodas and waters. Even the top-shelf liquor was kept in the locked kitchen cabinets when meals or cocktails weren't being served. I hurried back to my room all the same to report the occurrence to whomever was listening on the other end of my microphone. Probably one of the cadets.

My bed was unmade, which surprised me. Not that day-old sheets had ever bothered me before, but I thought for sure that the cleaning staff would have been by while I was in counseling. I had hidden anything potentially incriminating just in case. Perhaps they didn't want to risk having Mrs. Vanders and a maid in the same room. I grabbed the pillows I had kicked to the floor sometime in the night and tossed them onto the bed. A dark critter scurried out of its hiding place and buried itself back under the sheets.

My city instincts kicked in, and I didn't even catch my breath. My mind quickly worked through the possibilities: a cockroach, a big one, a water bug. I've only encountered the prehistoric-looking water bug a few times in my life, and aside from being an ugly son of a gun, he's harmless. I took a shoe in my hand and shook the sheets, hoping to coax him to the floor. A black pincer revealed itself, then retreated. *A black pincer?* My mind readjusted: a beetle, a big one, a mutant beetle. This time, I took the corner of the sheet in my hand and tugged it up forcefully, sending the invader to the floor on the other side of the bed. I crept around, shoe in striking position. The scorpion was not happy about the disturbance.

He moved his six-inch body with surprising speed, and my retreat wasn't fast enough. The stinger hit me in the ankle, and I went down with a shriek. I batted him into the wall with my shoe, where he was stunned enough for me to stumble to the door and out into the hallway. A staff member was running in my direction, and I panted to him not to go into the room. I'm not sure if he fully understood, but he nodded and checked my pulse as I slid down to the floor.

"Mrs. Vanders, are you all right?"

I shook my head no, but was too shocked to explain. My ankle felt like someone was pressing a brand into the flesh. I wrapped my hands around it and rocked until the nurse came and pried my fingers back. I didn't resist and instead concentrated on not passing out. I was cold and shaking, but sweat beaded on my forehead and above my lips.

Scorpions are not native to the Northeast, so I was unsurprised—though no less panicked—when the nurse did not recognize the sting. I managed to explain, even though my tongue felt as if it were covered with fur. The nurse indicated that I should lie down, and I was more than happy to comply. The wool carpet soaked up my sweat as something was slid under my ankle to elevate it. I couldn't have looked to see if I'd wanted to, because my vision was slowly giving way to black spots. I shut my eyes against them and lost consciousness.

⟞⟝

"Kennedy."

Our thirty-fifth president was waving from the open-air backseat of a limousine.

"Kennedy."

"Ask not what your country can do for you—"

"Can you hear me?"

I struggled up through the fog and blinked into a puke-green hospital room, complete with ominous beeping monitors and an IV bag. I followed the tube to the crook of my elbow where it was attached, then looked down farther to my hand, which was being held by a much larger hand. I enjoyed the contrast in skin tones for a hazy moment, my olive summer color against pink. The hand was connected to Ellis, who was mouthing my undercover name again as a reminder. I swallowed and was relieved that my tongue no longer felt like a squirrel, but it was still dry. And I was livid. Utterly exhausted and livid.

"It turns out you're allergic to scorpions, darling," said Ellis, patting my forearm in a forced way. I narrowed my eyes at him, and he darted his toward a hovering man and back to me.

"Mrs. Vanders? Kennedy? Can you sit up?"

I glanced at the hovering man, but couldn't make out much beyond the white lab coat. I maneuvered an elbow underneath myself and pushed. I had to pause halfway there, but I made it into a sitting position and leaned back against the pillows. The doctor asked me to open my eyes, and I complied long enough for him to flash a light into both pupils.

"Good, good," he said. "You're out of the woods now. My name is Dr. Dawson. I believe you met my wife Delores yesterday."

Mrs. Vanders or not, I wasn't up for small talk, so I nodded at the man. I may have muttered something about ice chips, because they arrived as the doctor began his spiel about ana-phylactic shock. He ended it with a warning to be careful, and it took considerable willpower to nod my head again instead of snap at him. Exactly how far away from Arizona do I need to travel to avoid scorpions?

"Your husband told me that your cancer's in remission. Congratulations."

"Thanks," I replied, keeping my expression as neutral as pos-sible. I ran my hand over my head and, as expected, found my short, real hair. It was probably the last thing I should worry about, but I prayed that my replacement Kathy Seasons/Ken-nedy S. Vanders wig had not been lost in the shuffle of my near-death experience. That would leave my supply thoroughly diminished, with only Kate, Katya, and Kiki left. And Kiki was a loaner, whatever Dolly said to the contrary. Or, if not a loaner, a special-occasioner.

When Dr. Dawson left the room, Ellis dropped my hand and stood up. He rubbed his face, and I wondered how long he had been awake and how long I had been out.

"Am I under observation?"

Ellis didn't respond for a second. "I didn't think it would be dangerous," he finally said. I could see that he was ambiguously angry. I had known that emotion before, radiating in every direction because you're not sure who the real enemy is, and you can't even rule out yourself. "Yes, you're under observation for a few more hours. They want to make sure your histamine levels really are stable."

"Am I going back to Whilshire Farm?"

"No way. We're going to find a way to subpoena the files."

"There's a whole other set in that cabin. They're unofficial, in a plain cardboard box, and no one's going to hand those over."

Ellis nodded and mulled over that new information. "We'll get a search warrant, then."

"There's no concrete evidence to link the facility to Samantha Evans's death. No judge is going to grant a search warrant."

Ellis shrugged, which wasn't an eloquent argument. It was more like an opening.

"I'll go back for another day and see what's in those files."

My voice cracked, and I stuck a few more ice chips in my mouth. As I crunched, I watched Ellis consider his options. He didn't seem to like the scrutiny, because he turned toward the wall to think in peace.

Somehow the term "anaphylactic shock" had a calming effect. Yes, someone had stuck a scary animal in my bed, but no, they weren't trying to kill me, only scare me off. If my voice could have taken the strain, I would have explained as much to Ellis, but he could figure it out himself. Top of our class and all that. I popped a few more ice chips in my mouth and waited it out.

"Twenty-four hours."

I slipped the IV out of my elbow and stanched the blood with a tissue. To his credit, Ellis didn't flinch, but opened up a couple of cabinets until he found a bandage. He taped it down over the puncture, then helped me out of bed. Surprisingly, my ankle looked normal except for a fierce-looking dot. "No harm, no foul" was my motto for the day. Ellis tossed me my clothes, which were neatly folded on the visitor's chair, and I threw them on as quickly as possible, being careful not to tear my bandage.

I linked my arm into his, but he slipped it around me and pressed my body against his while we walked down the hallway. The nurse at the floor station fluttered helplessly and tried to stop us, but Ellis put on his best Mr. Vanders impression, which, even if over the top, seemed to do the trick. Nurses and attendants were cowed, and we made our way out to a familiar-looking Lexus. When Ellis opened my car door for me, I laughed.

"Meeza insisted."

Meeza had also insisted on leaving me flowers, a bouquet of lilies that occupied the entire passenger seat.

"She's thoughtful," I said, inhaling the scent before positioning myself under them. My wig had been tossed carelessly onto the dash, and I pulled it toward me.

"Who is?" Ellis asked, climbing behind the wheel. The seat moved into a pre-programmed position. He glanced at the bouquet, then back to the road. "Oh yeah, she is."

I wondered when Ellis had called Meeza and what they had talked about. To be frank, I didn't like the idea of them conversing behind my back, swapping stories about Kathleen being duped by a veterinarian or Kathleen making stuffed foxes float. Were depressing thoughts a side effect of allergies?

We drove back toward the retreat in silence until I fiddled with the satellite radio and found a classical station. If our college classmates could have seen us, driving a Lexus, listening to what sounded like Bach, they would have beaten us up. Thankfully, there was no one we knew for miles around except for the crackpot staff of Whilshire Farm. I slipped my unharmed Kennedy wig back into place.

"This must clear me, right? I mean, I wouldn't sic a scorpion on myself."

"You didn't know you were allergic." He paused and glanced at me through the lilies. "Look, right now, the others are taking my word for you."

In other words, they were doing him a favor. The unspoken obligations he was under in return weighed on me, and I didn't ask any more questions.

We had worked out a pretty basic plan that involved me heading out to the cabin around midnight, a good four hours before Dr. Goldman started working. I wasn't exactly looking forward to plunging back into the woods, but at least I now had a compass and a destination. Plus, I had an hour-long massage to put on the NYPD tab.

CHAPTER EIGHTEEN

Slicked up with a variety of scented oils, listening to what I like to call "waterfall music," I should have been thoroughly relaxed, catatonic even, considering the events of the past day. Instead, I was running down a list of possible enemies as I watched a pair of perfectly painted toes through the massage-table headrest. Delores Dawson acted like my best friend, and I couldn't exactly see her rustling up an Arizona Bark and letting it loose inside a guest's—a wealthy guest's—room. There was Dr. Goldman, but we had bonded over gin, hadn't we? And he had also absolved me of my domestic-abuse sins. There was the cleaning and other service staff, but I honestly couldn't believe the residents' dirty laundry was publicly aired. Of course, people talk.

The masseuse worked on a knot in my neck, pushing it down as far as possible. It hurt, and I had to remind myself that this was good for me. When she went to work on another knot, though, I added her to my suspect list.

After a shower to wash off all the fragrances as well as the dried patch of blood on my arm, I dressed in a long-sleeved blue chiffon dress and paired it with heels and pearls. I knew I was going to be the belle of the ball that night, i.e. the primary source of gossip, so I made sure to smooth down my wig and put on a coat of lipstick. My eyes were just a little too large and gave off an air of naïveté that I didn't think Mrs. Vanders would have, even in a crisis. I added eyeliner, which helped a little bit, and gave myself a few reminders: my character would enjoy the attention, but not the cause. A trip to the emergency room showed weakness, and Mrs. Vanders was above weakness. I almost convinced myself, then added another coat of eyeliner just in case.

As expected, the dining-room occupants turned to stare at me as I entered. I raised a hand to my two buddies, the Caveres. Mrs. C. was ecstatic that she could be included in my circle of notoriety, and despite the smells of *coq au vin* wafting from the kitchen, I was reminded of my high school cafeteria, where I'd tried to stay out of the spotlight but watched girls rise and fall in the game of popularity.

"Oh, you poor dear! How are you feeling?"

Mrs. C. linked her arm with mine and led me over to their table, where three eager faces looked up. The three stumbled over themselves in introductions, and I decided it wasn't exactly popularity that made me a desirable dinner companion: it was boredom. With every whim catered to at Whilshire Farm, the conversation couldn't typically extend beyond weather. These definitely weren't my senior-year classmates with their STD scares and experimental drugs. Having something to talk about over meatloaf was never a problem.

I concentrated on the task at hand and dismissed the concern pouring from my table. "Oh, it was nothing. Just a little shock, is all."

"I heard it was a snake that crawled through the window."

I turned toward the woman who had spoken. She was so small that her clavicle bones looked like weapons, and I could have circled my fingers around her bicep without touching her skin. She was delicate to the degree of a sparrow. Another woman at the table nodded in agreement, but not Mrs. C.

"No, I heard it was a bee. You're severely allergic. Right, Kennedy?"

It was more than I could have hoped for. No official announcement had been made, meaning speculation ruled the roost.

"That's right, just a carpenter bee. I am violently allergic, though I haven't been stung since childhood."

"Imagine that! A carpenter bee in September."

The emaciated woman sat back in her chair to daydream about the possibility. She twirled her spoon in her soup, but didn't bring any of the liquid to her lips. I, on the other hand, was famished and tore into my chef salad as soon as it arrived.

The others swapped stories about their own allergies, ranging from good ol' ragweed to strawberries. One had gone to grammar school with a girl who wore an emergency necklace. Another had a brother who couldn't fly for years when peanuts were still being served on commercial flights. My attention waned, but I murmured enough to seem interested between bites of ham and egg. The chicken arrived soon after, making my level of interest drop even lower, but everyone except the sparrow lady grew quieter as well. Sorbet, a cognac, and I was headed back to my room, fearful of what I might find.

I really wanted my Smith & Wesson, but Ellis had vetoed a gun since I didn't technically have a license to carry. Without any other option, I turned on the overhead light and did a quick survey of the room. Nothing looked amiss, but I shook out the sheets and checked the closet. Sleep would have been a problem even if I hadn't needed to get up in two hours.

I wasn't convinced that midnight was late enough to avoid run-ins with the staff, but I also wasn't sure how much time I would need for the files. The good news was that my insomnia cover story would seem even more believable considering my traumatic day. So at the witching hour, I pulled on black yoga clothes, adding a cardigan this time, and wandered out into the hallway. Ellis had obtained the architectural designs of the building, so I now knew of another way out. I wound through connected hallways until I got to a staircase that took me to an illuminated exit. I didn't see any signs of an alarm and, sure enough, when I pushed on it, the door swung open sound-lessly. It had to lock from the inside, though, so I looked for something to wedge into the crack. There was nothing within arm's length but dirt, so I took off the sweater. *Well, that didn't last long.*

I was expecting the horror-movie symphony this time, but I still didn't like the cacophony of sounds. Thankfully the moon was bright enough that I didn't even need a flashlight. I pulled out my compass and headed ten degrees northeast, which I was promised would take me straight to the cabin. The incor-rect word turned out to be "straight," because I had to veer off course to navigate brush and trees. I could feel nettles stick into my pants, but there wasn't much point in pulling them out only to make room for new ones. When I tripped over a fallen branch, I stayed on the ground for a second to catch my breath.

In the pause, I could hear something moving toward me in the dark. Whatever it was didn't move stealthily, so I figured it was either too scary to care or human. I hunched down behind a tree and peered in the general direction of the noise. When a figure came into view, I wasn't entirely surprised; I never trusted anyone with a manicure that good.

Of course, Delores Dawson's manicure didn't really fit her nighttime image. She had replaced her pantsuit with jeans, a flannel shirt, work boots, and a rifle. What's more, she looked comfortable holding her firearm. If I'd had to guess, I would have put her path as ten degrees northeast. She came within a few feet of me and stopped. I held my breath and thanked the cicadas for not seeming at all deterred by the intruder. I would never complain about their buzzing again. Delores drank from a canteen, then took off again, stomping through the woods. She may have looked comfortable with that hunting gun, but I couldn't imagine any creature remaining in a one-mile radius. When I thought it was safe to follow, I proceeded in her general direction. Within five minutes, I was at a familiar clearing, watching a light flick on in the cabin.

I watched from a distance for a minute or so, but curiosity got the better of me and I crept to the closest window. When I peeked inside, Delores was putting the cardboard box of files on the table. For a moment, I thought her intent was to burn them, but instead she flipped through until she found a piece of paper she wanted. She tucked it into her pocket and flipped off the lights. I scrambled toward the other side of the house until I heard stomping coming from the woods and knew she was retreating.

I moved swiftly around the front and into the building. I didn't dare turn on a light, so I hauled the box of files over to the counter where moonlight pooled through the window. Unlike the variety of portfolios in the central administration office, these were all whisper-thin like Samantha Evans's. They all had admittance and discharge dates with a handwritten receipt stapled in the corner. No bills for scorpion food or ammunition. I reported as much to Ellis through my attached microphone.

"I'm going to see if I recognize any names."

There were a few hundred files, so my progress was not as rapid as I would have liked. Moreover, there was no identifiable system of organization whatsoever. I pulled out one at a time, looking for, well, anything at all. About ten minutes had passed when I pulled out Colt Hamilton's file. That wasn't too astonishing, since he must have known about the place to send his girlfriend there. A number did catch my eye, though: $2,450,000. That's a lot of massage oil.

On closer inspection, the paper stapled to the corner didn't seem to be a receipt but a deposit slip. There was a smaller number underneath the millions: $245,000. What could that 10% be exactly? I flipped back through the files I had dismissed while looking for familiar names and inspected the deposit slips. Some of the amounts made sense, but others were astronomical. Hundreds of thousands of dollars here, a million or two there.

"Turn around slowly."

I jumped at the sound of Delores's voice and turned to face the barrel of her Winchester.

"You're trespassing," she said calmly, and it was clear she had spent too much time mollifying customers. Her voice had a happy lilt to it when it should have sounded menacing. It was no less frightening for the sugary timbre.

"I couldn't sleep." My own voice was not as confident as I wanted and curled up at the end into a question. The real question was, how had this stomping madwoman snuck up on me? I glanced down at her shoeless feet and congratulated myself on solving that mystery at least.

She gestured for me to sit at the table, and I obeyed. Unless she tried to physically restrain me, I figured my best bet was to stick to my cover.

"It's a bit dusty in here. You should send someone out to clean it."

Delores ran a finger across the counter and shrugged. Some gunk lodged itself under her red fake fingernail, and I glanced down at my own. I avoided fake nails whenever possible, but Mrs. Vanders didn't seem like a person to be caught dead in a slapdash coat of Tickled Pink Wet n Wild. My French tips were securely in place.

"Did you find anything interesting beyond dust?"

I shook my head. "I was out here the other night with Dr. Goldman." I struggled to recall one of Meeza's sexual euphemisms and settled on "extracurricular activities." Delores wasn't buying it. With Ellis Dekker posing as my husband, I couldn't blame her, but I tried for a little girl talk.

"Oh, you must know how it is with the handsome ones, Delores. They only care about *their* needs."

There, I had worked her name into the conversation. At least if I ended up shot in the head, the NYPD would have a pretty good lead.

"What's in the files, Mrs. Vanders?"

"Nothing of interest at all. I was hoping to find some dirt on my friend Samantha, but you guys must really take the whole privacy thing seriously. There's nothing at all on those sheets."

Delores crossed the room and put her face two inches from mine. Her intent was to intimidate me, but all I saw was opportunity. I sprang up as fast as possible and launched myself directly into her chest. She fell back, hand still gripping the rifle, but its barrel was pointed toward the ceiling. I sprinted to the door, yanked it open, and ran in a diagonal pattern back to the woods. A shot was fired and lodged in a nearby tree as I disappeared from the clearing.

My wilderness skills fall somewhere on the spectrum of slim to none, but I figured I was safer there than back at the facility. I scrambled in whatever direction put the farthest distance between me and the psychotic director. When I thought my lungs might come up out of my mouth, I hauled myself onto the lowest branch of a tree. I couldn't hear anything, but that didn't mean that Delores hadn't entered the woods without her boots.

As a city kid, I had never actually been in a tree, but I figured I could imitate what I had observed in movies. I climbed as high as I could, ungracefully but with some success, then leaned back against the trunk. The tree still had most of its leaves and while I could see the ground, I couldn't see much else. I hoped that meant I was camouflaged, because my plan ended there.

My body wanted to gulp air, but I breathed as quietly as possible. I wasn't sure how much of the one hundred acres of Whilshire Farm consisted of forest, but I guessed most of it, especially since the place was clearly a front. Why waste money on expansion? Nonetheless, my attacker surely knew these trees better than me, and there were at least five hours until sunrise. That's a long game of hide-and-seek. My job often requires me to stay still for long periods of time, so I had that going for me. Of course, I had never been treed before, but there's a first time for everything.

Why did Hamilton and many others give this place millions of dollars? I shuffled through the usual suspects when large sums of money are involved—extortion, ransom, drugs—and settled on laundering. Whilshire Farm was the perfect setup for cleaning large sums of money, because they already made large sums of money. What's a few extra million to a company raking in, say, fifteen a year? The $245,000 could be the Farm's commission, which meant that Hamilton was involved in something larger than we had previously speculated, something that would leave him with over two million dollars he didn't want showing up on his tax return.

My palms burned when I tried to adjust them on my branch. I spit into them, probably adding countless germs, but at least the stinging dissipated. I listened as intently as I could before pulling the microphone out of my shirt and holding it up to my lips to whisper.

"Wolf," I said, then decided it was not the time for jokes. "I really am lost this time."

Both legs had fallen asleep by the time I heard the sirens. When I tried to climb down, prickly pain shot up my calves, but I ignored it and managed to get back to the lowest branch when I sort of fell into a heap at the base of the tree. I was back on my feet as swiftly as possible, sprinting in the direction of the sirens and lights. I didn't bother to zigzag, having no way of knowing where my hunter was, and made it back to the driveway much faster than I had made it to the cabin. I ran all the way to Ellis's squad car, where I leaned over and heaved until the air began to flow more normally into my lungs.

Ellis watched me with a mixture of concern and amusement. Finally, amusement won out, and he barked out a laugh.

"I'll take up jogging, I swear, if you stop laughing at me," I gasped.

"What happened? You used to be better than that."

Used to be. It was as if he had slapped me, and I didn't bother to respond. No matter that Marco had said the exact same thing to me a week ago. I felt that I had progressed in the last week, from peeping Tom to serious investigator. Also to murder suspect, so I probably shouldn't get my tail feathers in a twist.

"What happened?" he asked again, but he wasn't referring to my workout schedule. The mirth didn't drain from him entirely, but it was overshadowed by professionalism.

"That lady tried to shoot me."

"Delores Dawson."

I nodded, and Ellis said something into his walkie-talkie. He opened the passenger-side door for me, and I tumbled in gratefully. I watched the German shepherds receive their instructions before heading into the forest with their human partners. It was that kind of day.

Ellis leaned his head into the open driver's-side window.

"Meeza's coming to pick you up. Are you going to be okay?"

"Yeah. I need to talk to you, though."

Ellis climbed in and shut the door behind him. "You think I'm handsome?"

"Shut up."

He listened as I explained my money-laundering theory.

"Do you remember any of the other names besides Hamilton? Your favorite mastermind, Salvatore Magrelli?" I shook my head. "I didn't make it through everything, though."

Ellis made a few comments into his walkie-talkie before turning back to me. "Our handwriting expert deciphered the signature on Samantha Evans's info sheet. It belongs to Marvin Creeley."

It took me a moment, but I finally remembered the hedge-fund manager I had visited. With his background, he could easily manipulate the numbers for Whilshire Farm and their real clients, setting up tax shelters as needed.

"Good work," Ellis said and opened his door. Before climbing out, he looked back over at me. "For the record, I could satisfy your needs."

He was out the door before I could decide on an appropriate response.

CHAPTER NINETEEN

W hen Meeza picked me up, she clucked disapprovingly. She wouldn't drive until she had administered
first aid to my various scrapes and bruises, and I
was almost convinced that she wasn't even worried about the
leather seats. When she pulled away from Whilshire Farm, I
looked at myself in the fold-down mirror. Sure enough, an ugly
sight greeted me. I had dirt, blood, and what looked like sap
stuck to my forehead. Vondya had taught me various foolproof
techniques for securing wigs, so mine was still in place but
resembled a nest for small creatures, possibly moles or chipmunks. My yoga pants were ripped in unseemly places, and I
had a gash on my forearm.

"No stitches," I said as we finally got back to the city and she
turned toward Columbia Presbyterian. "I just need a shower."

Meeza made more clucking noises and may have mumbled
something under her breath, but she followed my directions
and parked in front of my building. I turned to thank her, but
she was already waiting for me on the sidewalk. As delicately
as possible, I followed her, wincing at the pain in my calves. I

was willing to admit that my injuries consisted of more than scrapes; I had probably pulled something and reminded myself to stretch before getting chased by killers next time.

"How is the Malik case going?" I asked.

It was a sufficient distraction, and Meeza launched into a sobering tale about her friend's husband bringing a woman home with him from his business trip.

"I didn't actually see them snuggled up, but it was obvious they were sleeping together."

"In what way?"

Meeza concentrated before answering me. "He carried her shoulder bag. Now, that's a sign of intimacy."

Who was I to argue with her logic? We stepped out of the elevator and walked down the hallway before I realized that Marco was leaned up against my apartment door, wearing pressed slacks and a button-down shirt, i.e. decidedly not undercover. Behind me, Meeza let out a small whistle of approval, hugged me gently, and disappeared. With his new clothes and a haircut, Marco was transformed. He had gone from gangster to regular guy overnight, and I was unsurprised that he looked slightly uncomfortable as himself, jiggling the loose change in one of his pockets.

"New friend?" he asked, watching Meeza retreat.

I ignored him as I stepped forward to unlock my apartment, but the day's adventures were not to end quite so easily. Tambo had replaced the makeshift pine door with what looked like reinforced steel. The new lock was shiny, and I didn't have a key.

"Couldn't handle a deadbolt?"

"I didn't want to scratch the surface," Marco said, but I knew that Marco the police officer would never break into an apartment without a warrant. I suddenly felt more uncomfortable, too, acutely aware that this was definitely the Marco I had cared about, not as easy to dismiss as the one who had visited me the week before.

I held up a finger that told him to wait and hobbled down to the basement. When Tambo opened the door and saw my state, he started.

"*Chat échaudé craint l'eau froide,*" he said.

My French isn't great, but I thought it probably meant something along the lines of "Look what the cat dragged in." I thanked him for the door and he replied, "It looks like you'll need it, *cherie.*" He handed over the keys, made sure I understood that there were no copies, and I reminded myself to bring him a thank-you gift. I was sure the door wasn't standard. Tambo had gone out of his way to get me something more secure, and I doubted he did that for many tenants. He had been the building super for thirty-some years and was friendly, liked to tell rambling stories about his boyhood days in Paris. I wasn't sure if they were true or not, but who was I to judge?

When the elevator door dinged open on my floor, Marco was still waiting for me. He looked me over, surveying the damage, and didn't say anything, which weighed in his favor. I let him follow me into my place and didn't object when he grabbed a soda from my refrigerator. He still hadn't said anything when I indicated that I was going to jump in the shower.

"I could join you."

"Or not." It wasn't a particularly witty response, but I was satisfied with the tone. I would characterize the cadence as downright icy.

"I saw you, you know. Try not to knock over the garbage next time."

This didn't ingratiate him to me any further, and I turned into the bathroom, locking the door behind me. Unfortunately, the bathroom lock consisted of a nail and latch, so it was more symbolic than practical. I loosened hair pins, ripped off tape, and threw my wig in the corner. It wasn't that my disguise had been unhelpful, but it was easier to blame the red strands than anything else. Crumpled, the thing looked like nothing so much as a blood-soaked scalp.

When I eased myself under the water, I swallowed the stings gratefully. They cleared my head, and I reviewed the facts as I understood them. Okay, so thoughts of Marco joining me may have hindered my train of thought, but I still suspected that Samantha Evans had never been at Whilshire Farm, that she was just an excuse for Hamilton to send money. I surmised that a lot of other patients had skipped out as well, trading cash for diplomas and untraceable offshore accounts. I had never heard of outsourced money laundering, but if my theory checked out, it was genius. Whilshire Farm took all the liability, but profited handsomely without actually getting their hands dirty with uglier crimes. What I did know for sure was that various people were funneling large sums of money into the establishment, and one of those was my very own number-one suspect Colt Hamilton. The real stumper was how Colt Hamilton and Stephen Kramer were connected. Was Hamilton fooling around with Gloria Kramer? I couldn't see boytoy-hungry Gloria going to Hamilton, however nice his suits, when she already had one of those models at home.

I washed the sap from my hair and cleaned out my various wounds. By the time I emerged, I smelled like mint and was hungry. A glance in the mirror told me I more or less resembled myself, but I was sure more bruises would bloom the next day. Marco had ordered a pizza, and I picked up a slice of pepperoni and stretched out as much as possible on my small couch, flexing and unflexing my calves to loosen them. Marco pulled up my desk chair and stared at me.

"If you're looking for sympathy, you won't get it from me," he said, but I didn't entirely buy it. He was looking at me with an emotion at least akin to pity. He really meant that he'd seen worse, and I nodded. I had, too, but that was a lifetime ago—where Marco himself belonged, if I was being honest.

"I'm out," he continued. "The big two I mentioned have been arrested, and I'm going to be the key witness."

I threw up my hands in disbelief, splattering sauce on my clean T-shirt. "You're going to be in more danger than ever if you testify."

Marco shook his head. "The father's not well-liked after he sliced up his wife and kids. I wasn't sure that this community had any lines left to cross, but mutilating your loved ones appears to be unacceptable behavior. Plus, this is going to be a major shakedown. I'll just need to lay low for a while."

I looked at him expectantly, but he didn't ask me to go with him again. It was implied, though, and I took a deep breath. I thought of his arms encircling the pretty Latina girl, and I turned jealousy and desire into the off positions where they belonged.

"I know it's part of the game, but you didn't seem to mind."

He shrugged. I couldn't tell if he was irritated or hurt by my response. There was definitely an unspoken accusation: *You of all people should understand.* Instead, he said "What's to mind" and picked up another slice.

"How long were you together?"

"Six months." At least, I think that's what he said as he popped a mushroom in his mouth.

"And you expect me to believe you don't have any feelings for her?"

"No, I don't expect that, because it's not true."

I flipped on the television, trying to find a sporting event, but it was only 11. We settled for a morning talk show and ate in relative silence, learning about solar-powered watches and expanded bike lanes. After the segment on trending cat memes ended, so did our truce. Marco rose to leave.

"I'm going to a safe house until the trial's over, three or four months from now. Then I'll be ready to hide away in some lush, tropical paradise. Sandy beaches. Palm trees. You in?"

He spoke deliberately, without apparent passion, but we were too much alike for me to miss the signs of exertion. His forearms were tensed as he swung them back and forth. I remembered wanting to reset my life when the Frank Magrelli trial was over. It occurred to me that Marco wasn't looking for a reset button, but a rewind one. As far as I could tell, those don't exist. Nonetheless, I was tempted. I'm not sure even now what made me shake my head. It was too simple, maybe, running away. Escape had long been my first-choice fantasy, but when faced with the reality, I balked. I couldn't quite muster up enthusiasm for leaving the embers of my life, however bleak. I had just managed to get them glowing again.

He was gone before I opened my mouth to explain. I lay down expecting to cry or ache, but instead fell asleep.

———

When my cell phone rang at four o'clock, my first emotion was unspecific panic that Marco was in trouble. The caller I.D. read "Restricted," though, and I figured it was either Meeza calling from our office or the NYPD calling from wherever. I cleared my throat before answering.

"Delores Dawson claims that you were trespassing and that she wielded her licensed gun in self-defense," Ellis said, dispensing with pleasantries.

"I was a guest at her rehab facility. And what about hunting me? Does she have a license for that?"

"Don't worry, Kathleen. The files are missing, but if Whilshire Farm is moving money in the amounts you saw, the IRS can handle it."

"And Hamilton?"

"We're keeping an eye on him. I'm going to stay at the bar myself tonight, make sure he doesn't leave."

From my cramped position on the couch, I could see the water damage from when my toilet had backed up and overflowed. There was an oval yellow stain, then a thin two-foot crack growing from the baseboard.

"You can't afford twenty-four-hour surveillance until the IRS exposes all the people using Whilshire for more than cattle-grazing or navel-gazing," I finally said, wondering what would happen if the crack reached the ceiling. Would the wall split in two?

"Cute. Listen, we'll find more evidence. Go occupy yourself with something else for a few days. I think we're almost finished here."

Ellis hung up, and I shut my eyes again. After five minutes, my mind was reeling. *Almost finished?* Hamilton was involved in something involving massive sums of illegal money. Payments, probably, but for what? Gloria Kramer suspected her husband of cheating, but his shady activities could have nothing to do with sex. A deal gone bad? I abandoned my second nap. When I stood, my muscles alternated between aches and stabs, and I decided to walk out the kinks in my life. A second shower seemed wasteful, so I replaced my sweatpants with jeans. I dug around until I unearthed an old bottle of nail polish remover to get rid of the ridiculous fake Kennedy Vanders nails.

The smell took me back to the Hamilton's basement and then, resignedly, to an earlier memory.

<hr />

Zanna was treating her rusted fire escape like a set of monkey bars. She had wrapped her legs around the rail and was dangling, head first, over the alley. We were on the fifth story, and I was panicking. I had her knees in my hands, trying to coax her up while she swung her body weight away from me again and again.

"Nino," I screamed into the apartment.

He and his friends had been watching a Mets game all afternoon, leaving me to deal with Zanna. She had snorted too much coke at a party the day before and had been a pain in the ass ever since. She had crashed around five in the morning, and I thought that would be it, but after a few hours of sleep, she had woken up in an agitated state. At first, she hadn't recognized me and had dug her nails in my arm. By mid-afternoon, I was ready to call my precinct and quit on the spot. Babysitting was above and beyond the call of duty.

"Nino!" I tried again.

"*¿Qué carajo?*"

Nino poked his head out of the window and saw his sister stretching her arms. "She wanna kill herself? Is that it?"

He was angry, but he was scrambling out onto the fire escape all the same. I kept my hands on her knees, and he reached over to pull her up by her arms. She wouldn't let him touch her, though, and started shrieking.

"Zanna, you stupid bitch. You need to calm down right now." He turned toward me for a second. "This isn't her fault," he said in a softer tone.

I didn't know what he was talking about, but I nodded my head. Maybe the Costas had a soft spot for addicts. He hung half his torso over the edge and got a grip on one of Zanna's flailing arms. He jerked her upright where she tumbled into me. We went down hard on the metal frame, but I was relieved that a few bruises were our worst injuries.

Nino and I got her inside and locked the window. Zanna wandered aimlessly around the apartment, moving from bedroom to kitchen to living room. The boys shouted at her when she blocked the TV, and she yelled some more. Finally, though, she curled into a ball on the floor and glued her eyes to the screen. Whether or not she could see David Wright taking a swing at an inside pitch was a whole other issue. One I didn't care about.

I pulled out a Bud Lite from the refrigerator and popped the top. Nino came in after me, and I thanked him.

"That shit was nasty."

"Yeah, I've never seen her act like that."

"Not Zanna. That shit she did last night. Apparently this new shipment ain't clean. It's got all sorts of, what do you call it, contaminants in it."

It had been a while since Salvatore Magrelli sliced me up. I had wanted out desperately, had even dialed my precinct number, but I would have been left with nothing. The brother of the boy Salvatore shot confessed to the murder himself, self-defense. What jury would believe my story instead? I hadn't even been in the room when it happened. Fast-forward one year and I was a fixture around the Costas, knew the hierarchy more or less. A bad shipment was an opening, I was sure. Adulterated cocaine could give people, even people as important as the Magrellis, a bad reputation real quick. The consequences could lead to concrete evidence, enough so that I could request to be taken out. My policy was never to ask for information, but I needed to at least keep Nino in the room. I opened another beer and passed it over to him.

"Frank's acting crazy too. His wife's got him on lockdown," he said.

Frank Magrelli's business philosophy differed dramatically from his brother Salvatore's. I had never seen Salvatore so much as smoke a cigarette or drink a beer. What he did with his money was anyone's guess. On the other hand, ask anyone about Frank, and they'd say he liked hookers and dog races.

"I'm glad I passed."

"Me too," Nino said. "I got bigger concerns, though."

Nino liked to puff himself up, but neither Magrelli brother trusted him with anything important. Still, he picked up information from time to time, and I waited for him to brag.

"We got to figure out what to do with this stuff. There's gotta be a way to make it sell, right?"

I suspected Nino was thinking about a plan along the lines of passing it off to unsuspecting college kids.

"You'll figure out something," I said.

Nino liked that answer. He winked at me and went back to the game. I took a gulp of my beer and set it down alongside the sink. The dishes were caked and starting to smell, so I doused them with detergent and turned the water on. As the bubbles formed, I ran back over what I knew about adulterated cocaine. At its worst, it could cause something called agranulocytosis, which affected the immune system. I wasn't worried about Zanna having it after one bad night, though. There had been less than five ounces left after the party, and I knew what they would do with that. You can treat it with an acetone wash as long as there's a dry place to store the treated cocaine overnight. Like a peanut butter jar.

Or a humidor.

CHAPTER TWENTY

I ripped off the fake Kennedy Vanders nails as quickly as possible and called Ellis back. He didn't seem happy to hear from me until I told him I had seen a gallon of acetone in Hamilton's storage closet.

"What are you saying?"

"That Hamilton could have been paid to clean adulterated cocaine. Maybe more than once in order to get a 2.4 million-dollar paycheck. Did you check the humidor for particulates?"

"No, we didn't dust down there. Let me get back to you. Don't do anything stupid."

Ellis hung up, and I tried to figure out what I could do that was stupid. I certainly didn't know how to check for particulates myself, so I headed straight to the office. I was keyed up, and I could at least do some prelim work on my open cases to keep my mind off everything.

I took the train down to 81st Street and walked across Central Park. It was the first time I had been there out-of-character in years, and I noticed how much the leaves had changed in a week. They weren't yet the brilliant reds and oranges of upstate, but the greens were definitely fading. Poet's Walk would soon be picture-book perfect, and couples would confess their undying love under the canopy of trees. I avoided that route and instead headed toward the carnival rides that would soon be replaced with an ice-skating rink for winter. The flying elephants and carousel were clearly designated for children, but they reminded me of Coney Island's more daring rides—the wooden rollercoaster, sky-high Ferris wheel, haunted house. All three of my favorites had survived Hurricane Sandy and been reopened for the summer.

It only took me about thirty minutes to reach my office. I was rewarded with a chipper assistant who had a lead on her client and was ready for action.

"Apparently Mr. Malik and his mistress meet at some sleazy motel most Saturday afternoons. Aren't I the lucky one?"

"Apparently. Do you want me to go with you?"

"No, but I was hoping to borrow a camera."

"Right, I need to get you a spare key for the supply closet. You can use whatever you need."

Meeza followed me into the office, chattering about how she had weaseled the information out of one of Malik's co-workers. She was so excited that I couldn't bring myself to tell her what it might be like to show the incriminating photographs to her friend. How I imagined it would feel as if you'd fallen off a ladder flat onto your back, wind knocked out of your lungs. I didn't have much experience with that exact situation, but I remembered from my halcyon days what it felt like to disappoint a friend. Actually, I had been disappointing Ellis every day since he had popped back into my life, and I could testify that it felt rotten.

I put my bag down on my desk and rummaged around until I came up with the small silver padlock key. When I swung open the door, Meeza's story cut off mid-sentence. She emitted a small shriek, then clamped her hand over her mouth. I looked to see what had caused such a reaction.

A strangled noise escaped my throat, and I bolted out into the shared space of the office building. I left Meeza standing in front of my ruined wigs, blood dripping onto the floor. It was splattered over everything in sight, from hangers to carpet.

Because it was Saturday afternoon, almost everyone had gone home. After I checked to make sure the bathroom and hallways were clear, I popped into the offices of the three people working late. I tried to sound nonchalant, but I could tell by the bug eyes that I wasn't succeeding. No one had seen anyone unusual wandering around.

"Kathleen." Meeza's voice was surprisingly steady, and I wished I could give her a raise on the spot. When I entered my office, I closed the door behind me. "Kathleen, it smells sweet."

She was right. There was no rusty scent in the air, only something syrupy. I went back to look at the mess and realized that neither of us had gagged, the normal reaction to gallons of blood. When I stuck my finger into a pool, I was fairly confident I knew what I would taste when I put the liquid to my tongue: maraschino cherries. I thought back to the shelves at Hamilton's. Looking around, I could see that in our alarm, neither Meeza nor I had noticed the dozen or so squished fruits scattered in the closet. Not exactly subtle.

Subtle or not, Meeza was shaken and called V. P. to pick her up. I called Ellis to send a forensics team and tried not to think about the differences between my assistant's life and mine. Let's just say that they didn't stop with her flawless complexion.

When V. P. arrived, he didn't look happy to see me. In fact, I was pretty sure he was glaring at me over the shoulder of his girlfriend as he hugged her. He may have mouthed an insult, but I can't read lips and let it go.

"Wait, what about Malik?" asked Meeza.

"I'll take care of it."

It was the least I could do. She told me the name of the motel and I wrote it down and waited for officers to appear. Ellis was first, and he didn't look happy to see me either. There were dark circles under his eyes that made him look like paid muscle, not the first-rate detective I knew him to be.

"Cherries?"

"Yep. Those sugary ones that go in cocktails. Hamilton had jars of them in his supply closet."

"They're not hard to come by."

"Can you dust for prints?"

Ellis spoke to two specialists, who began testing the door-frame and shards of glass that had settled at the bottom of the closet. Someone else photographed the process, and it was clear that my priority level had risen since my apartment break-in.

"You really shouldn't be here while they work," Ellis said.

I weighed the odds of retrieving my camera from the mess and decided they weren't good. I would have to pick up a disposable on my way across town.

"I have to get going anyway. I have an appointment at the Pink Lady Motel."

A forensics worker whipped around to get a better look at me, and Ellis's eyes crinkled at the corners as if he might want to smile. I didn't stay long enough to see the final result.

———

On the way to the fleabag motel, I formulated a hole-filled plan to nab Naaif Malik and be a hero twice over that day. Murderer and adulterer, check and check. I crossed my fingers that I was early enough for my plan to work as I smeared on some red lipstick. My jeans and T-shirt didn't really scream "rendezvous," but you have to work with what you have. I knotted the shirt right above the band of my jeans and folded my jacket across my arm to hide the gash. When I entered the motel lobby, I looked around curiously as if expecting someone.

"Can I help you, miss?" the receptionist asked. She was dressed in a maroon uniform that had been washed enough times to leave little pills of material on the sleeves. She had clearly worked here a while and had probably seen Mr. Malik before.

"Yes, please. I am meeting a friend. Naaif Malik."

"Mr. Malik hasn't checked in yet. Would you like to wait at the bar?"

She gestured toward a nondescript room I had passed without noticing. Through the doorway, I could see a small, poorly stocked area. The bartender didn't bother to look up from his newspaper when I entered. Actually, he didn't bother to look up when I ordered a drink. He managed to pour and keep reading simultaneously, a feat I deemed "natural talent." Of course, he looked ninety-five if he was a day, so perhaps ignoring customers was a skill developed over time.

"Thank you," I said, pushing a ten toward the bartender. He responded by mumbling something about kids and dope and "back in '82" without ever glancing up. I retreated to a faded velour couch in the darkest corner of the room. I could see the lobby door, which was the extent of my plan. The glass of wine I ordered was too sweet, and I shuddered when I took a sip, reminded of the cherries. Frankly, the motel didn't look that different from the dozen or so Manhattan hotel lobbies I've canvassed. Maybe a bit more tired, but lobbies are mostly unimpressive unless in fancy midtown establishments. The new boutique hotels are catching on, attracting partygoers and Europeans, but even they would look uniform without the neon lights and water features. And the guest rooms are still the size of port-a-potties.

Malik pushed through the revolving door. He looked slimmer than he had been in the provided photograph, but was still easy to identify as my man. Or Meeza's man, I should say. After a few seconds passed, he entered the bar, glancing at the patrons one by one. The hostess had obviously told him that someone was waiting for him. His survey didn't last long. There was a businessman nursing a whiskey and an older couple poring over a subway map. Malik glanced in my direction, then went back out, opening his cell phone simultaneously. I couldn't hear the conversation, but I could imagine it: his lover was on her way. Then he disappeared from sight.

It wasn't hard to guess the lover's identity, although Meeza hadn't left me a description. The woman appeared to be in her forties and, while well-dressed, fiddled self-consciously with her purse as she struggled with the revolving door. She grinned tentatively at, I could only assume, Malik. I took a quick photo with the disposable camera, careful not to wind the film and give myself away. Disposable cameras are outré for several reasons, not least of which is the duck sounds they make when the plastic wheel turns. I hoped the pair might have a drink before heading upstairs, but no such luck. The only way to get a couple shot was to wait in the parking lot. The more pressing question was how to sneak by the receptionist.

A quick visit to the ladies' room revealed a window just wide enough for a small person to squeeze through. I clambered onto the toilet seat and pushed up the window. My shirt got snagged halfway through the process, but the ensuing rip was a small price to pay for a clandestine escape. I swung myself out and dropped down to the pavement. I tried to guess which car belonged to my target so that I could stay away from it, but it was pointless considering that he could have come via taxi.

I settled on a space between a 90s model Chevy Blazer and a brand-new Chrysler convertible parked close to the front entrance. I squatted down and waited.

After half an hour, my cell phone rang, and I dropped it while trying to find the silence button. "What," I hissed into the mouthpiece as soon as I recovered.

"Hamilton's prints were on the jar. It's circumstantial, but we can hold him until bail's set. He'll be occupied for the night, at least."

Before Ellis blew my cover, I hung up and switched my phone to vibrate. I wasn't ungrateful, though. In fact, despite my cramped position, I felt lighter already. Hamilton wasn't a flight risk, so bail would be set, but he would be behind bars for a day or two. And Delores Dawson was miles away and headed for a prison cell herself when the IRS got ahold of her. Even better, Malik emerged from the building arm-in-arm with the woman and, yes, kissed her as I snapped off a couple of photos. They weren't money shots, but would be enough for divorce proceedings if Mrs. Malik went in that direction.

After their romantic good-bye, the woman walked toward the avenue, and Malik headed in my direction. I scrambled backwards and renewed my game of "Guess the Right Car." I was heading in the opposite direction when Malik turned the corner and spotted me, squatting awkwardly and clearly up to no good. I didn't know the first thing about the man, so I wasn't sure how this would play out. My gut impulse was to lie like a felon, but I had a couple of photos. Honesty was the other way to go.

"Mr. Malik," I began, standing up straight.

"Yes?" He took a couple of steps away from me, and I was sure I looked positively deranged with my torn shirt and scraped face. For good measure, I was shaking my right leg for circulation.

"I was hired by your wife to ascertain your whereabouts on Saturday afternoons. Would you like to explain what you're doing at the Pink Lady Motel?"

As if she had been patiently awaiting her cue, Mamma Burstyn came into view, hands on her hips, and I fought back an urge to run.

"I should ask the same of you, Miss Stone." I cringed at the use of my real name, but didn't say anything. Mr. Malik started to cry, and I heaved out a sigh.

"Just doing my civic duty, Ms. Burstyn."

"Uh-huh. Harassing my customers, more like. Or didn't you know that all the Pink facilities are mine?"

"No, I didn't know that."

"The Pink Parrot, the Pink Lady, the Pink Pirate's Ship. I am a damn mogul. You didn't know that?"

"No," I mumbled, though perhaps somewhere I had heard that Big Mamma was expanding.

She held out her hand, and I dropped the cheap green camera into it. "No, what?" she asked.

"No, ma'am."

"Uh-huh." We watched as Mr. Malik swiped at his eyes and climbed behind the wheel of the convertible. Mamma leaned her substantial body over the driver's-side door.

"You were lucky this time," she said to him. He nodded in agreement as she finished. "Miss Stone is good at her job. I wouldn't test her abilities twice."

He nodded again as he started the engine. She turned toward me, and I tried to look dignified. "You are good at your job, aren't you?"

It wasn't my finest moment of detective work, that's for sure, but I knew how I could get back on Mamma's good side.

"Did you hear about Colt Hamilton?" I began. "Any minute now, he'll be in custody for, at the very least, breaking and entering."

I could still hear Mamma laughing as I got to Tenth Avenue and headed toward the train.

CHAPTER TWENTY-ONE

O n my way to the detention center, I had been feeling downright giddy. No longer a murder suspect, I was mentally rehearsing my best Mamma Burstyn impression to share with Ellis, who had asked me to sit in on questioning. Hamilton's lawyer had conveyed that his client wanted to trade information for a deal. By the time I emerged from the subway, a deal didn't seem likely, though. I had a new voicemail from Ellis telling me that Hamilton had been attacked in the holding cell.

When I arrived, the front-desk staff was frantic, trying to contain the story. It looked like Hamilton might not make it, and that would reflect poorly on everyone from the Commissioner to the warden to the office secretary. I had time to look around because the young man behind the front desk didn't notice me for several minutes. When his panicked eyes met mine, he slapped himself forcefully on the head.

"Detective Stone? Detective Dekker is waiting for you. I'm glad you made it here before—" He didn't finish his sentence, and I didn't press him. I pulled out my state identification, a real one, no less, neither denying nor confirming my status as a detective. While the man made a photocopy, I took deep breaths.

"Here you go, ma'am. Jerry will escort you."

If he had played professional football, Jerry the Guard would have had a nickname like "Jerry the Giant" or "The Fortress." The top of my head didn't reach his shoulders, and when I followed him through the series of buzzing doors, I was certain no one could see me. Despite the obvious advantage of his size and position, Jerry was twitchy. His hand went to his gun several times with no apparent provocation. The hollering and banging that echoed through the place sounded consistent to me. I was grateful that we didn't have to walk past any cells to get to the medical facility.

Jerry opened the final door and grunted for me to enter before shutting me in. There was another, smaller guard on duty inside the room, but the handcuffed patients didn't look like a rowdy bunch. In addition to Hamilton, two other men were present, one the color and smell of urine, the other emaciated to the point of no return. This was a room for the hopeless.

I expected the sight of Hamilton hooked up to an IV to be more satisfying. He was sleeping, and I felt an unexpected stab of tenderness. The crook of his elbow resembled a peony where a nurse had tried several unsuccessful times to stick the needle. His head was tilted to the right, exposing the row of stitches where the shiv had entered his neck. This was no warning; this was a clear attempt to end the man's life. After allowing me to take in the scene, Ellis told me that they were moving Hamilton to the prison's hospital ward in the morning.

"That's good, right? That he can be moved?"

Ellis paused. "It's hard to say. Whoever wanted him dead probably isn't satisfied with fatally wounded."

"Fatally?"

Ellis didn't respond, and I hazarded another look at Hamilton and thought, of the two states, I would prefer to be dead. The IV dripped some kind of liquid, which I assumed was morphine.

"What do you know?" I asked.

"It happened less than half an hour after he had been processed. I was letting him wait in the holding cell—"

Ellis faltered here, and I knew that he was feeling guilty.

"It was the right decision, Ellis. Give him time to worry."

Ellis nodded and continued in a monotone voice, explaining that someone in the holding cell had a four-inch piece of scrap metal. The only explanation was that one of the guards slipped it to him.

"I wonder what he got in return."

Ellis knew I was talking about the attacker, but he didn't seem to like the question. He slammed his hand against the wall, causing me to jump back. This time, no vase shattered on the floor, and I didn't run away. For a split second, I thought back to that other time and wished I hadn't run away then either. How would things be different? *It doesn't matter now*, I told myself. The on-duty guard looked at Ellis, but quickly resumed his relaxed position.

"Who knows. Money? Blackmail? The deal must have been conveyed in a note, but we can't find it. Most likely swallowed," Ellis said.

Whoever instigated the attack was powerful enough to have a guard in his or her pocket plus enough leverage to persuade a stranger to murder someone. I thought back to Hamilton's willingness to make a deal. He was clearly going to rat someone out, probably the drug dealer whose cocaine he had been cleaning. I could name the big cartel players in town, and only one had any connection to this case. We knew that Stephen Kramer's assassin had worked for Salvatore Magrelli at some point. My mind stayed on task, but my body shivered in revolt. I tried to stay calm long enough to help Ellis reason through the available evidence.

"We still don't know who killed Samantha Evans," I said.

"I think we're looking for someone who's rebelled. Someone who found that hiring a hit man was a waste of money. Someone with a tie to—"

Here, Ellis paused again, and I knew he wanted to say Salvatore Magrelli.

"It's okay. I think it's him too."

I looked around the room, half-expecting the man to appear on an express elevator from hell. Of course, he wasn't in hell, and that was the problem.

"Right," Ellis continued. "Someone who has a connection to Salvatore Magrelli, but not a close one. I think the hit man was a recommendation, a favor. Maybe Salvatore wasn't happy about how that favor was used, or maybe he didn't care. In any case, the guilty party decided he'd give it a shot himself. How hard could it be, right? To pull a trigger."

I thought about the sizzling grill on Samantha Evans's brand-new back porch. She had probably thought things were looking up. Her boyfriend had given her enough money for a down payment. He was arriving any minute for a relaxing evening.

Ellis continued. "I don't think Hamilton killed Kramer, and definitely not Evans. From everyone I've talked to, he liked her, and she wasn't asking for any more money. He knew we checked the humidor this morning. He knew that the lab report would show trace amounts of cocaine. I think he wanted to make a deal about the drugs, I.D. the person in charge."

"Let me guess, there were multiple prints on the jars?"

"Yeah, at least two others who worked at the restaurant. That stunt looks like nothing more than a shoddy framing attempt."

"Something to spook Hamilton?"

"Exactly. Look, Kathleen, I'm not sure there's anything we can do about Salvatore right now. Unless this one makes a miraculous recovery, we only have circumstantial evidence tying him to any of this." Ellis tilted his eyes toward Hamilton, then back to me. "But there's someone else involved here, and I think we can get that one, whoever he or she is. I think we're looking for a personal connection. Maybe Kramer was involved in the drugs too? I don't know. We're still looking for a link between the bar and Kramer."

Ellis looked like he might take another throw at the wall, so I reached out and touched his arm. He recoiled, and I took a step back.

"I don't need your sympathy. I need your help."

Ah. There it was.

A plea to get myself involved in the very scene I'd run screaming from three years ago. It was evident that Ellis was trying to guess my answer, but he should have known I couldn't walk away now. True, I didn't appear to be a suspect anymore, and at one time I may have been too tired to care what happened to Salvatore Magrelli, but not anymore. I wasn't smacking walls, but I was angry, too. To be honest, I had been angry ever since Salvatore led me into the Costas hallway. The anger was part of me, embedded deep in my gut and more tenacious than any tumor.

"I'm on board," I said, as if I had a choice.

⟞✦⟝

The next day, I called Meeza to apologize for blowing her one case, but she stopped me mid-sentence, proposing dinner with her parents instead. Apparently, she was dealing with her nerves via curried chicken, a reasonable stress-relief method.

I took a rain check, then swung by an ATM to deposit a real check that had been folded and unfolded enough times to wear down the material. It was at risk of splitting in two, and the amount needed to be transferred to my bank account as soon as possible. Gloria Kramer's connection to the murders was tenuous at best, and if I was going to catch her husband's killer, I needed a new disguise. The NYPD certainly wasn't going to cover my expenses. I wasn't going to be much use to them as myself, particularly if that self was living on the streets, unable to pay her rent. I replaced these merry thoughts with ones of a brunette pageboy and new personality as the F train approached Brighton Beach.

When the doors opened, salty air whipped inside the car. I was glad for my jacket even though it had hurt to put it on over my forearm gash. It seemed like ages since I had climbed a tree to escape the Manicured Menace, but it had only been yesterday. When I left the station, I could see Coney Island in the distance, standing strong despite efforts to dismantle the carnival-esque atmosphere in favor of a more conventional boardwalk. Not even a record-breaking hurricane had slowed her down for long.

When the bell above the door jingled, Vondya hissed through her teeth. I wasn't sure if it was my scrapes and bruises or my naked head that elicited this response, because it was followed by indecipherable Russian as she ushered me into a salon chair. When I reached into my bag to retrieve my mangled Kathy wig, I knew the situation was going to deteriorate further. I shielded my eyes and held the thing out to her like the carcass it resembled. Instead of hissing, there was silence. Ominous silence.

I peeked between my fingers to see Dolly coming up the stairs and said a small prayer of thanks. Vondya wouldn't lecture me too harshly in front of her best customer. Instead she mumbled something that sounded like "Why me?" Dolly laughed as soon as the door shut behind him.

"Blowdryer, woman, seriously. They sell them at the drug store."

I looked at myself in the mirror and was pleased to see that all the tree dirt had washed out. The meticulously cut bangs were cowlicked, though, and I could see Dolly's point.

"Why blow-dry when I can wear one of Vondya's specialties?"

I made the comment in my most saccharine voice, but Vondya was unimpressed if even listening. She had filled a basin with cold water and was busy dunking my Kathy wig into a soapy mixture.

"*Chyort voz'mi.* I'll be with you in just a second, sweetnez."

Dollars to doughnuts she wasn't talking to me. Dolly told Vondya to take her time and flipped through a catalogue on the coffee table.

"What are you thinking this time? Another Davy Crockett special?"

"No, that particular wig managed to survive the train wreck of my life."

"I heard you got your man."

While the reputable newspapers weren't printing much, a few online rags had run a story connecting Hamilton with the murders and alluding to a violent incident. There was clearly a leak at the detention center. Someone had probably decided it would look better for a guilty man to get stabbed than an innocent one. I forced myself to grin, hoping I didn't look as grim as I felt.

"Don't I always?"

Dolly snorted and folded down the corner of a page. I got up and glanced over her shoulder at a chin-length, cobalt blue number that no one but Dolly could pull off. Vondya wouldn't like it because it was synthetic, but she could dye a human one. Dolly must have been thinking the same thing because he flipped through until he found a similar style in white-blonde.

"To bring out my eyes."

I looked at Dolly's chocolate irises and didn't argue.

"There. Now we condition," Vondya said, interrupting our stare. Her voice held relief, so I crept up beside her to apologize for the extra work. She swatted me away.

"The last time you were here, you told me you met a man. Nice divorcé, you zaid. Where did you meet him? Mud wrestling?" This made Vondya cackle.

"I got rid of the pistol, at least."

Okay, so it wasn't exactly voluntary, but the gun was gone, sure enough.

Vondya patted my hand and told me I was a good girl. That's when I knew there was no permanent damage to the hairpiece. After she placed it on the wire frame, she showed me how to comb from the ends to avoid breakage, and I turned my attention to the tangles. Vondya fussed a little bit over Dolly's choice, but Dolly was persuasive, particularly with an open tab courtesy of the Pink Parrot.

I flipped through the magazine myself, showing Vondya and Dolly a pretty shoulder-length one that would cover enough of my face to prevent anyone from recognizing me at Hamilton's. Ellis had asked me to cozy up to the staff. My wig choice was more like a suggestion than an order, though, and Vondya paraded out three possibilities, securing them on my head and consulting Dolly for a second opinion. I might as well have been a mannequin, and they might have preferred a plastic version of me. Less wiggling, more still-life. In the end, they decided on the longest brunette, though I objected to the length.

"Will it even look natural?"

Vondya crossed her arms in front of her, and I wished I had held my tongue. I was fast becoming her least favorite customer, but at least I was still a customer.

"Trust us, this is Kay," Dolly said, christening me. Sure enough, before I paid my bill, I was already imagining her, a jewelry designer from Poughkeepsie maybe. I could even visit the town to obtain a few believable details like favorite restaurant and bike path. She was probably vegetarian, and that accounted for the shine in her long, healthy hair. I shook myself from this reverie. There wouldn't be time for field research.

Kathy had to dry, so Vondya set her under the apparatus and told me to take a walk. Dolly exited with me, but stepped into a nail place for a manicure. I passed a tempting discount store boasting five-dollar towels, but managed to resist and make it to the boardwalk. The wind off the Atlantic stung my eyes, and the smell of beef stroganoff made my mouth water. I felt instantly more relaxed. There were dessert stands and souvenir shops, but mostly Brighton Beach felt homey, and I was sure the families eating picnic-style on the park benches would agree. An old woman even smiled at me as her granddaughter careered into my legs, oblivious to the threat of strangers.

The wooden slats under my feet were familiar and took me toward the Coney Island lights in the distance. The boardwalk crowd thinned, then swelled as I got closer to the year-round carnival. The clacking of the Cyclone greeted me first, followed by the inevitable screams as the wooden roller coaster shot down the slopes. The predictability of the noises made it more appealing somehow, the sound of safe abandon.

I passed an aquamarine and pink mermaid mural that made me think of Bridget Barnaby's lascivious snails. Then I entered Astroland Amusement Park and headed for the arcade, my favorite childhood spot. It was hard not to imagine my father spilling change into the skeeball machine, but the memory was more sweet than bitter that day, so I left it alone. The photo booth was filled with teenagers. They reeked of booze and maybe a hint of vomit. I hurried past and found an attendant who turned a ten-dollar bill into a mound of quarters that I carried around in a plastic cup like a retiree playing the slots. The coins felt infinite, and I didn't deliberate on the best games, I just played. I tried to make a dump truck release its bounty by hitting a bullseye; I used a claw in an attempt to rescue a green plush bunny; I maneuvered rubber balls into acrylic slots as the pig mascot oinked at me. In the end, my ticket count exceeded fifty—not a bounty, but nothing to sniff at either.

I had turned to use my final quarter on Skeeball when my cell phone vibrated. I figured it was Vondya calling to tell me my wig was ready, but I didn't recognize the number. I cupped my hand over my exposed ear and tried to hear above the din. The voice was still garbled, though, so I shouted for the person to wait and pushed my way out of the crowd. Of course, outside the arcade, barkers tried to lure customers to their booths, but at least the sounds could echo into the open air.

"Sorry about that. Who's calling, please?"

"This is Hank Stonebrook, you referred me to a client?"

The name didn't sound familiar at first, but then I remembered pawning James Clifton off on my one-time real estate agent. Gratitude made me disposed to like him.

"Right, of course. Is everything all right?"

"Not really. The guy you had me call? Said he only wants to work with this Kathy Seasons person. He practically hung up on me. Listen, I've Googled and I've called around, but it's like she doesn't exist. That's where you come in to save the day."

Hank may have laughed, but I felt my stomach sink.

"He only wants to work with Kathy Seasons?"

"Yeah, he won't even meet with me."

I dropped the phone. It cracked into a dozen or so pieces when it hit the pavement, and someone said "Tough luck" in passing. I bent to scoop up the remains, but my hands were shaking as I scanned the crowd.

"Calm down," I said aloud to myself.

"This will calm you down, Miss! Come play the horses."

I jumped up at the sound of the barker's voice. His game consisted of water guns aimed at various targets. I shook my head and turned away to smack into a human-sized, ceramic cobra. When its red eyes flashed, I started to run.

CHAPTER TWENTY-TWO

There were enclaves of people to navigate, but many stepped out of the way when they saw me barreling toward them. I dropped my tickets somewhere, and a delighted child grabbed them. I could just make out her squeal as I turned right by the arm-wrestling game and hurled myself forward. I had entered the park near the Wonder Wheel, and if I could make it back to that landmark, I could get my bearings.

As soon as I had connected Clifton to my former real estate agent, I had pushed him out of my mind. His refusal to work with anyone but me was more than suspicious. Who wouldn't want a more experienced person managing a multi-million dollar sale? Clifton was the personal connection between the bar and Kramer, I was sure of it. It even made sense that he had engaged me in conversation at Hamilton's just long enough for a hired gun to corner my client in the bathroom. Had Clifton been following me since I'd been following Kramer? I shuddered and kept sprinting for the park exit.

The booths became more elaborate as I descended into the belly of the carnival, my boots slapping a pavement slick with beer and funnel cake.

"Step right up, ladies and gentlemen!"

"A winner every time!"

"Shoot straight! Win big!"

"Go home with a panda!"

The booths and words blurred together. Then I saw the Wonder Wheel ticket window, and the ride towering above it. I slowed down enough to push through the crowd with a few "excuse me's," receiving a few "watch out, lady's" in response. The exit stood twenty feet in front of me beside an antique fortune-telling machine. It was spitting a card into the outstretched hand of James Clifton. He wasn't looking at it, though. He was looking at me.

I stumbled backward into a trashcan, but thankfully it was bolted to the ground. I used it to steady myself and kept running, no longer looking for an exit but a place to hide. Unfortunately, no climbing trees popped into view, and I considered the various rides. Cars went in a circle on something that blasted rap music and looked like the Himalaya. Cages spun high in the air on a spider-like contraption. The only enclosed ride was the haunted house, and I ducked inside as the attendant made a half-hearted attempt to stop me. Minimum wage doesn't produce impressive loyalty.

Inside, cars wound through a variety of grotesque props. I stayed to the side and avoided the tracks as much as possible. When a set of cars approached, I screamed, "Get help!" A few passengers pointed, but they thought I was part of the fun. In the black lights, I certainly looked crazy enough to be some sort of vengeful ghost. My only choice was to continue.

My shoes were inaudible over the atmospheric music, but that meant Clifton's would be as well. I held my hand out to the pine wall and touched slimy substances whose origin I tried not to consider. I let the wall lead me deeper into the house, but I knew it couldn't be that large—maybe a thousand square feet. Behind a mummy springing out from the wall, there was an opening, but when I tried to wedge myself inside, it was too small. I continued my panicked search until I found a door that swung open when I shoved it.

It was dark inside the room, but light crept in from the gaps in the structure. Two spare cars were pushed to the side, and there were paint cans, tarps, and tools spread around. It was some sort of repair shop, specifically for the spook ride. I picked up a clawhammer and flattened myself against the wall next to the entrance, hoping that Clifton hadn't seen me choose this particular attraction. It was too much to hope for.

I fiddled with the remains of my phone, but it was useless with a busted battery, and I focused my attention on any strange sounds. Of course, they were all strange: wheels in need of grease screeched; demonic voices erupted systematically from the PA system; teenagers shouted curses over the music, "This blows" and "Fuck this." After a few minutes, though, something creepier entered the arena: silence. Not total silence. I could still hear the sounds of the crowd and rides outside, but inside my personal hell there was no noise. The ride had been shut down. Lights flicked on underneath the door, and I knew that someone was hunting me for the second time in a week. Only this time, I knew for sure that the hunter was a killer.

A shadow flicked underneath the door, and I tightened the grip on my makeshift weapon.

"Kathleen, open up," said Clifton. "I don't like that apartment after all."

Running a background check on Kathy Seasons wouldn't have yielded anything useful, but somehow he'd figured out my real identity. Fingerprints from my wine glass? That's what I would have done.

When he laughed, it wasn't staged, but downright cheerful. Underneath my fear, there was a thread of disappointment in myself for liking this man. I wondered how I could ever have compared him to my absent-minded but good-hearted father. Then I didn't wonder anything at all because the door opened, and Clifton stepped inside. I threw myself at his silhouette, landing a glancing blow to the side of his head. The howl was followed by a pft-pft noise, and I threw myself on the ground to avoid the bullets. As if the odds weren't unfair enough, the hammer bounced away from me and the door slammed shut. I flipped over and kicked out blindly in front of me and felt Clifton stumble. I clambered on top of him, wrestling with the gun, trying to keep the end pointed away from me. He used his free hand to punch me repeatedly. It was clear that he wasn't used to fighting left-handed; nonetheless, I could feel blood trickling down my jaw. Inspired, I bent down and bit hard into his knuckles, and the gun dropped out of his reach. In the darkness, it would be difficult for either of us to recover our weapons. Clifton tried to use both hands to pummel me, but I covered my face and pushed myself off and away. I spat blood onto the floor—a mixture of his and mine.

"Do you want to know what my fortune said, Kathleen?"

I was sure that I never wanted to hear my real name again. He lunged at me, and we both hit the floor.

"Pharmaceuticals not enough for you, Clifton?"

It hurt to speak, but if I stalled, maybe the attendant he had paid off would be caught shirking his duties. A manager might insist he turn the ride back on, and someone would find us.

"Oh, there's money in prescription drugs, all right, just not as much as Charlie. You of all people should know." His nonchalant tone—as if he knew how this would end—made me furious. I wanted to tell him that he should know no one used the term "Charlie" anymore. "Blow," yes. "Coke," fine. But not Charlie or any other cutesy names like bubble gum or Florida snow.

He started to laugh again, but I wasn't amused. I was forcing images of a past life out of my mind to concentrate on more pressing matters like getting to my feet.

"But not enough to go around," I said.

This stopped the laughter, and I moved warily in a circle, keeping his looming frame in front of me. My ears were ringing, and my knees felt weak, but I examined his arms, throat, and bleeding head as much as possible in the ambient light. He reached into his pocket and pulled out old business cards and something that glinted. Nothing could have chilled me more than the sound of that switchblade.

"Stephen Kramer and his wife didn't need the money," he said. "They had gobs of it, lying around, waiting to be spent. Me? I worked for every dollar I made. I sweated over the cost of aluminum, the height of shelves, how to decrease package size. Twenty years in canned goods."

My mind quickly adjusted to the fact that I wasn't the only one lying about professions, mixing a little truth in with the lies. This man had obviously never been in litigation. His rumpled suits didn't indicate a devil-may-care attitude toward fashion. They indicated what the Tribeca property manager had known at a glance: he didn't fit in among the Kramers of the world.

"What does Kramer do," he continued, gesturing with the blade. "Flies on a private jet to a beach resort. Spends a day looking at diamond mine plans and flies back. He wasn't even there for the first shipment. He didn't even pop the cherry."

I was pretty sure no one used that term anymore either. At least, I hoped they didn't. Circle, circle. The head looked like my best bet. Not for a killing blow, but for enough pain to cause a distraction, let me make a run for it.

"What about Samantha Evans? Didn't she work every day?"

"Oh yeah, it's hard work sucking the boss's cock."

I wanted to argue with his tone, but didn't, and he kept talking. "Hamilton was always a putz and worse with money than me. And yet somehow his bar rakes it in. You'd think a dead body in the bathroom would decrease customers, but no. He comes out smelling like roses, even pays off his girlfriend to keep quiet. Stupid and sentimental. And you, you couldn't leave well enough alone," he sighed.

If Clifton hadn't seemed like a hunter in the mood lighting of Hamilton's or the fluorescents of my office, he seemed like one now. Somewhere along the way, he had mastered the stalk and was ready for the kill. He was playing with me, and I was sorry that I had underestimated him in the ways that counted. I should really know better by now.

There would never be a right moment, so I flung myself at Clifton's outstretched arm, pushing the knife away from me. He stumbled, but didn't let go and didn't go down. He even managed to maneuver the blade into my forearm, but I knew he couldn't cut very far from that awkward angle. I ignored the flash of pain and kicked him hard in the knee. *Every tough guy knocked down.* The kneecap popped and he keeled over, putting his head in striking distance. I kicked again for all I was worth.

⸺

When I stumbled, bleeding, into the daylight, the attendant backed away from me, his eyes as wide as cue balls. My appearance must have spelled "trouble" to him, because he disappeared into the crowd. I hobbled toward the arcade, looking for a friendly face or a payphone. Perhaps unsurprisingly, the payphone came into view first. I dialed 9-1-1, then blacked out. I woke up with an ice pack on my face, staring up at Ellis.

"James Clifton."

"We recognized him from the surveillance tape," said Ellis. That meant Clifton had been arrested, which was a relief as well as an incentive to sit up. I tried, but the effort was too much. I nodded instead, and Ellis continued. "This is what we can piece together. Hamilton was using his basement to clean adulterated cocaine, as you suspected, then laundering the payment money, first through the bar, then, when they had millions to hide, through Whilshire Farm. It's being shut down as we speak."

"Where will the Caveres vacation now?"

Ellis grimaced, then stood up to talk to the EMTs. They weren't for me, even though my face throbbed. They were carting off an unconscious Clifton, handcuffed to the gurney, so I assumed I hadn't killed him. That caused mixed feelings, which I decided I could sort out later.

"Sweetness, I will never give you a hard time about your hair again."

Dolly bent down to squeeze my hand. I started to ask how he had found me, but he waved off the question.

"I just followed the ballyhoo," he said. He brushed my bangs away from my face, and I knew I must have looked bad because Dolly looked angry. I'd never seen him look angry before, and I may have imagined it, because a smirk quickly appeared on his face. "They want to hire you," he said.

"Coney Island?"

He rolled his eyes, then apologized. "No, New York's Very Finest."

I didn't bother to tell him I'd been there, done that. Instead, I made a second, more successful attempt to sit up and examined the milling police officers, their hard-set jaws, hands on flashlights. The youngest one looked about fifteen, though I knew he had to be at least three years older than that. He kept glancing nervously in my direction, trying to puzzle me out. "Get out while you can," I wanted to shout, but then looked at Ellis, intimidating camera-happy spectators with a few choice words. He knew who he was now even more than when he was acing exams and climbing the ranks at breakneck speed. As a detective, he was in control, and the appeal wasn't lost on me.

A paramedic approached, but I waved him away.

"Just bruises," I choked out, covering the slash on my arm.

He didn't look convinced, but he left me alone when Ellis seconded my diagnosis. He handed me a blue slushy drink and squatted beside me on the pavement. I could have said that I knew my adrenaline levels would drop soon and I would need the sugar, but honestly, the drink looked appetizing despite being the color of Dolly's forthcoming wig. I gingerly sucked on the straw and waited for the question. It didn't come right away.

"Hamilton had been paying the usual mob protection fees when someone—maybe Salvatore Magrelli, maybe not—approached him. He was in over his head, so he brought in Kramer and Clifton. He knew them both from the bar. He decided that a man who ran diamond mines wouldn't object to some slightly illegal undertakings. And he knew that Clifton was in pharmaceuticals—or at least claimed to be—and could help with the chemical process."

I nodded, my new go-to move.

"Hamilton asked Brad Messer to hide the surveillance tape because he didn't want the bar investigated. The dumb kid never knew what he was hiding, thought it was dirty pictures or something. Most of the money was being sent to Whilshire Farm to be cleaned, but there would still be income discrepancies if anyone bothered to estimate the bar's income on a quarterly basis."

I took another small sip of my drink, then held the thing up to my swelling skin. I hadn't seen myself in the mirror, but I knew that this was the best disguise yet: Quasimodo. I tucked the knowledge away for future reference. Maybe it could be recreated with a little less drama, a little more makeup.

"What do you say? And before you answer, think about how satisfying it would be to put the other Magrelli away. No more looking over your shoulder ever again."

"You said you didn't know if it was Salvatore."

"True, but if not him, someone as bad. We just don't have the evidence, yet."

And won't for a long time, I wanted to add. We had won a round, though, which was something.

"Clifton knew I worked undercover in drugs. Maybe he did the apartment. He could have followed me." It was a strain to form complete sentences, but I wanted to tell someone.

"Maybe Magrelli didn't know you were involved. That's comforting, right?"

I had opened my eyes to take all this in, but I closed them again in protest. Surely Ellis didn't want me to answer right that minute, did he?

The truth was, when I wasn't getting my face bashed or my arms scratched, there were moments when the old spark flared up, and I remembered what had brought me to law enforcement in the first place. Often, the collusion of doing good while being bad was the only thing that made sense. Let's just say I wasn't the women's club type. Soup kitchens were out. Ditto animal shelters and bake sales. The old arguments were present, of course, about my life being safer, about not having to lift weights or run miles. But maybe, if I returned, I could get one more very dangerous guy off the streets. As I had been reminded several times recently, I used to be better. While I would never say it aloud, I used to be valuable, and maybe

I could be again. I had caught James Clifton, hadn't I? Yes, I would have preferred an easier capture, but however poor the execution, he was in handcuffs, not me.

The commotion caused by an ambulance and squad cars paled in comparison to Coney Island's everyday commotion. People noticed a criminal being carted away and a woman applying Icee to her bruises, but they lost interest quickly.

A barker shouted, "A winner every time!" on a loop. I knew it was a real person, not a recording, because sometimes he would put the emphasis on "winner," sometimes "every," and sometimes inexplicably "A." I wondered what that winner would get. Nothing impressive, I figured. Maybe a stuffed frog or an inflatable baseball bat. I had seen a cheap-looking dolphin mirror at the arcade. And yet that little knickknack might be given a place of honor, on the bed or on top of a little league trophy. In this way, some eight-year-old would add to his or her identity: Winner of Carnival Games.

Children are often the best shapeshifters, cruising easily from daughter to student to athlete to fan to bully to victim. They can reinvent themselves in a ten-minute car ride. But I wasn't so shabby myself, ducking in and out of realms, imagining that the next incarnation would be the one to stick. Or maybe not. Maybe the joy was in the reinvention, and that, at least, I knew I could do.

ACKNOWLEDGMENTS

How lucky can a lady get? First, I found my wonderful agent Penn Whaling who not only believed in this book, but once sat in Brooklyn's most humid basement to hear me read. Then I got to work with talented editor Maia Larson who made this story better with every note. I am grateful for the entire Pegasus team, including Charles Brock who designed the super-cool cover. I wrote this book on the sly despite my high school motto, *Noli Res Subdole Facere*, yet a few people back my writing endeavors with blind faith that I do not deserve. (By which I mean, my family and friends are the best.) Most importantly, my mom and dad are almost as excited about Kathleen Stone's adventures as I am, and they haven't even read them yet. My writing co-conspirators Ricardo Maldonado and Matthew Pennock make me keep my chin up when I don't want to. And Kristen Linton, Tayt Harlin, Toral Doshi, and Katie Meadows always believe in me too. See, lucky? Thank you to Eric Hupe for double-checking the Italian and to Navin Shah for helping with the Hindi. Finally, this book is dedicated to Adam Province for his support, which he gives with just the right amount of humor (a lot).